SCORNED EVER MORE

A LADY FORSAKEN (BOOK THREE)

Christina McKnight

La Loma Elite Publishing

Dedication
To My Daughter~

Life isn't always fair...
Sometimes you get knocked down...
But, never give up on yourself and your dreams!

Your future is what you make of it...never settle for less
than EVERYTHING!

And if someone stands in your way, you have my
permission to punch them in the nose.

Love, Mom

Prologue

London, England
1788

The rules had always been the same:
1. The girl must be of noble birth,
2. The taking must be in clear sight of all men competing, and, finally,
3. Further attachments resulted in the loss of all points garnered.

A one-point penalty would be assessed if the female were married, and beyond that, if her husband or father were present during the tryst then extra points would be awarded.

Andrew Penton, the newly proclaimed Marquis of Drake, was hedging on a monstrous thirteen points being added to his running total, even with the penalty due to Mrs. St. Augustin's married status. The only way he could muster more points was if the girl were an innocent, and although his reputation as a rakehell of the first order was true, he did not relish taking the virtue of a young girl, no matter how willing she appeared.

"Surely, I cannot." The woman before him feigned innocence at his plight. "I must return before the performance begins."

"Come now, Pearl," Andrew coaxed. "It is only a few moments within my box. You truly must see the view. I guarantee it is far superior to the baron's seats below."

With little more effort expended, the baroness followed him willingly into his box, the door shutting soundlessly behind them.

"My lord," she gasped, "you were correct." Pearl moved from his reach toward the edge of the box, overlooking the general crowd below.

"Come here, my pet." Andrew hadn't followed her to the edge. "Come sit with me."

He took a seat just out of the shadow's reach, enabling Chastain, his dear friend and competitor, a clear view. He glanced at Chastain across the theater and winked as Pearl returned to sit next to him. Andrew nibbled the woman's neck, her moans barely covered by the dramatics of the production.

Chastain, always the most brazen of the pair, had already relieved his female guest of the top portion of her gown. If one could peek into the darkened corner of Chastain's theater box, one would behold a succulent breast exposed for the world to see. The young girl, most likely pushed into Chastain's arms by her own marriage-hungry parents, clawed at Andrew's friend's shirt as if her very life depended on what he could give her. Fortunately for the girl—and unfortunately for her money-seeking family—Chastain would offer nothing beyond this one night.

Their games of seduction had not only progressed in their scandalous nature over the last couple of years, but had also lost their ability to thrill Andrew. Only two years out of university, and already high society had lost its luster. Therefore, their games were always evolving. No more could the tryst take place in a private setting, nor would either man take the word of the other that the deed was, in fact, done.

His seduction and taking of the Honorable Mrs. Pearl St. Augustin would be made far less problematic if he could coax her from her seat, push her up against the back wall of his box, and lift her dress. He would take her swiftly, be done with it, and be at his gentleman's club before the night's performance ended... He may even return her to her husband's box. He wasn't a complete scoundrel devoid of the manners suiting a marquis, despite his years out of university.

But he knew he would forfeit points if their tryst happened anywhere but in plain view of Chastain. To top that off, Andrew had fallen severely behind in points as of late. With the renovations currently underway at his country estate and his withdrawal from town for an extended period of time, he'd been unable to make the acquaintance of London's newest crop of debutantes. This gave Benjamin—Lord Chastain—a clear advantage, since he'd spent the holiday season traveling from one house party to another, gaining introductions to the crème de la crème of the season's freshest faces.

That simply meant Andrew would have to appease himself, and his needs, more often...since every time he bedded a widow or married matron he earned fewer points.

Curse Chastain and his ever-increasing lead.

"Oh, Andrew," Pearl simpered as he took her earlobe between his teeth and gently alternated between nipping and sucking it. "Can we go somewhere? Anywhere?"

The desperation in her voice dampened his lust further.

He released her lobe long enough to answer. "I am afraid not, my pet. I have a very busy evening and only have a few moments to spare. Though, I would deeply relish a complete night in your company," Andrew encouraged. He needed this—not only for the points, but also for his own release. He'd denied himself too long, focusing on the responsibilities to his lineage and not his own body.

It was time he concentrated on what truly mattered—besting his friend at his own game.

Chapter One

London, England
February 1799

The Marquis of Drake, Andrew Penton, leaned casually against the wall bordering the gardens. Anyone who stumbled upon him might think his pose nonchalant and tranquil. Yet inside, his discontent festered just below the surface.

There were numerous places he'd rather be, many obligations to which his time would be better devoted. Instead, he flitted around yet another *ton* gathering, acting the self-indulged lord with nothing better to do than discuss the weather with simpering young debutantes, and argue the merits of the war to be waged against their French counterparts.

He'd fled the overcrowded ballroom only moments before when his latest dance partner, pushed upon him by their hostess, had stepped on his booted foot one too many times. That was not the only injustice he'd been dealt during his brief time this evening. Another chit had held him so securely during their promenade about the dance floor that her hands had left sweaty stains on his linen shirt.

He wondered if young women today were properly trained in the art of the quadrille, or if they were sent into the wilds of society wholly unprepared.

And all the time, Andrew's dear friend Benjamin chuckled at his unease.

It had been far simpler when he hadn't tried to be a respectable lord; when he hadn't given a feathering about what others thought of him or his antics about town. The days when he'd only cared about spending his coin and who would warm his bed that night seemed so long ago.

Now, he hid from potential bedmates and begrudgingly paid the new income tax levied against him to help offset the cost of financing British troops fighting in the Napoleonic War. Two shillings per pound was a trifling amount compared to what he'd spent to set up his last mistress in her own London townhouse.

It was past time he returned to the ballroom. The evening would end shortly, and he could return home or to his club for a drink.

Andrew pushed away from the wall, his position hidden from view of the main drive, and started back to the side entrance he'd exited a few moments before. It had been fortuitous that the lord who owned this home had a door leading from his study and onto the drive.

"…we have gone over this several times."

The words floated on the light breeze, meeting Andrew as he stepped inside the study door and the warmth of the house. Pausing, he strained to hear the rest of the conversation, if only to delay his return to the ballroom.

Andrew pushed the doors closed, leaving it open only a crack as footsteps approached on the outside walk. It would not do to be caught eavesdropping.

A trio stopped outside the door, their features obscured by the darkness, though Andrew saw enough to know the group consisted of two females and a well-dressed gentleman.

"See that you follow the instructions given to you." The man took the arm of one of the women and walked on, leaving their third companion behind.

Without the pair blocking his view, Andrew took in the sight of the woman before him. She was gowned in the darkest of blue to match the color of the night sky, her hair piled atop her head, leaving her neck exposed…almost vulnerable.

As he watched, she brought her hands to cover her face, and her shoulders shook ever so slightly as if she sobbed; yet no sound broke the silence of the night.

The urge to step back outside, comfort her when she was clearly upset, was strong—but that was a familiarity he was not comfortable with. If someone happened upon him alone with a young female in the shadows of the front drive, there would be many questions. Questions he was not suited to answer.

Instead, he kept her in view.

The least Andrew could do was ensure that she caught up with her party and entered the ball safely.

After a few moments, her hands fell away from her face and rested at her sides. She squared her shoulders and called, "Do wait for me, *Pere*." And with quick feet, she hurried to catch up with the pair who'd left her behind.

As speedily as she'd moved toward the front

entrance, Andrew closed the study door and made his way back to the ballroom and his place beside Benji on the fringes of the dance floor.

"Where did you run off to?" his friend asked.

"I was hoping our great host had something a bit stronger than sherry stashed in his study."

"Ah, very clever of you." Benji patted him on the back in sport. "And tell me you found an exquisite bourbon or scotch."

Andrew wouldn't share what he'd actually come across or his true reason for escaping the merriment around him. "Alas, it seems our hostess has hidden the good stuff." As he spoke, he kept his gaze trained on the entrance to the ballroom, waiting to see the woman dressed as night descend into the crowd.

"Do not look so despondent," Benji said. "Your side of the wager is nearly fulfilled and you can depart."

"I do not look despondent." Though, if he had to dance with one more simple-minded girl, Andrew was prepared to put himself out of his misery. "Besides, I have already satisfied our wager."

"The devil you have!"

Andrew looked about as members of the *ton* turned their looks upon them. "Do keep your obscenities down."

"Our wager stipulated the first to six dance partners without being approached by their sires after wins ten pounds. You most certainly have not met the number to conclude our wager and take the purse."

Andrew thought back. "There was the cross-eyed chit, the homely creature solidly on the shelf…" He held up his hand, counting the fingers as he went. "…the young girl with the horridly orange dress, oh, and do not forget the sisters who each demanded their turn."

"Ah-ha!" Benji said in triumph. "Only five. It so happens I myself am at five, as well."

It was then that *she* entered the room—and all thoughts of wagers, coin, and his dear friend fled his mind.

"Enough," Andrew commanded his partner to silence. If only every person in the room would do the same so he could behold her in peace.

The glow from the candles lining the walls and hanging from the ceiling showed her beauty for what it truly was: stunning. Exquisitely refined. And utterly dissimilar to any and all women he'd met recently, far surpassing them not only in beauty but poise.

She appeared nothing like he'd expected from her silent sobs and hunched shoulders cloaked in the darkness.

Now she stood tall—exuding a firm confidence that he at once admired and envied. The gems hanging from her neck and ears further enhanced the glow her presence cast on the room. Never would he think her capable of such a vulnerable persona as what he'd seen only moments before from his hidden vantage point in the study doorway.

A quick glance around the room told him that he wasn't the only one enthralled by her sudden appearance, as a few others took in the sight of her.

She spoke to the pair beside her, all serious as they descended the few steps and blended into the crowd. The older couple were likely her guardians, judging from their similar features and complexion—though their outward display of self-assurance aligned, as well.

Would she be as captivating when she spoke as she

was by sight alone? He could not help but wonder. On so many occasions, a pretty turn of the lips or a coy glance caught his attention only to be followed by a disappointing one-sided conversation, or worse yet, blank stares without a word uttered.

Andrew kept his eyes firmly on her, urging her to look his way—or better yet, walk in his direction.

His previous need to protect her fled.

The woman radiated poise and composure as she took in the room, as if not a thing in the world could dampen her night, her eyes traveling across the crowd, never lingering too long on any one person or group.

It was then that Andrew realized he wanted her. In his arms—and in his life.

And he would stop at nothing to have her.

# # #

Lady Lorelei de La Valette took in the scene around her. Elegantly gowned women danced with smartly dressed gentlemen, young debutantes hid amongst the palms on the fringes of the dance floor, and servants hurried to and fro with trays overflowing with food and drinks.

She loathed their superior attitudes, yet simultaneously envied them their excessive lifestyle.

After many years of travel, it seemed to her that she should feel no sense of unease when entering a room wherein she knew not a soul, but even to this day, she longed for a familiar face.

"You know how important this night is," her father, the Comte of Epernon, hissed in her ear once again. "These people will compliment your beauty, all while despising your French heritage."

"We have been over and over this, *Pere*." She used the French term and waited for the scolding she knew would follow.

Yet, it came from her mother, which was unexpected. "Lorelei, what have we told you?"

"I am to appear as nothing less than a lady born and raised amongst London's upper crust. I am to blend in with other debutantes and not give reason for anyone to remember me." She only hoped her moment of weakness before entering the ball did not show on her face. The tears had receded before they'd fully started, and she'd hurried to catch up, the night covering her seconds of doubt.

"Very good, my daughter," her father said. Though many would see his words as harmless, Lorelei knew them for what they truly were—a threat. The consequences if she failed would not only impact her, but also her parents.

She was tired of running. If she complied with what was asked of her then it was possible her sires, as well as herself, would come into favor and a new fortune. They were here for a specific task, which could be accomplished in little time, and then they would spirit her off back to France. Her mother's hope was that none would remember her presence.

"Smile, *ma petite*," her mother whispered as she stepped back and the trio moved farther into the grand ballroom.

Lorelei wanted to ask why they trusted De Pez and Bonaparte—and wanted particularly to know how being in his favor would benefit any of them. Instead, she lifted her chin in defiance and pasted a smile on her face, hoping no one could tell it didn't reach her eyes.

Her entrance into the room had also been carefully staged to maximize her exposure. They'd arrived late—after the receiving line had disappeared—but before the gentlemen had retired to the card room off the main ballroom. Her hair was swept and gathered high upon her head to reveal her slender neck and highlight her dark, exotic coloring. Her eyes, the color of moss, were outlined by a thin line of coal. Her lips held a hint of color, though not enough to start gossip. And her dress, conservative and outdated by French standards, favored a high neckline in the front but plunged in the back to show off her gracefully arched back. The midnight-blue satin clung to her tall frame, smoothly gliding to the floor and pooling about her slippered feet.

A delicate strand of cultured pearls hung around her neck, and teardrops dangled from each ear. They were the preferred stone of the English, and that suited Lorelei.

Taking the final slow step into the crowded ballroom, her parents blended into the background and Lorelei took a champagne flute from a passing servant to steady her shaking hand. Peeking over her shoulder, Lorelei confirmed that the comte and comtesse had indeed given her a bit of space, yet they still kept pace with her. It would not help her to have them shadowing her all eve.

It was known that Benjamin Davis, Lord Chastain, held a fondness for women, and Lorelei had no reservations about preying on that weakness.

Lorelei moved through a part in the crowd quickly, hoping her parents lost sight of her. The group of ladies stepped close, effectively covering her movements, and Lorelei switched directions, traveling parallel to the comte, successfully assuring she had a few moments to herself.

She knew not a soul in the room—nor all of London.

And that terrified her.

For a brief moment, she contemplated whether she'd be able to follow through on the task given to her. The stark reality was, she hadn't a choice.

She tilted her glass to her mouth in hopes it would cover what she was actually doing—searching the crowd.

The British stood on pomp and ceremony, which meant no man would approach her without a proper introduction. The comte had insisted she leave the introductions to him, as he was convinced many lords would flock to his side to discuss the ever-changing governmental systems and the key players in their home country. The political situation in France was strained, particularly in their interactions with England, for the War of the Second Coalition still raged on.

Though who these men and women thought the comte loyal to, she cared naught.

She would not pass on the opportunity to sample life in London society; it was a place she could belong. Amongst the finery, she could find the home she had been lacking, even if only for a short time, though she also understood the dangers of falling in with the wrong people. A group of established wallflowers adorned in every shade of pastel imaginable lined one wall. Lorelei knew to steer clear of the group, or she'd likely end up amongst the palms with them. Nor should she attract the attention of the wealthy, elderly gentlemen currently escorting the most well-to-do debutantes and elite courtesans about the dance floor.

No, she sought the notice of only one man.

She'd studied his portrait thoroughly on their journey to England.

His every feature was imprinted on her mind: the roundness of his cheeks, his fashionable sandy brown hair, and his penetrating stare. She wondered if, when they eventually met, she would feel any tenderness for him, or if he would take a genuine liking to her.

Her research told her he was an avid horseman who craved excitement, but also lavished himself with the finer things in life.

She searched the crowd once more.

Lord Chastain—Benji, as he was commonly referred to by his consorts—stood with another man just outside the room that would hold the evening's card game. He gave off the exact impression she'd expected: an entitled rakehell who stood on the fringe of society by choice. Both he and his friend stood tall and wore tailored suits that would rival the fashions in Paris. He was as handsome as his miniatures portrayed, but she found her gaze drawn to the man beside Chastain, who appeared equally at ease at the center of the crowd. She noted how other partygoers gave the men a wide berth.

Benji had the reputation of a womanizer and gambler, though there was nothing particularly extraordinary about his appearance to suggest either designation. Lorelei had expected a jovial man, but he laughed only at his companion's remarks and barely acknowledged anyone else who walked past.

However was she to attract his attention if he never took his eyes from his friend, she wondered? Truly, he looked nothing like a man she would ever call 'Benji,' which had always struck her as a child's name.

Her sires thought to accomplish—with all due haste—exactly what they'd journeyed to London for: unlimited access to Benjamin Davis, Lord Chastain, keeper of the plans to the fortified city of Carcassonne, located on a hilltop between the Atlantic and Mediterranean Sea. It had been long held that when Lord Chastain's father had fled France, he'd taken the only set of plans to Carcassonne—which also happened to be a detailed map outlining the best possible way to lay siege to the great trading city.

Lorelei, her glass in hand, moved along the side of the dance floor as the men conversed. While the room was filled with marriage-minded matrons and fortune-seeking fathers, she noted that no one approached the pair, and neither man put their name upon any girl's dance card.

How would her father obtain an introduction if both men kept so much to themselves?

Lorelei had decided even before their carriage arrived that it would be necessary for her to break free of her mother and father and seek her own introduction. Even then, she sensed her father had again spotted her and was currently staring daggers at her across the crowd as she maneuvered herself farther from him and closer to Chastain.

Though he would be angry with her, she'd gladly accept his wrath later, for he would never cause a scene in public.

Chastain's associate took in the milling crowd. His eyes landed on her briefly, then returned to her for a longer inspection. It felt as if his earnest gaze penetrated to her very soul, uncovered all her secrets, and found her wanting.

She sensed she should turn back and approach Lord Chastain when this man wasn't close, but something drew her attention back to him.

Lorelei smiled.

To her amazement, he smiled back, turned to Chastain and said a few words…then started in her direction.

The crowd moved out of his path as he walked toward her, his eyes never releasing hers.

It was then that she felt her first hint of trepidation. The man was stunningly handsome—not to mention, a friend of Chastain's—and he was coming straight for her, a smile still upon his face.

"I can do this," she mumbled to herself as panic set in. The lady next to her turned a pointed look at her before taking a step away, putting distance between herself and the young lady talking to no one. Lorelei would have done the same had she been in the woman's position.

Before long, the man stood before her. His eyes, while intense, were the softest hazel she'd ever seen.

"Good evening." His voice was a rich, deep baritone. "May I have this dance?"

She hadn't heard music playing, nor the voices of the great number of people surrounding her.

She had only eyes for him.

Shaking her head gently, she snapped from her daze. "Ah, well, it is by chance I have a free space later in the evening."

He smiled. "That is a shame, for I find myself without a proper dance companion at this very moment. Pity."

He made to walk away, but she touched his sleeve

ever so lightly, pulling her hand back before anyone saw. "I believe a spot may have opened only just now."

She needed more than a brief moment with this man, though he wasn't the one she'd originally sought.

"Then allow me to ask once more—but only once more," he said. "For I do not find myself in the habit of begging for dance partners. May I have this dance?"

"You may." She smirked. "If it so pleases you, your lordship."

She wanted to giggle at the pompous tone in her own voice. The English were not known for their candor, and a sense of intrigue settled on her at his forthright nature.

He reached toward her, and Lorelei started to retreat before she realized he only sought her dance card, tied loosely at her wrist. He held the card in his large hands and wrote his name upon the first line.

The Marquis of Drake.

The letters were written in a thick, bold script that seemed an embodiment of his masculinity and borderline arrogance.

"Shall we?" he asked, holding his arm out for her to take.

"I would enjoy nothing more, your lordship." Lorelei worked hard to suppress her accent. An import, as many were likely to call her, she did not wish to attract attention for her French blood, as many took offense knowing their countries battled and lives were lost every day. "It is a pleasure to make your acquaintance."

He spun her on to the dance floor, settling one arm around her lower back. "The pleasure is all mine, I assure you."

As they moved to the light strains of music floating

through the room, Lorelei caught sight of her father, only a few feet from Chastain. He should be pleased with her progress, aligning herself with someone close to Chastain, opening up the possibility for an introduction.

"May I inquire as to the name of my beautiful dance partner?" the marquis asked.

She returned her attention to him and her breath caught at the sight. Forcing herself to exhale, she answered, "Lady Lorelei de La Valette."

"Ah. While your accent is subtle, your skin tone gives away your French heritage, no?"

"*Oui.*" With her father out of hearing distance, Lorelei let herself fall into her native tongue, fearing naught from the marquis. He did not show himself to be a man entangled in the war between their nations.

"*Charmante.*" His skillful pronunciation had her smiling. He continued to look upon her. "I have not seen you about town. Are you newly arrived?"

"Correct, your lordship."

"Please, call me Drake or Andrew, as my *amis* do."

"That is not proper, your lordship."

He chuckled. "But what do you see as *propre?*" He paused, as if scouring his brain for any other French words hidden there. "A *femme* is most *captivant* when they are themselves, *non?*"

She took her gaze from his, knowing she blushed a deep crimson. No man had called her captivating that she could recall. "You are *juste*, your lordship." She hoped the couples swirling close by did not notice her embarrassment.

"*Je suis toujours juste, mademoiselle.*" He once again paused. "I fear that is the extent of my knowledge of your language."

"Well, you did very well, indeed."

"You have a much more solid grasp of English than I French."

"It is only *juste*, as I have spent many years learning about your country."

Something about him turned her back into the shy schoolgirl she'd been before her parents had changed her whole world. While she was well-traveled and highly educated, Drake gave the impression he'd seen and experienced more than was possible, given his youthful appearance.

"What brings you to my fair city?" he said, lapsing back into English.

"Oh, to escape the dreaded heat of India." It was an effort to keep a straight face, particularly when the marquis willingly continued with the farce.

"Is the land as wild as I have been told?" he asked, appearing equally serious.

It had been a while since she'd enjoyed such an enjoyable exchange. "There are parts still untraveled!" When he only stared, she continued, "—and I will not go on about the inconveniences of outsmarting the monkeys who seek at every turn to rob you of your food."

"From France to India and now England? I dare say, you must be appallingly exhausted after such feats of bravery!"

As they continued round the dance floor, she allowed herself to laugh. "I assure you that it takes more bravery to enter a crowded ballroom than to face down a lion determined to steal my boots and gnaw on the leather."

"Lions? Gnawing on your boots?" he said with bewilderment. "I do agree, I would rather face a whole den of tigers than one marriage-minded matron."

"What always helped me was my ability to scale an elephant and make off before any harm was done." She was enjoying her outlandish tale as much as it appeared he was.

"I must remember to request your counsel when I travel next."

"I would be more than happy to guide your expedition." She paused before continuing. "That is, if I am not indisposed at the time."

"I am sure you will find the time to help a friend. But might I inquire why you'd be indisposed?"

"Well, I may be exploring the colonies at that time."

"India? The colonies? By heavens, you put most English gentlemen to shame with your geographical exploits."

Lorelei forced herself to stop the banter, recalling the reason that she was here this eve. Their conversation, while amusing, did not suit her main objective. "I fear I am not as well traveled as I appear, though I did have the pleasure of visiting India in my youth, and do plan to sail for the colonies someday."

"As long as 'someday' is not today." He increased his hold on her, bringing her closer to him as they danced. "Back to my original question."

She'd completely forgotten how their conversation of exotic lands had started. "Which is?"

"Why are you in London, Lady Lorelei?"

While he asked one question, Lorelei expected the answer he sought was to another one altogether. "Not to find a husband, if that is what you wish to know."

"My suspicions about you were correct: you are the forthright kind." He looked at her appreciatively, and she relaxed once more. "And I must say, I am very disappointed to hear you are not on the market."

"And why is that?"

"Because I find myself with a lot to offer one such as yourself." When she continued to stare, a smirk on her face, he continued. "You see, I am titled, wealthy, handsome…and dare I say, charming?"

"Oh, you are very charming." Lorelei wanted to laugh but held back, not wanting to offend him. It was not that she feared hurting Drake's feelings, only how it would appear to others around them. "You will be happy to know, if I were not here on a political errand with my father, I would find you quite suitable."

She should rein in her flirtatiousness with the marquis and focus on an introduction to Chastain, but she was unable to stop herself. It was the first stimulating conversation she'd had since her departure from France. In her mother country, her parents' ever-changing residence was always open to educated men and woman who enjoyed discussing the evolving regime from King to Directory to the man who it appeared would be their next leader, Napoleon Bonaparte. Though the topics might bore another young lady, she found any subject with the potential for debate highly interesting. She'd usually been clever enough to persuade her father's associates to her way of thinking.

During one such conversation, she had even devised a method for solving the horrid stench from the crowded and polluted Paris streets—yet her father called her plans idealistic in nature, no more than the easily dismissed musings of a woman.

No one here in their rented London household spoke to her, and the men who came to see her father avoided her, knowing she was committed to a higher cause and thus not open to their advances. As any woman would, she enjoyed the marquis' undivided attention.

Though they hadn't discussed any subject of great import, his intelligence was clear in his wit.

The music stopped, signaling the end of their dance. "Thank you for restoring my wounded pride. May I request another dance later in the evening?"

"I am sure that would cause gossip of the worst sort, your lordship," she said formally, dropping in a shallow curtsy. "But as I do not much care what society deems proper, I would entertain another turn about the floor with a dance partner as skilled as yourself."

"Until then." He brought her hand to his mouth and pressed his lips to her fingers. After several long seconds, he released it. "May I escort you to your chaperone?"

Looking up, she noticed several sets of eyes on them, some couples stopped in mid-promenade to take them in, though she expected the gawking had more to do with the marquis than herself.

"Oh, that will not be necessary." Lorelei's father was close, she could feel his stare. She needed an introduction to waylay his scolding over straying from their plan. "I find myself parched. Would you be so kind as to escort me to the refreshment table?"

She'd handed her last glass to a passing servant before taking to the dance floor with Drake. Their walk would force them to pass by Lord Chastain, not having moved an inch since she and Drake—Andrew, as she now thought of him after their brief conversation—had taken to the dance floor.

As they walked the perimeter of the room, Andrew peppered her with questions about her trip from France, how she liked his wonderful city, and if she had plans to travel to Bath after the season ended. Lorelei gave him as many noncommittal responses as she could muster in an attempt to give him no useful information about herself or her family, while still hoping to keep his interest. She was pleased to note that their continued conversation had caught Chastain's attention.

The duke, her original intended target, stepped into their path as they drew close. She'd seen the look on his face before from other suitors, and prided herself on her ability to distract men from their own base thoughts upon meeting her for the first time. This night, she'd only planned to gain an audience with him, possibly pique his interest, and hope for him to call upon her soon.

"Drake," Chastain greeted them and turned a slight bow in Lorelei's direction. "My lady."

Lorelei couldn't believe her good fortune. She'd been in the room less than thirty minutes and now stood face-to-face with Chastain. She could only imagine her father's reaction as his child, a mere female, had gained an introduction before him.

Her mind whirled with the possibilities of gaining more ground than they'd planned for this evening, perhaps even a private conversation.

"Lord Chastain, may I introduce Lady Lorelei." Drake's words sounded guarded and not at all happy. "Her family is new to London."

Chastain smiled, a smirk that could only be described as smug. The pair had appeared to be friends earlier, but something about the way they now assessed each other led her to believe otherwise. She hoped that played nicely into her plans, which as yet were limited.

She coyly eyed Chastain from lowered eyelids as she

curtsied. "Lord Chastain, I am honored to make your acquaintance."

The marquis moved closer to her side.

Her words gained the response she sought. "The honor is my own, Lady Lorelei. Drake and I have been friends for more years than either of us can count."

The tension that had shadowed the trio moments before was alleviated, and both men smiled as they chatted about inconsequential topics.

"If you'll excuse us," Drake said as he again settled Lorelei's hand in the crook of his arm. "We were just on our way for refreshments."

"I find myself in need of another glass, as well." Chastain turned toward the table several paces behind him, not to be dismissed. "I shall accompany you."

"That would be delightful, my lord." And exactly what Lorelei had hoped he would say. She needed to find a way to speak privately with him without insulting Drake. While she very much enjoyed the marquis' company—and he was extremely pleasing to the eye— she had other matters on which to focus.

With sherry in hand, they moved toward the terrace doors. She knew the darkened gardens would be a perfect spot for a quiet conversation.

"Lady Lore—"

"Ah, there you are, my daughter."

Her father's voice sounded behind her, and she turned to greet him. His icy stare chilled her faster than the cold winds that moved across the English Channel.

"Father, may I introduce the Marquis of Drake and Lord Chastain, his dear friend." If her father's thought was to steal Chastain away before she had an opportunity to speak with him, he had underestimated how badly she wanted to impress him. "These fine London gentlemen were explaining to me the marvels of England's unpredictable weather patterns. A lady must be prepared for showers every time she leaves her home. How tiresome!"

"Very true, Lorelei." Her father turned to Chastain. "My daughter is very interested in London culture."

Her father, the Comte of Epernon, had never been a man with tact. He was used to getting what he wanted, when he wanted, at no cost of time or money to himself. But London was not France—and his foreign title meant little to the *ton*. Even if her father failed to realize this, Lorelei knew at least that much.

"Father, please!" Regretfully, she slipped her hand from Drake's arm and moved to Chastain. "Now is not the time for dreaded government talks. I believe Lord Chastain was about to escort me to the terrace for a spot of fresh air." She gave her father a pleading look, hoping he'd take the clue and keep Drake occupied.

"Very well, but please bring her back after she cools down a bit." He finally acknowledged the marquis. "Your lordship, I believe they have finally opened the card tables. Would you care to join me?"

Drake gave her one last lingering look before bowing and wishing her a wonderful evening. He'd wanted to stay and dance again, she could sense it, though he was too much the gentlemen to deny Chastain.

She watched her father and the marquis walk side by side to the card room. Though his back faced her now, the memory of Drake's stare lingered. Never had a simple look dug so deeply, making her question the consequences and lasting cost of her mission. There was nothing left to do but allow Chastain to guide her outside and into the cool night air.

Chastain, while every bit as well dressed as Drake, lacked something. From where her hand rested on his forearm, she did not feel the tight, corded muscle of a man who spent hours at his fencing club, and she suspected he did not possess the sculptured legs of a skilled horseman, as she'd been told. His tailor should be commended for the fine cut of his coat, which no doubt covered what he lacked beneath.

It was truly a shame that the marquis was not the man she sought, for after only a few short minutes in his presence, her interest had been significantly piqued.

But her word was her bond—and her allegiance lay not with her own needs and wants, but with what would garner her family approval from the man many said would take control of France. "Shall we, Lord Chastain?"

"Without further ado, my lady."

They walked arm in arm toward the terrace door. All the while, Lorelei refused to glance over her shoulder.

Chapter Two

Andrew stopped outside the card room and dared a glance in the direction from which he'd come. He regretted it immediately, as he was helpless to do anything but watch Chastain escort the enchanting Lady Lorelei out to the terrace and the secluded gardens beyond.

Whatever had bothered her earlier had clearly been pushed from her mind, something for which Andrew was grateful.

He hadn't the faintest idea why he cared. She was beautiful, of course—tall and slender in her blue gown. But he hadn't counted on her wit and intellect when he'd first seen her. A dance with a striking young woman was all he'd anticipated, but from the instant she'd spoken that had changed. He wanted more than a mere dance. He wanted to continue their conversation; to learn of all she'd done and where she had been in her short life.

Instead, he meandered about inside while Chastain had the pleasure of a few moments alone with her, which irritated him to no end. They'd been best friends since Benji had moved to England as a young child, the two attending school and university together and spending their seasons in London while their fathers fulfilled their obligations in Parliament, but still, Andrew was hesitant to trust him. After the early death of his father, the previous Lord Chastain, something had changed about Benji—he'd become more reckless, less wary of consequences. Their games had evolved from simple bets at White's Gentlemen's Club to risky investments in the shipping trade to even riskier ventures with women. Lots of women.

While Andrew had lived a rather untroubled existence thus far, he still cringed at how outlandish their friendly bets had become. It was no secret that both men appreciated the fairer sex—and what they could do for them—but Andrew had never set out to ruin his conquests. Toy with their emotions, perhaps. But Benji never shied away from it.

Damn Benji and his games.

And Lady Lorelei was not the type to be played with. What it was that made her different from others they'd occupied their idle time with, he couldn't say yet. Possibly it was her sophisticated nature—she'd been privy to more than just England, had beheld exotic coasts, seen much more than Andrew could claim. She was not one to be trifled with. From the way she held herself, Andrew suspected she was used to doing the toying. One day, she would find a man who would treat her as she deserved to be treated: a lady of the first waters, a woman to be cherished and cared for.

Neither he nor Benji were that man. Both would seek to possess her for their own purposes, whether it was financial gain or carnal pleasure, yet neither of them could ever deserve a woman such as her. Though she presented herself as educated and well-traveled, he had no doubt that she was pure.

Part of him wished to be the man for her.

They were too old for this type of tomfoolery, but it seemed only he realized that fact. His mistakes of the past had been difficult to move past. Chastain could only keep at it for so long before his past came calling—as Andrew's had ten years earlier.

Suppressing the memories—a woman shamed and a child he'd been forced to forget—he turned back to the card room. If he'd thought there was anything he could do to right those wrongs, he would have done so, gone to any extreme to prove he'd changed…for the better. But it had been made clear to him long ago that neither his attentions, nor his wealth and title, were needed.

But tonight wasn't about dredging up the past or planning a new future, he reminded himself. He put the past where it belonged, behind him. Forgotten. He couldn't change it. Nor could he go back in time and live up to what had been expected of him then, but now was different. He'd worked tirelessly to improve his standing, not cause any more heartache to others. Even though Chastain sought at every turn to pull him back into their philandering ways, Andrew resisted.

"Marquis?" A servant asked. "Will you be playing this hand?"

He looked up to see a full table staring back at him, awaiting his move. The men surrounding him tolerated him because of the title he held. He was unable to escape the legacy of goodness his father had left for him. It was a responsibility he'd been too young to accept and fulfill with any measure of success, nor had he wanted to in his youth.

He needed to shake off his absurd attraction to the woman. His life—that of a confirmed bachelor and semi-reformed scoundrel—wasn't the kind one brought a woman into. The need to settle down and start a family was definitely not something he'd ever dreamed of, nor wanted—though Lady Lorelei was beauty personified, and her wit and intellect had him second-guessing the future he'd planned for himself. It would not take long for the rumors about him, most of them true, to reach her family, and then she would turn away from him, no matter how he felt about her. It would take work to convince her otherwise, and that was the exact reason he couldn't further their acquaintance, whether he wanted her or not.

His thoughts were ridiculous and illogical. The Marquis of Drake, a previous rakehell and philanderer, did not fancy having any feeling other than lust for a woman. There was no other feeling he could be experiencing after a mere few moments of dancing.

But the need to protect her from Chastain and his less-than-noble intentions was strong, even though he knew they shouldn't be based on his own feelings for her.

"Oh, yes." Andrew reached into his coat and pulled several billfolds out, laying them on the table. "Please, deal me in. I am ready for a spirited game, gentlemen."

The only man at the table he was unfamiliar with was Lady Lorelei's father, the comte, but if his pockets held riches the likes of his fine suit, then Andrew would have a very fruitful evening indeed. Though it would be nothing short of appalling to set his sights on Lorelei's father's coin.

He needed to keep his mind on the game at hand and not the game Benji was playing on the terrace.

Women were a luxury that he could not afford to possess, at least during hours before the midnight bell.

Andrew played hand after hand, winning more than he lost and managing to amass a sizable stack of money. The comte, alternatively, bowed out more often than not, claiming the cards were not in his favor. His folding didn't unsettle Andrew. He much preferred not to best Lorelei's father.

After a few more hands and two more drinks, Benji joined him, taking a seat recently vacated by a baron who'd lost the small amount he'd joined the table with. Andrew eyed his friend, barely stopping himself from denouncing the man as a reprobate to everyone sitting at the table, including the girl's father.

"Gentlemen." The comte stood. "Thank you for a rousing game, but I must remember my duty to my wife and daughter. I look forward to another game soon, as France lacks the spirit of the conquest at the gaming tables. Until next time." He bowed curtly and went on his way.

"Tell me you did not," Andrew accused as both he and Benji watched Lorelei's father depart the room.

"Why, I haven't the faintest idea to what you are referring."

The smug smile on his friend's face told him the man knew exactly to what he was referring and that he'd most likely done exactly what Andrew hoped he hadn't. "Do not toy with me."

"I would not dream of any such thing." Benji needlessly adjusted his intricately knotted tie. "Particularly when there is someone nearby I would so much prefer to toy with."

"She is a lady," Andrew whispered venomously.

Several players at the table eyed the pair. A crowded room was not the ideal place to start a verbal confrontation. "Lord Chastain, may I interest you in a walk about the main hall? I have heard that our host has the most enthralling art on display."

Once alone, his friend turned on him. "What has you all in a lather? It cannot be solely due to the fact that I escorted the lovely Lady Lorelei to the terrace before you'd had the opportunity to do the same."

"You know perfectly well it hasn't anything to do with you escorting her outside, but all to do with your behavior once you were out of my sight," Andrew fumed.

"I know our wagers well enough to know I cannot garner any points for what occurs out of your viewing."

"That is exactly it: nothing should happen out of my viewing—or in my view, for that matter."

"Why ever not?"

"Because Lady Lorelei is not just another young debutante."

"You have that correct. The woman is incredibly alluring."

"…and rich…and foreign…and not for either of us to touch."

"Who says?" Benji asked.

"I say!" he shouted.

Benji stared hard and then his brow cocked. "Ah, I see. You are captivated by the woman. Another of your obsessions, I presume."

"I most certainly am not captivated by her."

"That was not a question, but a statement of fact. She is no different than any other silly chit we've taken a liking to…and furthermore, your obsessive nature is highly unattractive."

"Obsessive nature? You haven't any idea of what you speak."

"Oh, I do not?" Benji questioned. "What about all this time and energy you waste at that pile of stones you call an estate?"

"What about it?"

"It is a waste, I tell you."

They squabbled like schoolboys. "That property has been in my family for generations and has needed repairs for over two decades."

"Then have your steward see to it."

"I do not trust his judgment in all matters."

"Ah-ha!" Benji pointed to the sky as if he'd come to some grand conclusion. "See? Infatuated you are."

The man's spot-on assessment shouldn't have angered Andrew, but it did.

Andrew was man enough to admit he was drawn to beautiful women, but add Lady Lorelei's adept mastery of conversation and her sharp wit—what man would not be instantly enthralled by her?

"And furthermore, I think a small wager will help you overcome your asinine obsession toward a girl you do not even know. Now, if you will excuse me, Lorelei—"

"Lorelei?" Andrew asked.

"Oh, yes. Did I not tell you? Lorelei suggested we forgo formalities since we are now *friends*."

Andrew didn't relish the way Benji emphasized 'friends.' And *furthermore* he wanted to cuff him and throw his friend against the art-covered wall. The sound of shattering glass and Benji's head thumping the hard surface would be rather satisfying, even if it didn't rectify the situation.

Though Lorelei seemed wise for her years, every instinct in Andrew screamed to protect her, do all he could to safeguard her from the likes of Benji—and the rest of society.

"As I was saying, Lorelei..." Benji obviously enjoyed his friend's dour mood. "...promised me a dance. But the evening is young and there is time for more than a mere dance, I should think. So I must not keep her waiting."

"You go too far." Andrew should have warned the comte about Chastain—though that would insinuate Andrew counted rakehells as his closest friends.

Benji pushed past him and started back down the hall to the ballroom.

"Chastain."

Benji turned. "I have told you, do not call me that. And do us both a favor and forget about Lorelei and whatever noble feelings or infatuation you've developed for her after one simple dance. She is naught to either of us, and most certainly nothing more than any other warm female body." His friend gave him a penetrating look and dropped his voice. "And we both know what we do with warm female bodies."

Andrew knew exactly what they did with them.

They used them until they lost their luster.

And that caused a wave of sickness in his gut.

"Do not wait for me to depart. I will see you on the morrow." Chastain resumed his stride, leaving Andrew behind.

If he pushed the subject, and his friend, then Andrew knew Chastain would only seek out Lady Lorelei with more vigor. It was better Andrew forgot about the woman. Then, perhaps Chastain would, too.

Chapter Three

Lorelei walked into the drawing room of her parents' rented London townhouse with all the grace and poise demanded of a woman of her age and social status. The daughter of a French noble, even though residing in England, was to carry herself above anyone perceived to be of a lower class.

At the moment, her poise had naught to do with rubbing her social status in another's face, but all to do with appearing confident and above reproach to her parents—for she knew they would soon bombard her with questions about the previous evening.

She took her customary seat next to her mother and across the small table from her father's armchair.

The trio sat quietly, awaiting someone to break the silence.

She wouldn't be the first to speak. Their carriage ride home the evening before had been silent as well, with each lost in their own thoughts. Her father had likely been planning his next move, and her mother probably dwelled on her own lack of suitable evening attire if they were to stay an extended period of time in London.

And Lorelei… She thought of all sorts of things that would certainly lead both her parents to lose confidence in her: the cut of the marquis' fine suit, his secure hold on her as they'd twirled on the dance floor, and the way he'd glared at her and Lord Chastain as they'd departed the ballroom to seek a breath of fresh air. The look should have sent off red flags of warning and cautioned her to keep her distance from the man, yet she still found herself drawn to him.

"Lore?" her mother's quiet voice called her back to the present. "Your *pere* asked you a question."

Distraction was the one thing her father simply detested. "Oh?"

"Did you spend your time wisely with Lord Chastain?" her father repeated.

"Wisely? I am unsure."

"Why is that?" the comte asked in French. He sat in his armchair, *The London Post* spread across his lap.

"We spoke on the terrace, but he did not appear overly invested in our conversation. Then he asked for a dance and said he must retire to the card room." The man's behavior had been suspect, especially when they'd had a moment alone—a time when most gentlemen sought to press their advantage with a kiss. "But once he came to claim his dance, he seemed to be very interested in every word I spoke and held me closer than was proper."

It was fairly obvious that Chastain's interest in her grew once they were in view of others, specifically the Marquis of Drake, though there was no reason to share that fact with the comte.

"His family is naturally an apprehensive lot, as well

they should be." Her father folded the paper he'd been reading before her arrival and set it on the table between them, crushing any hope she'd had of avoiding their questions until she knew more. "Did you secure a continued acquaintance with him?"

She thought of their conversation on the terrace. She'd stood close to him in the shadows, trying to appear agreeable to any advances he might attempt, possibly even a stroll into the dark gardens below. She'd complimented his intricate necktie, ran her fingers down the sleeve of his coat, and even spoke of the infallibility of his lineage, but naught had drawn the man in.

"It is a simple question," her mother clucked.

What her mother didn't seem to remember was that men—at their basest nature—were unpredictable. Her parents had spent too many years together and had come to know each other well—far beyond most couples. They worked and lived together; on the surface, they trusted each other implicitly. Part of Lorelei wished for a connection such as theirs, easy and straightforward. Yet, what her parents lacked was love and genuine affection for one another. She'd never seen them embrace nor share a kiss. She often wondered where each would be if their previous government hadn't seen fit to demand the comte and comtesse further their relationship.

"We spoke, we danced, and I assume he will not be able to fight his natural maleness. He is interested, that much is clear. I've no doubt he will come to heel and either give us what we seek, or we'll find he has no knowledge of his family's past and the treasures entrusted to them." Lorelei hoped her voice sounded firm and unwavering because inside, she dreaded failing. Not so much for her country—as her parents did—but for her parents, who had invested their time and energy in training her. And, while unspoken, they all feared displeasing the man coming to power. Her father had insisted it was integral to their survival that their new allegiance be demonstrated in a way that could never be questioned by De Pez or Bonaparte himself.

Her mother smiled while her father settled back into his seat to read his morning paper.

"And what about the other man with whom you danced?" her mother asked. "He seemed quite smitten, as well."

"I danced with many men, Mother." She attempted to push off the inquiry.

"The first man—what did you say his name was?" She looked to the comte for the answer. "He was speaking with Lord Chastain when we arrived."

"Drake." The comte huffed and returned to his paper. "The man is harmless."

Lorelei kept silent, waiting for the topic to change.

"He is anything but," her mother, Camille, countered. "He kept a close eye on her all evening."

"I agree with *Pere*. The marquis was nice and a good dancer, but that is all."

"A woman's intuition, you both shall see."

Lorelei hoped her mother's sixth sense was off, and the marquis would not seek to further their *friendship*.

"Do we know anything about the man?" her mother continued to prod. "There is the possibility that Chastain knows exactly what he has, and has informed someone of its existence."

The idea was absurd, and Lorelei only hoped her father thought the same. "The marquis is a friend of Chastain's, that is all." She cast an uninterested glance between her parents. "Besides which, the Chastains have always been loyal to their pact with France. They did our country a favor removing the plans from within our borders—and might I remind you, we only seek to find the plans and remove them from Chastain's hold to deliver them to De Pez. We are not here to harm anyone, out a French loyal, nor cause a scandal." Though she questioned their methods daily.

"Well stated, my daughter!" Her father praised her. "You remember all we've instilled in you. You will make a fine French asset for years to come."

The pride in his tone grated on her nerves. She was a young woman with her whole life ahead of her, yet her parents were determined to sign her over to Napoleon Bonaparte, a man set on taking France as his own—reserved and resigned to giving up the chance to continue the de La Valette name.

Lorelei knew if she continued in her parents' footsteps, she would not have children. The thought of subjecting a husband—which her government would hand select for her—and her children to a life at the mercy of a fickle government and their ever-changing agenda was something she could not abide.

She'd spent many afternoons pondering the possibilities of a different future. Maybe handing over the plans and walking away, never to be bothered again. Dare she dream of her parents coming with her? Oh, to live a quiet life, mayhap find a patch of land to call her own since her father's title and supposed wealth hinged on the generosity of the Directory or whoever successfully wrested power from it.

Lorelei held no stock in the ability of Bonaparte to keep control of France, nor even to keep his own head upon his shoulders.

A light knock sounded at the door, and all three turned, fearful of being overheard. When they'd traveled to London, they'd done the socially acceptable thing by hiring local servants to assist in their townhouse. Her father worried bringing their own trusted kind would call attention to them and negatively impact their acceptance within the *ton*.

They'd been relegated to a life of being watched continually and fearing servant gossip would ultimately be their downfall.

"Enter." Her father switched back to English and focused on his paper once more.

"Comte," their butler said in greeting. "Lady Lorelei has a caller—a gentleman."

"A caller?" The light note of her mother's words cheered the room. "Do show him in."

Maybe she'd brought Chastain to heel sooner than she'd expected.

"Well, I do not see how I ever doubted your charms, Lore. You are as beautiful as your mother ever was in her prime."

"Thank you, *Pere*." Lorelei wondered if her father realized the insult to both her and her mother in his words. She turned, catching her mother's wounded look seconds before it was replaced with a prim smile.

Footsteps could be heard coming from the hall— two sets, to be exact.

Lorelei stood to greet her guest, but was startled to see the butler come through the door with a bouquet of the most beautiful blue flowers she'd ever beheld.

"My heavens," she whispered.

The butler moved to set the arrangement on the

long table behind the lounge her mother sat upon.

Lorelei turned back to the door, ready to welcome Lord Chastain, but was surprised to see another man standing just within the door.

"Lady Lorelei, thank you for seeing me unannounced," the Marquis of Drake said as he bowed to her. With a smile, he moved farther into the room and took her mother's hand, bringing it to his lips. "Comtesse of Epernon, I hadn't the pleasure to make your acquaintance last evening."

Lorelei stood, frozen in her spot, as she watched her mother blush at Drake's attention. He was every bit as entrancing in the daylight hours as he had been in the low lighting of a ballroom. He wore riding attire of the darkest ebony, fitted perfectly to his muscular thighs. His coat strained across his broad shoulders in what was the latest London fashion. While tight garments were unfitting to gentlemen of a more portly nature, they suited Drake.

"Comte, it is a pleasure." The marquis issued a curt bow.

Her father only eyed Drake, not saying a word.

"Oh, my lord, you have brought the most handsome flowers. Wherever did you find such blossoms at this time of year?"

"I traveled to the far reaches of the continent to find flowers that were worthy."

"Just since we last danced?" The room and everyone else in it receded.

His green-flaked hazel eyes sparkled mischievously, much as she'd expect from a child caught with their hands on the pie cooling in the kitchen window. "Alas, I only sent word to my country estate."

"Is your world truly so small?" she asked.

"My world seems trivial at the moment in the light of your radiance."

"A-hem." Her father cleared his throat, effectively extinguishing the warm tendrils of need that had started to creep through her at the marquis' words. "Would you care to have a seat, my lord?"

"No, thank you." He took one last look at her. His gaze offered much more than she could ever want. "I must be going. I only wished to bestow Lady Lorelei with a gift that is but a fraction as lovely as she."

His words were the height of impropriety, and would only be overlooked when spoken by a couple already betrothed. The marquis spoke as if he courted her, yet she suspected he was not the kind. After their dance, she'd overheard gossip about the marquis and Chastain, both known scoundrels and confirmed rakehells. They'd spent years shocking the *ton* with their less-than-honorable escapades. Despite having researched the duke, she hadn't realized the extent of his rakishness.

"I will bid you all adieu." He bowed to the room at large. "I hope to see you again soon, Lady Lorelei. Comte and Comtesse, do have a fair day."

With those words, he strode from the room, the sureness of his step never faltering. Their butler followed, closing the door behind them.

"A woman's intuition is never wrong," her mother hissed and fell back onto the chaise lounge. "Whatever are we to do? His attention cannot be rewarded or encouraged."

The comte sat in silence, and Lorelei suspected he awaited her response in order to gauge her interest in the marquis. He was a wise man, her father, who knew the best way to feel out any person from whom he sought answers. Silence was usually the superior method, allowing the person in question to out themselves and their intentions.

Lorelei recognized his methods well. And she also knew better than to show any amount of interest in Drake, his extravagant display, or his future activities. "I suggest we discard the flowers posthaste in case we have any other callers this day."

Her father eyed her, no doubt judging her every word, but most of all her actions. "Very well, again wise."

"...and while we are at it, inform the butler that the marquis is to be turned away if he calls again." Lorelei grabbed the bouquet of flowers, nestled in an expensively engraved vase, and made to leave the room.

"Where are you going?"

"To dispense with this atrocious display. No need to have the servants gossiping any more if we ask one to throw them out with the noon-day scraps. You can be certain word would reach the marquis." The arrangement was heavier than it appeared. Her arms strained under the weight. "If you don't mind, I will return shortly."

Her mother smiled. "Very well," she said approvingly.

Lorelei walked down the hall, but instead of turning toward the kitchen, she continued straight and veered to the left, pushing through a swinging door to the servants' stairwell. The passage narrowed as she climbed the two flights of stairs, forcing herself upright under the increasing weight of the flowers. Thankfully, the passage was deserted at this hour, most servants busy cleaning various bedrooms and the main hall.

Pushing the door at the top of the stairs open

slightly, she looked both ways down the hall. It was more likely she'd run into her maid in her suite, but Lorelei had come to trust the girl since she'd been assigned to her the previous week. Her maid, Isabelle, had youth on her side, but little else. With deft fingers and a chipper disposition, she attended to all of Lorelei's needs. When she was assured that no one was in sight, Lorelei quickly hurried to her room and placed the flowers upon her dressing table.

Her mother and father rarely called on her within her own rooms, so she had little worry that they'd discover she hadn't disposed of the arrangement. Besides which, she liked the sight and smell of them. Never had anyone given her a gift, beyond the small trinkets her father bestowed on her during the winter holidays each year. Even her birthday was not a day of celebration.

She sighed. It was time she returned to the drawing room, but she truly wanted to rush after the marquis, thank him for calling and for the beautiful gift, and tell him that if things were different, she'd welcome his attentions. His coach would be gone by now, however, taking him and Lorelei's hopes for any sort of future with him.

These thoughts had no place in her life. There was no point in wishing and dreaming of things that would never be hers—the Marquis of Drake especially. He was a man of extreme wealth, title, and passion. He could do far better than tying himself to a woman embedded in his country for the sole purpose of espionage and treason.

She shook any thought of him from her mind and rubbed her hands together to be rid of any trace of the flowers she'd just carried.

She could change little in her life at the moment.

Once she'd found the plans—and thus demonstrated her parents' allegiance to the new ruling faction—the opportunity to escape her current life would present itself, she was sure of it. Her mother and father could be made to understand her desires for more than the life they'd chosen for themselves. It included a home—not a rented townhouse in a foreign city, but a stable home with a garden in back and a large hearth. Where? She could only guess as of now. She enjoyed the liveliness of London, however. Mayhap her parents would decide to remain here.

Wandering to the window, she drew the curtain aside and stared at the street below her second-story opening. Neat brick homes lined the lane with a cobbled road between, barely wide enough for two carriages to pass one another.

One such carriage sat parked before her townhouse even now.

Squinting, Lorelei wondered who could be visiting her parents. No one sat on the driver's box of the phaeton, only big enough for two, with a pair of smart-looking, matching grey horses hitched to it. She scanned the walk and front steps below and, sure enough, the marquis strolled the walk.

The man continued to surprise her. First asking her to dance without so much as an introduction, and then appearing with flowers. She wondered who had shared her directions with him.

Maybe there was enough time to ask him just that question.

#

Andrew lingered outside the comte's townhouse, taking a few moments to calm his nerves. The last twelve hours had been spent giving orders and rushing about to make sure his flowers looked perfect. And now he hesitated to leave, for he had nowhere to go. He'd thought about going to White's for a meal, or popping into his fencing club for a quick match, but neither appealed.

He'd expected more from his visit with Lorelei. A private moment was out of the question, but possibly an invitation to accompany them to a ball or dinner party. His hopes had been dashed when she'd accepted the flowers and the comte had made clear he wasn't welcome to stay.

There was little chance of his gaining her favor, or advising her on Chastain, if he wasn't able to speak with her.

Staring up at her townhouse, Andrew sighed.

It was past time for him to depart, for it would do him no good to be observed lurking around their house.

Before he could climb onto the box seat, the front door opened. He froze.

"Your lordship?" Lady Lorelei said. She shielded her eyes from the glare of the late-morning sun. "Is something amiss?" She lifted her gown and stepped down to the walk. The home across the way blocked the sun, and she was able to lower the hand.

Andrew instantly took it in his and raised it to his lips, sweeping a light kiss across her wrist. "Lady Lorelei," he said. He released her hand and stepped back, hoping she didn't notice the nervous perspiration on his palms.

"Everything is wonderful."

"Is something wrong with your carriage?" She glanced over his shoulder, taking in both horses and rig. "We have a stable in back if you require assistance with anything."

"All is as it should be, I promise you." The location wasn't ideal for warning her against Chastain, but at least the walk was abandoned, and the door behind her only stood partly ajar. When he saw a flash of material in the crack, he knew a butler hovered inside. "I should be going. Thank you for accepting my call without sending my card round first."

She smiled, tentatively, appearing as nervous as he. "I am happy you came—and thank you for the flowers, they are beautiful."

Nowhere near as beautiful as you, he thought, but kept silent, afraid to look the unexperienced lad with his first lady love. Which was preposterous, for he'd only come to warn her about Chastain's less-than-honorable intentions.

Though he would admit, the way her dark hair cascaded down her back, as though her maid hadn't had time to arrange it before she'd left her chamber, drew his notice. And her olive eyes, shadowed by her dark lashes, had him drowning in a sea of green.

"Your lordship?"

"I beg your pardon," he replied. "I was…" Lost in your eyes? Imagining my fingers running through your hair? "…thinking of the many engagements I have today. I really should be going."

Her puzzled expression almost had him reaching for her hand again, but he clenched his fists at his sides, resisting the temptation.

"I see." Lady Lorelei crossed her arms, closing herself off from him. "Do have a lovely day."

He regretted his words immediately. "And you also. Might I interest you in a ride through Hyde Park?"

"Now?"

"Oh, no." He was making a mess of things; it would be best if he turned tail now and fled before he said something truly embarrassing. "Possibly tomorrow—or any day after."

Any man who knew him would be giddy with laughter over the mockery he was making of himself.

"I should enjoy that greatly, your lordship." She smiled. "I will have to inquire with my parents—"

"Naturally," he cut in.

"—but I would find pleasure in that. I have seen very little of your city since my arrival."

A man cleared his throat and they both looked in the direction of the step, where a young lad stood, a satchel slung over his shoulder. "Morning post, my lady."

"Oh, thank you, Gustavo." The lad beamed at her words and handed Lorelei a few envelopes. "I will bring them to father right away."

Andrew felt a sliver of envy for the way Lorelei looked at the boy. There was little to be jealous of, for he'd only danced with her once and brought her flowers. He had no designs on her—nor would he ever. He was not looking for a wife. He reminded himself that he'd only come out of a need to protect her.

Lorelei glanced through the letters when the post boy moved on to his next delivery, an awkward silence falling on them.

"I will bid you farewell." He bowed, but she continued to stare at the envelope in her hands, her knuckles white from grasping it so tightly. "Are you unwell?"

At his words, the butler opened the door behind her and glanced out.

Finally, she looked to the marquis once more, but her former ease was gone, her shoulders tensed and her eyes wide with concern.

"I must go," she said, not waiting for his response before she fled into the house. The door slammed behind her—no doubt the butler conveying his suspicion of Andrew.

Chapter Four

Andrew stepped down from the carriage in front of his townhouse and flipped the reins to his waiting footman before straightening his overcoat. His morning had taken an odd turn, but nevertheless, Lady Lorelei had received him and she'd loved the flowers. The comte had been gracious, though not overly welcoming. No member of the *ton* would look unfavorably upon their daughter being courted by a marquis, even if said marquis had a less-than-stellar past.

He'd thought long and hard the previous night about forgetting the woman, continuing on as if they'd never met and sparks hadn't flown between them. He had little doubt it would have been for the best, yet instead he found himself rising to send a servant to his hothouse for the perfect flowers to present to her. Giving a woman flowers was not something he was used to doing. A shiny bauble here or there, of course. Silky scarlet-red undergarments, most definitely. But flowers? Heavens, no. They did not benefit him in any fashion.

It nagged at him the way their visit had ended. He

should have followed her back inside, if only to make sure she was well after receiving the letter in the post.

His most significant failure, however, was neglecting to warn her about Chastain. Now, he reasoned that the likelihood of her ruin decreased significantly if he simply remained close to her.

"Good day, Alfred," he said when the front door opened.

"Good day. Lord Chastain awaits you in your study."

It was almost as if his thoughts had conjured the man. It was early for Chastain to be about. At this hour, he was usually entertaining his guest from the previous night, ensconced in her bed.

His friend paced before the hearth, facing Andrew when he entered the study. "Where have you been?"

"I was out." He wasn't about to tell him he'd been at Lady Lorelei's townhouse. "What are you pacing for?"

"We were to leave first thing after morning meal for Sasha's annual festival at Eggerhart Quarry." Benji threw up his hands like a petulant child denied a sweetmeat. "If we do not depart with all haste, all the choice girls will be picked over."

He'd forgotten the one thing that both he and Benji lived for: Madame Sasha's annual masquerade ball at her country estate. It was a fortnight full of debauchery during which Madame Sasha introduced a new crop of courtesans to exclusive men of the *ton*. Her guests were encouraged to sample the Madame's goods and make offers on any girl they found to their liking.

Each year, Sasha delivered on the promises made in her invitation. Men left their wives, children, and responsibilities behind to flock to the country house party for several nights of delight with the chance of returning to town with a new mistress.

Other men, like Benji and himself, enjoyed the diversion, but were less likely to settle on one girl for more than a few nights. They much favored Madame Sasha's London establishment—Craven House—to meet their needs.

"Please, temper your urgency." Andrew poured himself a drink and, upon second thought, gave Benji one, too. He was on edge and could use the heat. "It is only a few short hours' journey, and within a day, you'll tire of the festivities and be ready to return to town."

Taking his glass, Benji downed the liquid in one gulp. "Let us be off already."

"I am unsure I can go."

"What? You jest, certainly."

"I fear I do no such thing. Something has come up and I must remain in town."

"What could have happened since last eve? Wait a moment…"

Andrew knew from the smirk on his friend's face that he'd reached the correct conclusion. "I have business—"

"Business… Lady Lorelei is business now, is she?"

"Who mentioned Lady Lorelei? As you well know, I have many responsibilities. I do not relish the way you squander your title and estate while you focus solely on indulging your own needs."

"You are bloody cunning," Benji said. "You still fancy the chit."

"And if I do?"

"She is captivating, in that exotic way." Benji tapped his forefinger against his chin in thought. "Eyes that look into your very soul. But if I am being honest, I only care about how heavenly it would feel to be embedded deep inside her—"

"She is a lady. Have a little respect." The concept was one neither man had ever thought much about, since their only true use for a woman up until then had been to afford them pleasure. A warm bed for the night—or several, depending on how welcoming her charms were.

Benji had a look of utter confusion on his face. "I will admit, I pondered the idea of gaining a private moment with the girl, mayhap spirit her off to one of the empty rooms above."

"All I mean to say," Andrew said, "is that Lady Lorelei is young and new to England. She deserves better than men who favor her only to get a glimpse of what her silk evening dress hides. We are not rutting boys, straight out of university."

His friend thought over his words before speaking. "Then I propose a truce."

"What type of truce, exactly?" he asked skeptically.

Benji was back to his easygoing, devil-may-care self. "Neither of us pursues her."

"Go on."

"No talking, no touching, do not even dream of her at night—a simple dance is out of the question altogether."

It was better than he'd hoped for—his desire to protect her would be moot, leaving him free to return to his daily life. "You would agree to that?"

And hope that Lorelei's allure faded with time.

"Most assuredly." Benji moved toward the door. "Now that that is settled, shall we be off?"

The man's agreement had come too quickly. Their

long acquaintance allowed Andrew the clarity to see past Benji's words to the heart of the matter. His friend knew he wanted something—whether it be a woman or a horse, mattered not—and therefore, in accordance with their good-natured rivalry, Benji would make sure he acquired it first.

"As I said earlier," Andrew said, "something with my estate has arisen and I cannot delay addressing the issue. But, by all means, please go and give Sasha my best. I do regret not attending."

"Very well," Benji said skeptically. "I believe I can manage without you this one year, but under no circumstances will I give excuses to Sasha for you. Send word yourself."

"Then I do hope you are overtaken by highwaymen on your journey."

Benji laughed. "And I will give them what-for and send them on their way, relieved of their own weapons."

"I expect nothing less."

"And it will highly impress Madame and her girls. My tales of unmanning an unsavory highwayman, all to reach them. Why, their corsets will untie themselves, I suppose."

His friend had one thing on his mind, and, thankfully, it did not start with an L—neither Lorelei nor love. Yet, those two words were all Andrew could think of.

Maybe it would be wise for him to spend time in the arms of a willing woman in order to forget about a certain girl.

Instead, he said, "Yes, I agree, they will fall to your feet in ecstasy when you retell your harrowing journey to deflower them. I truly wish I could be there, but I must meet with my steward posthaste."

"Then I will not keep you. Shall we have dinner at White's upon my return?"

"If I have returned from my country estate, for certain."

"I will think of you during my time of debauchery."

"Please, do not," Andrew called after his friend as he left the room.

He despised lying, especially to someone he considered as close as family. That he did so with Benji, agreeing to a truce with which he had zero intention of complying, set him on a path he was reluctant to go down. He'd worked hard to mend the ways of his youth, putting his transgressions behind him.

With Benji out of town and away from the rumor mills, Andrew could advance his relationship with Lorelei in a proper way, if he were so inclined. Part of him feared her allure extended beyond the competition with Benji for her attention—that she was more than a prize to be won.

Mentally, he made a list of things one did when courting a woman. His list fell decidedly short as he was at a loss after flowers. He realized he was not versed in much past lifting a girl's skirts and giving them pleasure. Without that, what drew a woman to a man? He was in over his head and knew it.

# # #

Lorelei paced her room—back and forth and then back again.

Days had passed, and she hadn't been called upon since Andrew had brought the flowers. Each day she attended a tea here and a dinner party there, all in hopes of gaining Lord Chastain's attention once more, but he'd been mysteriously absent as of late. Her family's contact in London had been working hard to procure invitations for the comte to all the finest homes with the most elite families.

Added to Chastain's lack of attendance was the fact that people avoided both Lorelei and her parents. Lorelei was ignored by young women, and gentlemen only approached her father. They were doing a dreadful job of appearing inconspicuous.

The envelope in her pocket almost burned a hole in her morning dress. It hadn't been meant for her, and keeping knowledge of its existence from her father would cause irreversible harm and distrust if it were ever discovered.

She slipped the letter, addressed to the comte, from her pocket for the tenth time in the last hour. Taking the thin piece of paper from the envelope, she unfolded it and glanced over the words. It was written in her native tongue to prevent the household staff from reading it, should it fall into the wrong hands.

Comte of Epernon,

I grow impatient with your lack of information and progress in a certain matter. If your efforts are not redoubled with all haste, do not think to return. As expected, assistance will be dispatched if you are unable to fulfill your obligations.

De Pez

A new hopelessness filled her. The threat was clear, and called her family to immediate action or face the consequences.

While the comte had advised his family of the necessity of their cooperation in this scheme to help De Pez in order to save themselves, Lorelei had little doubt that De Pez would gain far more than her family would once the plans were safely handed over. The comte and his wife were known sympathizers of Louis XVI, and thus must demonstrate their support for Napoleon if they wished to return to France. Anything short of that meant they would never be safe from those who would turn them over for the bounty that would surely be on their heads.

If she hadn't intercepted the letter, she was certain her father would have never shared it with her. His years of protecting her from the volatility of his chosen life needed to end. Lorelei was as much a part of their present situation as the comte and comtesse, or had they forgotten about signing over their only child?

She wasn't a pawn to be used but not entrusted with secrets.

She'd given up the hope—or at least the immediate hope—of a home and family, instead pledging herself to her parents. Did they realize the sacrifices she'd made with little thought to her own happiness?

All their lives stood in jeopardy—from both their past allegiance and newfound alliances.

What most frightened her was the question of whether they had chosen to side with De Pez and the wrong party.

She sat at her writing table, a clean sheet of parchment before her, and pondered her options.

She could hand the letter over to her father and face his wrath for opening his personal correspondence and then hiding it from him. Or, she could devise her own plan.

If Lorelei came forward and admitted her deceit, then she would have the added burdens of not only her father's scorn, but also of appeasing De Pez. Very little thought went into her decision as she picked up the quill pen and dipped the pointed tip in the ebony ink to her right.

She hadn't many options left to her.

She scrawled the words across the page in her well-practiced, elegant script.

Lorelei didn't allow even a moment to consider her decision before dusting the paper with sand, folding the note, and ringing for Isabelle. The letter she'd penned hadn't requested a reply—for she could never have awaited it patiently. All that was left to do was prepare for her evening...and find a way to escape the townhouse unnoticed.

Chapter Five

Lorelei wrung her hands as people moved past her. Many looked her way, but averted their gazes quickly. She knew how she appeared to them, and it was the thing she despised most about England. She was a female standing unchaperoned at Covent Garden. They undoubtedly mistook her for a lady of the night awaiting her benefactor.

She was awaiting someone—but she wasn't a harlot, and he would never be her benefactor. She was actually nervous that he wouldn't show up, or that he hadn't received her missive at all.

It had been quite daring and forward of her to send word directly to his home, but time was not on their side, and she needed to assert her interest in him before it was too late. Or rather, establish that his interest in *her* was not unwanted. She had few other options with his recent absence from all social functions.

She only hoped that with Isabelle's help, her presence at home went unnoticed and she could slip back inside without anyone aware. She would inform the comte about her outing on the morrow, and hopefully have good news for him. Then, perhaps the letter could be forgotten.

Vendors hawked fruit and sweetmeats to attending noblemen and their companions as women who'd soon perform sashayed through the crowd. They giggled when men whispered in their ears, curtseying to women who wished a word, and accepting all gifts of flowers and trinkets. This night—and place—belonged to them.

Blending in with the crowd should have been simple, yet she'd chosen a dress that would entice him, and, in turn, it attracted much unwanted attention. She'd selected a gown of the richest green, so deep one could mistake it for onyx. With her neck, ears, and wrists dripping in pearls, Lorelei was the envy of every woman who passed. Part of her wondered if the marquis would find her attire to his liking, then quickly dismissed the thought. The marquis was not why she was here.

She stood as still as possible, so as not to expose the daring slit up the side of her dress that reached clear to her mid-thigh and revealed her black stockings below, complete with bows just above her knees.

She sighed with relief when he finally approached, appearing from the crowd as if out of thin air. As he walked, she noticed his eyes wandering, touching on several provocatively dressed women.

"Lord Chastain." She dropped a slight curtsey. When her eyes focused on his feet, she noted the high gleam of his boots and, as she straightened, took in his attire all the way to his carefully combed hair. He was one with expensive taste, and not a strand stood in defiance to that.

"Lady Lorelei." He grasped her hand and brought it

to his lips. She feared they created a spectacle when he held her fingers there for an untoward amount of time. His lips pressed to her chilled hand fell on the side of mush—nothing as firm as the marquis' touch. Finally, he released her and smiled. "I am only recently returned to town, and I must say I was taken aback."

"Why ever so, my lord?"

"It is only that you seemed to favor the marquis over myself."

She wondered if he tested her. She'd danced with both men that evening, yet accepted a second from only Chastain. It was quite possible he knew of the marquis' visit to her that next morning. They were friends, after all, and she expected they also shared confidences.

Her stomach turned at the thought of the marquis hearing of her very inappropriate invitation to Lord Chastain to meet her at Covent Gardens. The reputation of the outdoor playhouse was known far and wide for its hidden nooks and dark corners. Trysts often transpired under the aquiline noses of all, but with no one the wiser.

The Marquis of Drake was likely skilled in that particular area, and she could almost envision him removing his overcoat—and then her dress, his hands moving across her heated skin, even as the actors upon the stage spoke their lines.

"That is foolish. I could hardly take my eyes from you." She pushed the erotic image from her mind and focused on Lord Chastain. His shoulders were not as broad, and his hair—while perfectly coiffed—lacked volume. His height was only just past her own, and she suspected the bottom of his boots were padded. She could not fool herself. He was a very handsome man, and was probably considered a great prize, yet he was short of something Drake had in abundance. That exact something eluded her. The men were very much the same: titled, wealthy, educated, and finely attired, so why she was drawn to one and not the other made little sense.

"I am pleased to hear that. Shall we?" Without waiting, he slipped her hand into his, drawing Lorelei to his side as they began to walk through the jovial crowd around them. "The evening is quite nice."

"Yes, it is." The last thing she wanted to discuss was the weather, it being mild or otherwise. "I hope I am not keeping you from a prior engagement out of town."

He chuckled. "Not at all. Well, yes, actually you are, but how could I resist your invitation?" She didn't know if he jested or was only trying to entertain her. Either way, his words irked her, though the same comment from the marquis would have drawn a smile.

They moved casually through the crowd with no direction. Lorelei felt him lead, but to where she didn't know. Perhaps he had a private box from which they would watch the play.

"Please, do not leave me to wonder. To what do I owe the pleasure of your company this night?"

"A woman would be mad not to seek more time in your presence, my lord."

When he smiled with satisfaction, she knew she'd given the perfect answer. Lord Chastain thought greatly of himself, and she'd known flattering him, stroking his ego, would ultimately draw him in. It was the first lesson her mother had taught her—and arguably, the most important she'd ever learn. Men sought admiration above all else, whether it was for their wealth—which normally had naught to do with them, but the many lords before them—or their prowess on horseback.

Lorelei considered what she hoped to gain from this evening. Hopefully, she would pique his interest enough to pursue her. Once they'd established their relationship, then it would not be looked upon unfavorably for her family to visit him at his home. A dinner party at his London home or a holiday at his country estate would enable her and her parents to find what they sought.

"I do, so thank you for forgoing your plans." She glanced up at him coyly from beneath lowered lids. She'd employed the look numerous times, yet it was a bit harder to pull off when the man beside her did not tower above her as so many others did. "Do you have a box we might sit within and talk?"

"Ah, yes, talk is exactly what I have in mind," he whispered. "This way."

He increased their pace and she noticed the crowd start to thin as they moved to a low-lit area of the gardens. The torches, which sat high above the path, became fewer, their scant pools of light leaving more dark nooks the farther they got from others. The chatter of people receded, and giggling mixed with heavy breathing could be heard from the darker areas just off the path. She could barely hear the soft music from the orchestra any longer.

Lorelei looked about nervously. It was too late to turn back now—to cry off would certainly leave a bad taste in Lord Chastain's mouth and he'd most definitely never call on her again, let alone allow her into his home.

"Where are we going?" she asked. "I am sure we have passed all the boxes with premium views of the performance."

"It is not much farther, I promise."

The number of lamps in the outdoor garden

dwindled the farther they got from the crowds, as did the maintained path they'd followed. The greenery lining the trail began to encroach on her walking space, snagging on her dress. The needles from the plants embedded in her silk skirts as she brushed past, urged ever on by Lord Chastain. Before long, her fine slippers became moist with the dew covering the ground. The moon overhead could barely be seen due to the towering trees looming above.

Chastain's hand tightened on her arm and he pulled her to a stop. She snapped around to face him, but his unyielding grip didn't lessen.

"Ouch." He'd hurt her, yet she only let the one word slip past her lips before forcing a carefree laugh. "My lord, wherever have you taken me?"

If he noticed the trepidation in her question, he showed no sign of it. "Oh, I assumed we could use a few minutes alone to get to know one another."

Lorelei couldn't make out the expression on his face in the dim light, and feared she wouldn't enjoy what she saw if she could.

Chastain pressed his body harshly into hers, his rigid stance forcing her to bend slightly back. The only thing keeping her upright was his hold on her arm, sure to leave a nasty bruise.

She was thankful for the darkness so he could not see the fear in her eyes, though many said you could smell terror upon a person.

"It would be lovely to learn more about you and your interests." She refused to show her fear. "But this is hardly a suitable place to talk about our families and hobbies."

His hand released her, and she stumbled backwards,

attempting to gain her balance. "Luckily for you, I have no family to discuss. Now, my hobbies…" Before she could move any farther back, his arms snaked around her and pulled her close. He ground his hips into hers, his erection evident through his fine evening garb. His hands moved lower and took firm hold of her derriere. "I would much prefer to show you."

Lorelei stilled herself, knowing as a gentleman of the *ton* his manners could not be so lacking as to take this situation much further. Angering him would only make her task harder to accomplish.

His hands squeezed ever more insistently on her backside, creating marks she knew would match the one on her arm.

"Kiss me, *ma cherie*," he said, mimicking her native tongue as he pressed himself against her, likely ruining the fine silk of her gown. "Come now. We both know you little French courtesans enjoy your romps as much as us English lords."

She wanted to scream, to lash out at him, to run. Yet she begged herself to remain calm—to think of her ultimate duty to her family's safety.

Instead of bashing him over the head, she forced a smile to her lips and her eyes to lower in subservience. "My lord, your words are the height of impropriety. Is all you demand a kiss?"

"Of course, my lady." He reverted to formalities, but the rigid length of his body didn't yield. "A kiss and my night will be complete."

A simple kiss. She had kissed several men in her short time out of the schoolroom, but those men hadn't forced themselves on her. Lord Chastain saw her as a debutante—and an innocent, yet he still pressed his advantage.

Chastain leaned in toward her, and she slammed her eyes shut, needing to get this over with, satisfy him for a time so she could depart. His breath fanned across her face as he came close. It was only then that she noticed the smell of liquor on him. His breath and clothes reeked of it. She'd been so focused on attaining what she sought that she hadn't noticed his intemperance.

No longer could she count on him to act the respectful gentleman.

At long last, his lips landed cruelly against her tightly closed ones. His mouth moved and his tongue sought to force her lips apart.

When she resisted, his hand released her derriere, moved up her side to her neck, and finally took hold of her chin. His finger clamped down and held her face still.

A whimper escaped her.

"Oh, I knew you would enjoy my touch." The words were whispered against her neck as his mouth attacked more than caressed the tender flesh there. "Do not fight this, my dear—or go ahead, it will only make this moment that much more memorable."

"Please…" she begged.

His lips crushed hers once more, and his fingers released her face.

A little of the tension left her. She could handle this brutal kiss.

That thought was barely out before her dress was suddenly being pulled up. Cool night air brushed her legs, covered in only sheer stockings and muddied slippers.

Panic set in once more.

She pushed against his chest, hoping he would realize his untoward behavior was not appreciated.

Instead, his arm once again wrapped around her waist to hold her close as his other hand grabbed at her breasts.

She struggled against his lecherous advances in an attempt to free herself.

When she heard material rip, she stopped struggling as her mind sought to comprehend what was happening.

"Come now, my little *putain*. I promise you'll enjoy this more than any you've had before."

"What…" He thought her a whore, a common chit with no reservations. "No—"

"It is too late now. You will see what teasing gets a girl like you." His words were cold as ice, and his eyes matched.

With little effort, he took her feet from beneath her and she landed in a small grassy nook a few feet from the seldom-used path they'd come down. He landed solidly on top of her, knocking the wind from her lungs in their fall. She'd terribly underestimated his strength and the muscle beneath his evening attire.

She pushed against him, tried to free herself, to kick at him, but her legs were twisted in her gown. He was all over her, tearing at the bodice of her dress. She felt her necklace snap from her neck and pearls burst everywhere, hitting her face, exposed chest, and arms.

"No." Her voice pierced the air. The thin thread of the word held no substance, even to her own ears. She did not want this… She hadn't asked for this.

The moments passed like a lifetime as she blocked out the reality of what was happening to her.

She ceased to fight, knowing his strength far surpassed hers.

Instead, she sobbed. Whether she wept loudly or her

violated moans never left her throat, Lorelei didn't know.

"I do say," a male voice could be heard only steps away. "One should learn to be more discreet with their trysts. What say you, John?"

Another man laughed before he spoke. "It is as if all of London is without manners of late."

Chastain haphazardly rolled off her with a small grunt, alerted to the presence of others.

She lay on the ground, her dress torn and in tatters around her, as he adjusted his pants and tucked his shirt in. Lastly, he straightened his cravat and mumbled, "I trust you can find your way home."

Warm tears streamed from her eyes and seeped into the earth around her. Her body begged to cry out at the injustice almost completed against her person, but she feared drawing attention to herself once more. Though the men who had happened upon them deserved her thanks, for Chastain would have surely finished the deed had he not feared discovery.

Instead, she remained quiet.

With a curt bow in her direction, the duke turned and headed back down the path in the direction they'd come. She watched his boots as they moved farther from her. Oddly, they remained clean and unsullied by the mud that clung to her so willingly. It was as if filth did not even want to be associated with the likes of him.

She'd highly misjudged the man with whom she was expected to become more closely acquainted. He was no more a proper English lord than she.

Chapter Six

Andrew swirled the liquid in his tumbler—exactly what he'd been doing for the last hour as he awaited Benji's arrival. He'd spent the hour before that playing billiards with Lord Storr and chatting horses with Sir Ryker.

At first he'd wondered if he had misread Benji's note requesting his company for dinner at White's. His interest in hearing tales of Madame Sasha's country party was minimal, but he could not turn down his friend's invitation.

Standing, Andrew walked about the room, leaving his half-empty glass behind. In the previous days, he'd had little drive to drink, which was a welcome change from the norm. The days had been spent in the company of his solicitor, planning future improvements to his properties, horse purchases for his stables, and negotiations about a new sea venture. All completely legitimate business dealings, yet they could have waited until after Sasha's party.

At last, Benji entered White's, blinking several times

and shading his eyes from the bright lights. It figured that his friend was still in his cups after his time at Madame Sasha's, where the barkeep was as generous as the women.

"Andrew." Benji fell into the seat across from where Andrew had been sitting, jostling the small table between them just enough to send the amber liquid over the rim of Andrew's glass. "I do apologize for my tardiness. I had a quick stop before joining you."

"I was beginning to think you'd fallen asleep and hadn't sent word you were not coming." Andrew laughed, reclaiming his own seat. "I am glad to see you had a thrilling time at Sasha's. Meet anyone interesting?"

Andrew mainly asked, hoping his friend would tell him he was distracted by a fresh pair of breasts, keeping his mind far from Lady Lorelei.

Benji signaled for a drink before answering. "The party was much the same as previous years—rousing fun, with lots of drinks and no sleep."

"I gathered that from your…" Andrew paused, taking in his friend's disheveled dress. "…less-than-stellar attire this evening."

Benji looked down at himself, as if noticing for the first time that his clothes were wrinkled and it looked as if mud clung to his white shirt, his neck cloth slightly askew.

"Mayhap a bath and clean clothes should have taken precedence over this dinner."

"No, no." Benji sat a bit taller. "We agreed to have dinner once I returned to town, and I find I'm overly curious about your time without me."

Andrew had no intention of sharing more than he had to, no talk of flowers or where his mind actually lay.

"This and that, all mundane things, I am afraid…but necessary nonetheless."

He paused when a manservant delivered Benji's drink and took their meal order.

With a fast tilt of the glass, Benji emptied it. "Another."

"Are you sure you should not take some time to sleep," Andrew asked. "Perhaps allow the spirits to leave your system?"

Benji eyed him. "When did you turn into my father?"

"It is just—"

"You have become quite rigid as of late."

"I most certainly have not," Andrew said defensively.

"Madame Sasha's?"

"What about it?"

Benji accepted another drink, but took only a sip this time. "You never would have missed the opportunity before."

"I told you, I had business matters to attend to."

"Yes, yes." Benji waved off his comment, leaning slightly in his chair. "Certainly something that could not be put off. I will say, I will never pass on the chance."

There was something off about the way his friend spoke, almost as if his life of ease and debauchery had consumed him entirely. Either the man was past exhaustion, or he truly was as drunk as he appeared.

Andrew laughed, in hopes of lightening the dour mood that had settled on this conversation. "I assure you I will not disappoint you again."

When their meal was set on the table between them, both men hurriedly picked up their silverware. Andrew was mainly focused on getting through the meal before Benji passed out. It was likely his friend hadn't had time for a decent meal in days.

"Madame Sasha asked about you," Benji said around a piece of meat in his mouth. "She is worried you have replaced her."

"I most certainly have—"

"And I am inclined to agree."

Andrew was at a loss for words. The tenor of their friendship had changed drastically over the last few years, and he seemed unable to alter its course. More and more he'd spent time alone or with his stewards. His evenings about town, visiting Craven House and such, had dwindled to only one or two per month. Frankly, he was shocked Benji hadn't addressed his lack of attendance long before now.

"Perhaps I do not favor such encounters any longer." Lorelei immediately sprang to his mind. He realized with something of a start that he would gladly spend every evening in her company for the rest of his years and be perfectly happy.

Benji stared at him as if he'd never seen him before. "That is absurd. What man does not favor an exquisite lady unclothed in his bed?"

Who did not, indeed?

But the only thing that ran through his mind was Lorelei, laid out naked on a bed he knew very well, smiling up at him as he lowered himself atop her.

"Hello?" Benji snapped his fingers before Andrew's face. "I know I am the one in his cups here, but you seem overly preoccupied."

"I am." He shook his head, determined to not let every word remind him of her…and how he longed to see her again. "I should go. I fear I am not the best company tonight."

"You will desert me?" Benji asked. "It is just as I thought."

"Whatever do you mean?"

"You think I cannot tell what is on your mind?" Benji set his fork aside, his plate empty. "You are still thinking of her."

"That is preposterous." Andrew sat back, his own meal forgotten. "I have much more on my mind than a mere woman. And what is this talk of deserting you?"

"Simple. One woman comes along, and suddenly, you are canceling plans with me." He picked up his fork and speared a piece of meat from Andrew's plate. "The chit is not worth your time—nor my own, for sure."

Andrew suppressed the instinct to come to Lorelei's defense. "It did not seem that way the other evening," he prodded. "Besides which, at some point our family obligations will overtake our friendship...even for you."

"You foresee a time we will not be as we always have been? And I should not need to remind you that *we* are the only family either of us have."

Andrew could not disagree with his friend, but the draw of something more—some*one* more—was strong. "You are correct. And it is best that we do not overextend ourselves where marriageable women are concerned."

The men raised their glasses in salute and drank heavily.

"Besides, she would most certainly choose me." Benji laughed.

"I highly doubt that, but it is good to know we are not in competition for this one."

"Very true, I find I am uninterested in the girl. I have

an aversion to women of a certain height."

Now it was Andrew's turn to laugh, the conversation close to old times between the pair. "Oh, you mean she nearly stands above you? I can see how that would be most off-putting for someone of your unnaturally modest stature."

"It is not I who is short, but she who is exceedingly tall." Benji kept the jest going. "But even if I do not care, that does not mean you can rush in for the taking."

"And if I did decide to court Lady Lorelei?" Andrew asked, testing the waters.

"Then I fear it would only cause you upset." Benji looked over Andrew's shoulder when the bell above the door rang to welcome another guest. "Ah, I believe we have company that will prove just my point."

Andrew turned in his seat, making eye contact with a middle-aged man.

He jumped to his feet and navigated the room to greet him. "Good eve, Sir St. Augustin," Andrew said in greeting. "I do hope the night finds you well."

The man hit him with a hard stare before responding. "Drake. I see not much has changed since our last encounter." He nodded toward Benji, who practically lay across the back of the chair Andrew had vacated. "You still consort with the most unsavory characters."

"Sir—"

"I have told you, do not approach me," St. Augustin cut him short. "As far as anyone knows, we have never met, nor will we ever."

"I only seek to learn if she is in good health."

"You lost the right to ask long ago. Now, let me pass." The man made to walk on, but Andrew laid his hand on his shoulder to stop him. "Unhand me."

They stood thus, neither backing down.

When a quiet clapping sounded behind them, Andrew let his hand fall from the man's shoulder, not wanting to create any more of a spectacle. St. Augustin had every right to despise him. Hell, if their places had been reversed, Andrew would have challenged the man to a duel.

"Drake." The intensity in St. Augustin's eyes dared Andrew to cross him once more. "Do not contact my wife or *my* child. You made your stance very clear years ago. They belong to me, a man worthy of their affection—not a drunken rakehell who gives little thought to others."

Every word the man said was true, and Andrew could do naught but stand aside and allow him to continue on to his evening's entertainments.

# # #

Lorelei slipped into her coat the moment she entered her waiting carriage. She wrapped the warm material about herself like a cocoon, covering the torn and mud-stained silk of her once-beloved gown. Her fingers touched her throat where her treasured strand of pearls had sat, nestled in the hollow of her neck. They'd been a rare gift from her father during a time of great joy.

Now, they were gone.

"Where to, my lady?" her coachman called from his seat atop the carriage.

"Home, thank you." She kept her sob at bay long enough to utter the words. At the moment, there was no place farther from her *home* than her parent's townhouse.

She was unsure if she considered France home either, however.

The sound of the carriage wheels on the cobblestone drive drowned out her heart-wrenching cries as tears streamed down her face, soaking the collar of her fleece. She pulled her coat tighter around herself and sunk further into the velvet, wishing it would swallow her whole and transport her to another place and time.

Time.

Before arriving in England, Lorelei had a sense that life was nothing but time, endless days, months, and years. Enough to do her parents bidding and have a spot of fun playing the spy, with time to spare for a family of her own. Now, everything seemed all too real. She ached to settle in a place long enough to make it her home. And friends—how she wished for time to make genuine friends, people who knew and cared for her.

Now she wondered if there would ever be enough hours, days, years to make herself whole again—pull together what little was left of herself and live: enjoy the sunrise, bask in the glow of the sunset, breathe in clean, fresh air, or feel the grass of a sparse grove beneath her bare feet.

She straightened in the seat, pushing her thoughts of self-pity deep, and brought her hands to her hair. It must look a fright. The drive from Covent Gardens to her townhouse was not more than ten minutes. How long had she pondered fleeing London and leaving her parents behind—along with the weight of the obligations forced upon her by De Pez?

Once again, time was not her friend.

She wiped the condensation from the windowpane and looked out at the passing street.

Two blocks remained.

Which left her precious moments to pull herself together—and prepare to slip unnoticed into the townhouse, same as she'd left earlier. With luck, her parents would still be out for the evening. She need only hold in her misery until she reached the safety of her rooms, then she would give in to her emotions. Her cloak would cover the disaster beneath and hide the dirt that clung to her arms and legs. Her hair could be blamed on Lord Chastain's eager hands during a sweet farewell kiss.

Her stomach lurched at the thought, recalling his horrid breath and viselike grip on her body. The image of his body pressed against hers for what seemed like an eternity soured her stomach, but could have been no more than mere moments before he'd been frightened off by the passing men. Those mere moments, however, could translate into her failed mission and her family's certain punishment. If this led to their failure and subsequent penance, then she would never forgive herself.

The moisture of his sickly sweat upon her was a cruel reminder—though she hadn't forgotten—that she'd tempted a beast, and now must live with the consequences.

Lorelei knew her sacrifices could not be in vain, as if she—her body, her mind, her very soul—did not matter.

Though her virtue was still intact, rage coursed through her at the intended injustice Chastain had planned for her. Why she'd thought meeting him without her parent's knowledge was a good idea, she did not know.

The carriage door opened, revealing only the hand

of the coachman to assist her down. "My lady, we have arrived."

As she extended her hand to allow the man to help, Lorelei saw the dirt caked under her once well-groomed nails and the smudge of filth marring the back of her delicate hand.

Appalled, she quickly pulled her hand back. "Thank you," she stuttered, shaken by the sight of herself. "Please precede me in and make sure my maid has prepared my room while I gather my things. I have misplaced my favorite gloves."

"Of course, my lady." Without hesitation, he turned from her and moved to the front entrance. The door was opened with a flourish, as only a true English butler could do, and the coachman conferred with the man before returning to his driving box.

The coachman cleared his throat, signaling his desire to depart round to the livery and be done for the evening.

Oh, how she wished unhitching the mares and brushing the sweat from their coats would mark an end to this terrible evening.

But pity was not something she felt for others, and especially did not extend to her own circumstances.

Lorelei raised her hood to cover her mussed hair and departed the carriage, pulling her cloak about her and digging her shaking hands into the deep confines of her fur-lined pockets to hide any further evidence of her disastrous liaison.

She held her head high—she would never hang her head in shame for anyone to see—and took the steps into the thankfully empty grand foyer.

Lorelei breathed a deep sigh of relief the moment she closed the door solidly behind her.

Sending word ahead to Isabelle had been shrewd. Not a soul would intrude upon her until first light on the morrow.

The first thing that greeted her upon entering her bedchamber was the last thing she wanted to see: the beautiful bouquet of flowers from the marquis.

They symbolized everything that would never—could never—be hers. The thought of a husband chosen out of mutual affection, a life full to brimming with the laughter of children, and most of all, a home, a stable place with an open hearth where their peace was never disturbed.

That was never to be.

The shrill pitch of the words in her head should have been enough to force the flowers from their perch on her dressing stand, but they stood still, unaware of the turmoil within the room—within her.

Before she knew what she was doing, she held the large, heavy display in her hands. Her fingers traced the etched glass of the crystal vase. There was little doubt that delicate hands had crafted the vessel.

Delicate hands…

Lorelei once again looked to her own hands. Hands that were once as delicate as those of any London lady, born and raised to be the center of every room they entered. Yet, now she recognized them for what they truly were—cold, mercenary hands that belonged solely to her crown, never herself. They would do any and all that her crown demanded of her.

No part of her was hers to command. But this moment—with the flowers held securely in her hands—was hers.

Rage. Anger. Disappointment. Alienation.

Loneliness. Fury. Shame.

She allowed her emotions to take full control and roll through her. It was an unfamiliar sensation, and she hoped numbness to it all would follow.

With little effort—born mostly of her pounding heart and aching soul—the vase flew through the air at the wall above the fireplace that warmed her room. It fell short and shattered when it hit the floor.

Deep down, she knew what her crown would demand of her:

Destroy. Conquer. Accept no resistance.

Glass splinters flew in every direction. The glow from the many candles placed around the room glinted off shards of razor-sharp crystal.

Her legs grew weak beneath her when the intense emotions continued to course through her, having not been dispelled as easily as she had hoped.

How *dare* the Marquis of Drake offer her any hope of a future—especially the future she dreamed of.

Chapter Seven

Andrew rode through Hyde Park, a light breeze in his face and his feet securely in the stirrups. Normally he abhorred the necessities society demanded of him: the balls, morning calls, afternoon teas, and evening musicales. All bloody irritating and time consuming, when he'd much rather be handling his many business engagements. There were always disputes to be settled for the tenants on his many estates, repairs needed…and then, he was also reaching the time when he could no longer put his duties to Parliament from his mind.

Regardless of all this, today he'd taken a different route home from his solicitor's office. He'd passed up main streets in favor of cutting through the park, even though it brought him into intimate contact with other members of the *ton*. Thought of idle talk of the weather and the season's grandest entertainments did not dissuade him this day.

He slowed his mount to a walk when he reached the path that cut through the park. Ladies and gentlemen dressed in the most fashionable walking garb strolled leisurely, waving to acquaintances and stopping to speak with friends.

Andrew smiled, expecting to hear a familiar voice call a good morning to him, but as he continued along the path, he noticed many averting their eyes or turning away from him to chat with another, giving Andrew their back.

How long had he been treated thusly, he wondered? It was something of a revelation to realize he'd done this to himself. He rarely danced at social gatherings, avoided any attachment to a particular female in order to discourage matrons, and he never invited people to his home—and neither did they arrive unannounced.

Without knowing it, he'd become a recluse by choice of his actions, a man society deemed unapproachable.

His mood threatened to turn sour.

Andrew pulled his horse to a stop and dismounted, deciding to try a new tactic. With the reins in his hands, he began to walk along the busy path, smiling at passersby and calling a good day to those with whom he was acquainted. A few people nodded in greeting, but none stopped.

A passing carriage held the Dovington family crest.

"Good day," he shouted. When the vehicle slowed to a stop and two women looked out of the open-air coach, he continued. "Lovely to see you, Lady Dovington. And you, Lady Eugenia."

Lady Eugenia, newly introduced this season, waved in greeting. "Good day, my lord."

"Marquis," her mother said cautiously. "I believe this is the first time we have seen you during our daily outing, is it not?"

Andrew was well aware that gaining an introduction

for their homely daughter would be a boon and mark the girl's coming out a success.

"Yes, well, I fear my physical activity is severely limited due to my hectic schedule," he responded. "But this weather is quite lovely, is it not?"

He'd resorted to talking of the weather, his smile forced, and the pair stared back at him as if he'd grown a second head. It was almost painful to keep his lips upturned.

They only nodded in return.

"Well, I will not keep you any longer." He issued a curt bow that matched his stiff smile and resumed his promenade when their driver called the horses into action. "Whatever am I doing?" he mumbled to himself.

"I was wondering the same, your lordship," a melodic voice called behind him.

Taken by surprise, Andrew dropped the reins to his horse and turned. "Lady Lorelei, what a pleasant surprise." He looked about for her parents, but only noticed a maid trailing behind her. "You always have the advantage of sneaking up on me. Are you out alone?"

"No," she said, gesturing over her shoulder. "My maid, Isabelle, is with me."

"I see. Can I interest you in a stroll?"

"I had hoped to have a spell to myself." He was unsure if the words were meant to discourage his company or not. "But I fear Hyde Park, especially at this hour, is not the place one comes to clear their thoughts in isolation."

"Shall we?" Andrew held out his arm. "Whatever could one as young as yourself need to clear their mind about?"

Lorelei stared up at him hesitantly, her eyes a very

clear green with the morning sun shining down on them. "Oh, I am sure my troubles are not all that different from other young women." She deflected the conversation to matters of a less serious nature—and he allowed it.

Finally, she set her fingers on his arm. He could have sworn they trembled ever so slightly before settling.

He would play along for the moment. "I am unaccustomed to the troubles of young women, please enlighten me."

As they walked, her soft grey dress brushed against his pants and she clung—a little tighter than necessary— to his arm. "Unaccustomed to *young* women? Do you not have any sisters or female relations?"

"I was cursed an only child, and my mother passed when I was in my youth." He hadn't spoken of his family in years. They were a distant memory he chose to keep locked away, a remembrance of happier times that never ceased to bring him great sadness. "It was just my father and me after that until he passed, no other relations to speak of."

"Ah, I see." She kept her head lowered and her eyes on the path ahead. "Your home must have been very quiet."

"Indeed," he sighed. "After my mother passed, I rarely saw my father, for he favored town life and took his responsibilities in Parliament very seriously. And what about your family?"

"Much the same as yourself, although my parents are still with me. No brothers or sisters…and my father travels quite frequently, so if I have much family I am unaware of them."

"Yes, well." He felt the need to make her feel better about her situation. "Traveling agrees with you."

"Thank you. And I am sorry for the loss of your parents." Her free hand patted his sleeve. "I would be lost without the comte and comtesse."

"I would think not," he disagreed. "You seem a very independent woman, one that embraces life."

She laughed, and Andrew felt his own grip on her tighten.

Andrew nodded to a familiar couple when they passed, but they didn't stop to make conversation, and he had no intention of sharing these precious moments with Lorelei. Instead, he steered her off the walking path and into the wide meadow that spanned the length of the park. The area was also a bit more secluded, with only the occasional horseman riding through.

"The other day, you fled into the house so quickly." He hesitated to mention it, but needed answers. "Did I insult you in any way?"

Her head snapped up and her eyes hardened. "You did nothing of the sort."

"Then why did you rush off?"

She fell silent for a moment, and their steps slowed before she spoke again. "I received a letter from home. That is all."

"But you did not appear happy…" he probed.

"No."

"May I ask why?"

"No." Her pace slowed as if she drug her feet in the ankle-high grass.

"I am sorry for pushing you," he apologized. "Do forgive my rudeness."

"I was only jesting, your lordship." She gave a strained laugh. "It was from my father's business associate. Nothing overly important."

Andrew got the sense the letter was very important, but he would not press her for information she did not want to share. Instead, he changed the subject. "So, tell me why you came to Hyde Park, of all places, this morning."

# # #

The Marquis of Drake was everything the duke was not.

Charming. Compassionate. Witty.

It only left the question as to why the two men were friends.

Lorelei hadn't wanted to take the marquis' arm. She hadn't wanted to speak with anyone, especially a man, after last night. Her body felt as damaged as her fingers, cut and bruised from the hours she had spent collecting all the shards of glass from her room. Thankfully, her swollen, nicked hands were concealed inside her gloves.

If he saw through her cheery demeanor, he was gentleman enough not to say.

"Lady Lorelei?" he asked.

She stopped walking and looked to him. "I fear my mind wandered, your lordship."

"Yes, you were distant for a moment. If you wish, we can walk in silence," he offered. "It was I who interrupted your peace, as it were."

"I was happy to see you," she confided. "London is a very lonely place."

He cheered at her words. "I have heard, but I have never been one to need a lot of company."

"But you and Lord Chastain are close friends, correct?" Lorelei took the opportunity to gather information, though she had to rein in her feelings to even say the man's name. "You only spoke with him that night at the ball."

"Benji and I have neighboring estates," he said, at ease talking about his friend. "Our fathers were friends, and in turn, we went to the same schools, attended the same entertainments. It only made sense we became friends. Though, to be honest, I believe we outgrew each other years ago."

"Why do you say that?"

"In recent years, I have grown, taken full responsibility for my estates and many business ventures. Chastain is still content being the carefree lord, happy to while away his days attending country parties and playing cards all evening."

"But you are not?"

"No," he admitted. "There must be more to life than pleasure."

"Indeed, your lordship."

Before she knew it, they stood in the middle of a grassy area lined with trees, flowers pushing up through the well-trod earth in many places. Her maid walked ten paces behind her, Andrew's horse not far behind that. The animal seemed to follow his master as if he were a hound and not a noble steed standing over seventeen hands high. A few paces away, she spotted another trail that wound its way back from whence they'd come.

She leaned in to him, thinking only of the pleasure he could likely give her—not the harsh touch she'd experienced previously or the severe kiss of an overly forward gentleman, but the soft, cultured touch of a caring man.

"Lady Lorelei, I..." His words sounded like they

pained him greatly. "It is improper."

The sound of pounding hooves and shouts had them pulling apart abruptly.

"Out of the way!" one man shouted.

Headed straight down the grassy stripe they now stood on was not one, but two buggies, racing at breakneck speed—and headed right for her.

Lorelei stood frozen.

Staring into the wild eyes of two sets of horses, the many decisions she'd made in the past months flooded her. The ample opportunities she'd had to turn away from her family's choices, and the stark reality that nothing she'd done as of late in any way resembled what she'd dreamed of for her future.

A cold gust of wind pushed the few loose strands of her hair about her face, and the pounding of hooves bounced around in her head.

Closing her eyes tightly, Lorelei braced for the impact and the pain she knew would come.

A heavy weight hit her, and Lorelei's feet felt nothing but empty space. Butterflies swam in her stomach as if she were falling a great distance, her arms pinned to her sides.

Her mind begged her arms to move—to lessen the collision with the ground that was inevitable.

Suddenly, she lay upon her back, the wind knocked from her lungs.

She fought, clawed at whoever held her down, kicked her legs relentlessly, pummeling the solid weight that pressed against her. She needed air, she needed to be free; she needed to be back on her feet.

A rock dug into her back each time she moved, and the pain actually calmed her. She could feel it, and she wouldn't push it away—this moment was happening, as if her nightmare were coming true once more.

Yet, it wasn't the same. The smells were different, her back was not moist from the mud, and somewhere, though it sounded miles away, someone called her name.

"Lorelei, stop, please," a voice pleaded. "Lorelei, you are safe, unharmed."

A horse neighed, and she heard weeping not far away. Was *she* weeping?

Finally, the weight lifted from her, and she was pulled to her feet, though arms surrounded her like a cocoon.

"Should I be getting her pa?"

"No." It was Andrew's voice she heard, and his arms that hugged her. "She is calming now. Lorelei…can you hear me?"

Her eyes focused, but all she saw was his chest, felt the fine lawn cloth of his undershirt pressed to her cheek, but the thick wool of his jacket on her forehead.

Lorelei's hands were trapped between them, and she pushed, trying to gain some distance as her heart continued to race. But no, it wasn't the racing of her own heart she heard, but the receding sound of hoof beats in the distance.

"Andrew," she called on a cry.

"I am here, my love." His hand caressed her head and moved along the length of her hair to her lower back. "You are safe, though a bit dusty."

My love? The proclamation was as surreal as the accident that had nearly taken their lives moments before.

When she remained quiet, Andrew pulled her close once more, his lips kissing a trail across her forehead while his hands moved up and down her arms, warming her. "You are so cold."

She was, but already she warmed from his touch. "I shall be fine, your lordship."

"Your lordship?" Andrew released her, searching her face, but she could only stare back.

She could not have any serious feelings for him, nowhere near how he felt about her. It would only cause them heartache in the end—for her family's plan did not include remaining in England for an extended time, nor would they willingly leave her behind.

"I must go," she whispered, breaking the spell. "My father shall worry if he discovers my absence." And to think, just moments before she'd prayed he would kiss her. Now she realized the consequences of that action would last longer than her mission allowed.

"Shall I accompany you home?"

She wanted to say yes, to extend the moments with him and bring his arms around her once more, but they couldn't be seen together. Particularly since it was Chastain she should be pursuing.

Lorelei nodded to her maid before she answered. "That is not necessary. I do hope to see you again soon."

It was time she returned to her senses.

Andrew bowed hesitantly. "Please, send word that all is well with you."

"Good day." They both stalled. Lorelei knew her reasoning for delaying her return home, but not why he seemed reluctant to be on his way. "Thank you again for the flowers."

There was little reason the flowers jumped into her mind at that moment, and maybe it was all that had transpired so suddenly, but she truly wished she hadn't destroyed them.

Andrew's horse gave a great neigh and nudged his shoulder to gain his attention. "I am being summoned, as it were."

"I, as well." She'd avoided any eye contact with her maid since she'd stumbled upon Andrew, for she would have likely received a look of concern. "Farewell."

"Until we meet next."

If there were a next time, Lorelei said to herself.

She had to be the one to walk away, or they would continue to stand in the middle of the meadow staring at one another until the sun set and they could no longer make out the other's expression in the dark.

With one final smile, she grasped her grey woolen skirt and rushed to her maid's side. It was either that or into Andrew's arms.

Chapter Eight

Lorelei descended the stairs to break her repast after another night filled with night terrors and tears. At some point during the long hours, she'd come to terms with her situation. Her path had been predetermined long ago.

And she would not forsake the obligations her parents had entrusted to her—no matter what she wanted for herself. If she did, Lorelei would not be the only one whose life would hang in the balance.

She greeted the butler, who stood not far from the door, as if expecting an early-morning arrival. "Good morning. Shall I find the comte and my mother in the morning salon?"

He bowed before speaking, "My lady, the comte is with a visitor in the study. He bids you have your morning meal before joining them."

Her parents were early risers, as the French didn't find the advantage in languishing about bed until midday as the English did. Still, a guest this early was uncommon. The person must have been sent from her own crown, and was seeking to escape the notice of neighboring *ton* members and servants.

"Very well." She inclined her head to dismiss the man and started toward the breakfast room. If her parents did not feel obliged to call for her when the crown sent someone to see them, then she would most certainly take her time breaking her fast. "Please, send word I will join them shortly."

"Of course, Lady Lorelei."

A knock sounded at the door as she walked toward the morning salon. She paused, recognizing the voice that sounded when the butler greeted their newest guest.

"I am here to see the comte," a cultured, masculine French voice spoke evenly. "Here is my card."

Her knees threatened to buckle as her hand went to her pocket to feel the letter she still kept on her person for fear someone would stumble upon it in her room.

Lorelei didn't turn to see the man standing there, for there was no need.

She knew the voice well.

After a pause, the butler said, "I am afraid the comte is unavailable at this hour, but I can give your card to him at his earliest convenience."

"Pardon my haste," the man continued, his voice calm, belying everything Lorelei knew. "But it is of great importance that I speak with the comte."

Lorelei turned, unable to allow the butler to intrude on her father, for the man was likely here because no response had been issued to his note.

"Monsieur De Pez," Lorelei called, making her way back toward the front door. "What an honor to see you. The comte and comtesse were not expecting you, I am sure."

"Lady Lorelei," De Pez purred, taking in the sight of

her. "I was unable to send word of my arrival in London."

"Oh, well, I am sure that is of no import." Lorelei turned to the bewildered manservant to explain. "This is my father's dearest friend, Monsieur De Pez. I will inform him of your arrival."

"His lordship, I mean the comte, has instructed that he and his guest not be disturbed under any circumstances," the butler fumbled, casting his eyes to the floor. "My apologies, Lady Lorelei."

"Well, I am sure my father would make an exception for his very dear friend's arrival."

"He was very clear that he and Lord Chastain not be disturbed."

Lorelei froze, the forced smile draining from her face. "He is with Lord Chas—" At this very moment, Chastain could be regaling her parents with tales of their daughter's wanton actions and her behavior unbefitting a lady. The man was despicable enough to spread falsehoods about their previous encounter, though she hoped the comte intelligent enough to see her actions for what they were: a means of gaining entrance to Lord Chastain's life.

"Lady Lorelei," De Pez cut in. "I have only arrived in town and may discuss my news with you, just as well as with your father."

She couldn't concentrate on anything he said, for her thoughts traveled to the study where her father spoke with Chastain.

While it put her on edge, the mention of Chastain had softened De Pez. "Very well, please follow me," she said to him. "I was preparing to break my fast when you arrived. Can I interest you in a morning meal? I assure you our cook is very adept."

"I would much relish that."

There were many things De Pez relished, food being at the bottom of his list, Lorelei was certain. In their limited association, she'd heard of De Pez's fondness for cruelty, intimidation, and violence. She hoped never to witness them firsthand.

Lorelei dismissed the servant attending them in the breakfast room and hurriedly filled two plates with an assortment of eggs, meats, cheeses, and bread. If she were lucky, she would have him gone before her father and Chastain were done in his study. If Chastain knew anything about his family's history with the French government, then he would recognize De Pez in an instant, bringing their charade to an end—and likely bringing her family's assignment to a most unsatisfying conclusion. De Pez was likely so shortsighted he would never think of the consequences for all of them should he be recognized by the duke.

After setting De Pez's dish before him, she took her usual seat at the table.

Lorelei took a deep, calming breath before speaking. "How may I help you?" she asked.

"You are so much like your father, my dear. Never one to mince words."

"I find those who do to be ignorant and oblivious to the important things going on around them," she replied coolly.

"Can I not try the meal you so graciously offered before we discuss," he paused, looking for anyone eavesdropping on their conversation. "...*enterprise?*"

"I apologize for my dreadful manners," she acquiesced. "Please, the food here, while not of the quality we are accustomed to in France, is nevertheless delightful."

De Pez speared a boiled egg and brought the round mass to his mouth, taking a large bite. His eyes closed as he savored the fresh taste.

Keeping a guarded gaze on him, she brought a piece of cheese to her own lips. The normally flavorful delicacy tasted of sawdust in her dry mouth, and she decided the farce could not continue. De Pez was not just any visitor, and she was not one to entertain her father's *friends*. At the moment, she didn't know which was worse: her awkward meal with De Pez, or her time spent dwelling on what was happening in the study.

"Why are you in London?"

"I have traveled far to see that you and your family are moving toward concluding your assignment."

"Did you not hear that Lord Chastain—at this very moment—is ensconced in my father's study?"

"Yes, I did. Yet, his attendance here could mean many different things." He brought another morsel to his mouth and chewed before continuing. "I do so hope to gain sight of the man before I depart."

"You cannot be serious… That will jeopardize all we've worked hard to accomplish here. You could very well ruin our entire ruse." Part of her screamed that that may very well be De Pez's goal in London. If Lorelei's family failed, De Pez would enact swift punishment upon them all. But what his plan could be surely eluded her. "My father would be most unhappy."

The idea was appealing, nonetheless. If De Pez were the one to alert Chastain to their true motive for being in London, then the failed mission would once again be due to his incompetence, and in no way her family's fault.

"Come, Lore, I only want a glimpse of him, to see if

he looks anything like his late father or grandfather before him. It is highly unlikely he would remember me, for he only saw me once, when he first arrived in England."

"You will address me as Lady Lorelei, Monsieur De Pez." She would not stand for the man's careless usage of her nickname, an informality she hadn't given him permission to use, nor ever expected to.

"Touché," he droned. "We have known one another for many years."

"I am aware of our past."

"And our future?" he asked.

"My father will never allow that to happen." Lorelei was not oblivious to the fact that De Pez had pushed her father for Lorelei's hand in marriage since she was no more than thirteen years of age.

"One day he may not have the choice of turning me away." He'd looked upon her with lecherous eyes ever since the day she'd stumbled on her father and De Pez deep in discussion in their study. She'd been eight at the time—and he, older than her father. Then, she'd been unaware of her father's connection to Louis XVI and had gladly joined the pair, accepting De Pez's invitation to sit on his lap as the men discussed business. It was only when she'd told her mother later that Monsieur De Pez must have had a large candy stick hidden in his pocket that the comtesse—in a rare moment of motherly affection and advice—had cautioned her only daughter and forbade her to interrupt her father while he worked, no matter that someone in the room beckoned her forth.

She'd heeded her mother's words ever since, never letting herself dwell on how her mother knew to avoid her father's business friends.

"Please, come forth and say what you've come to

say," Lorelei pressed. The man, seeking the favor of a new shining light in France after his exile by Louis XVI and the Directory's unwillingness to consort with men associated with the executed King, was determined to bend all to his will. "We both know that is the task you've been assigned."

Once he'd said his piece, Lorelei could go back to worrying about what was happening behind her father's closed door.

"If you insist," he said, sitting straight in his seat and setting his fork aside.

"I do."

De Pez pushed his plate from him and crossed his arms upon the table, leaning in her direction. "I grow impatient with your family's lack of progress."

"We have only been in town a short while."

"Be that as it may, if the task had been assigned to me, I would have gathered what I needed—by force if that's what it took—and returned to France with all due haste."

"Is that how you accomplished your previous mission with the Chastain family? With brute force?" That had been exactly how he'd completed and failed his previous mission under Louis XVI—and why he hadn't risked accompanying her family to London in the first place. "Did killing the previous Lord Chastain allow you to find what our old government sought?"

She didn't need an answer to her question because she already had it.

And from his cold stare, he hadn't forgotten his publicized failure, either.

"No?" she asked, keeping her mocking grin at bay. "Well, since you and Napoleon Bonaparte gave my family this mission—confident in our methods—I will insist you allow us to do it in the fashion we deem appropriate."

"Are you fully aware of what is at stake?" His steely eyes drilled into hers.

"Of course," Lorelei snapped. "My *pere* has been very forthcoming with everything."

"So you know, then, that I was against including you in this delicate matter."

She wasn't surprised in the least. De Pez was from the old way of doing things, preferring to use women only when seduction was needed… But hadn't she essentially proven him right and bargained her body to Chastain?

"I do hope my *delicate* nature and sensibilities do not jeopardize your neck, monsieur."

"I hope not, either—for your sake and the comte's." Quick as the tide turns on the Channel, De Pez was all business again, putting at bay his threats. "And you know what you are looking for?"

She'd gone over and over this with her father. "Yes, the plans to Carassonne should be housed in a small cylinder no longer than a tall vase, leather in construction." It had taken Lorelei some time to figure out exactly why De Pez sought to present the plans to France's greatest fortified city of trade to Bonaparte, but it made perfect sense. Bonaparte looked for a way to take the country willingly, and if that did not come to pass and the citizens of Lorelei's country fought his rule, then he would take what he wanted by laying siege to France's most vulnerable city, in essence crippling and starving its people from within until they submitted to his will.

Lorelei sat back, not realizing she'd leaned toward De Pez. "Will that be all?"

De Pez stood, knocking his chair over in his haste,

bringing a servant scurrying into the room.

"Everything is fine," Lorelei said, dismissing the woman once more. "It was lovely seeing you, and I did so enjoy your tales of my home country. I am sorry my *pere* was waylaid and unable to see his dearest friend." The words were for the benefit of the woman standing just outside the room, as was her own use of English during their conversation. But she gained great satisfaction from the look on De Pez's face at her curt dismissal.

One day she knew she would have to pay for her gross mistreatment of De Pez, especially if he did indeed come to have his own power under Bonaparte. But the look of rage on his face, knowing he could do naught to her at the moment, would be worth the pain she'd likely suffer at his hands.

"Do tell Mathis I was here." De Pez hurled the threat as calmly as any man with his expertise could before he left the room—and the house—without so much as the slamming of a door.

Yes, the man was well-versed in his role, not letting even the insubordination of a woman rile his outward appearance.

He would come to learn that Lorelei had developed her own mask to hide her true feelings.

She took advantage of the empty, quiet room to calm herself before joining her father and Chastain.

Her anxiety rose once more.

She'd tarried long enough, and keeping the comte waiting was not in her best interest—especially if Lord Chastain let slip what had transpired between them. Would she have the fortitude to tell her parents what she'd done?

The error in her actions was clear, and her folly was

only hers to remedy.

She paused for a fraction of a moment before entering her father's study, running her damp palms down the front of her skirt and then lifting her chin.

Lord Chastain may have cruelly misused her, but she'd be a damned fool to allow him to see her broken.

So it was that with a serene smile she grasped the knob and turned, pushing the door open to greet her parents and their esteemed *guest*.

"Good morn, father, mother." She nodded to the pair who sat in a matched pair of high-backed chairs. Turning, she curtseyed to Chastain, who had stood from the sofa he'd likely been sprawled upon before her entrance. "And a very lovely morning to you, my lord."

She couldn't fathom his reason for calling on her parents after the way he'd treated her.

"Lady Lorelei." He smiled slyly and made to take her hand, but she snatched it back and hid it in the folds of her dress. His stance stiffened, noticing her discomfort. "Your father and I have been discussing a topic most serious and deserving of your opinion."

She eyed him suspiciously. If he thought inviting her to the conversation *and* insinuating that her stance on the matter at hand would impress her father, Chastain had sorely misjudged the comte and his regard for women. If they actually cared for her opinion, they would have requested her presence earlier.

Lorelei realized she frowned at Chastain and quickly replaced her downturned mouth with the placid smile from a few moments past. "How can my limited female mind be of service to you?"

Her father laughed—a deep, throaty sound—that had her turning to him, no doubt a look of shock on her face. He grinned back at her. Next she looked to her mother, hoping the woman would impart something of use, but the comtesse kept her eyes on her hands, knotted in her lap as if she hadn't been a part of the conversation at all. They looked at odds. Her father never smiled.

She had most assuredly missed something of great importance.

"Father?" she asked.

"Come, my daughter." He held his arms wide. Grudgingly, she moved to him and allowed him to embrace her. "You have done well, my child," he whispered for her alone.

She pulled back and looked to him for clarification. "What have you done?"

He brought her close once more. "You will remember your pledge—and wipe that dour look from your face. This is a joyous occasion."

"We are to be wed," Lord Chastain said behind her. "I have spoken to men in powerful places and banns are to be read with all due haste. We shall be married not long after."

Marriage? Reading of the banns? All due haste?

"Surely you jest."

The words bounced around her head, causing a splitting headache within seconds.

Her whole body screamed no. She should feel elated by the news, renewed in her mission knowing De Pez's threats were unfounded.

While she hadn't done so in a very long time, at one point in her youth, she'd envisioned herself walking down a long aisle with hordes of onlookers. She'd be gowned in a dress befitting a queen, with yards and yards of material spanning the length of a large cathedral. The only thing lacking from these dreams was her intended. Never had she so much as gotten a glimpse of the man's face, though she was sure he wasn't Lord Chastain.

"Do you not have something to say to the duke?" her mother prodded.

There was much she longed to say to *the duke*.

Though none of it was appropriate to say in polite company, nor in front of her unsuspecting parents, for she hadn't only been keeping De Pez's letter a secret— they had no idea she'd deviated from their plan and snuck out to meet Chastain.

Lorelei would delight in railing at Lord Chastain, diminishing his manhood. Or questioning the stock of his blood, for no man raised a true gentlemen would take such liberties with an innocent.

Rage flared in her. The nerve to show his face here and ask for her hand in marriage. And why? That was the burning question—why her?

"Perhaps they need a few moments to speak privately," the comte finally said, ending the awkward silence that had befallen the room.

She would not be left alone in Chastain's company.

She looked to the duke, and his smile faltered. Her eyes narrowed and her fists clenched at her sides, her passive expression having melted from her face at Chastain's mention of marriage.

Had he awoken from his stupor, realized the grave mistake he'd made with her, and come to make things right? If so, marriage made little sense, for he didn't look about to apologize.

"I fear, Comte, that I haven't the time for an extended social call," Chastain said. "I have things to attend to before our announcement is read by one and all in the papers tomorrow."

Tomorrow? Lorelei wondered if her father had ever planned to ask her if she were willing to marry Chastain. It was too much to ask, even for her country.

"Camille." Chastain bowed before her mother. "It was lovely to meet you. I must say your housekeeper prepares fine tea. You must send instructions round to my kitchen."

"Thank you, my lord." Her mother blushed, actually turned a soft crimson at the man's compliment. Lorelei had never seen her mother so openly display her emotions.

Next he stood before her, every inch the gentleman, and stared at her intently. "Lady Lorelei, we shall suit well, I have no fear."

"If you say it is so, I am sure it will be, my lord."

"May I call on you?" There was little emotion in his words, almost as if he were saying what he thought was proper for the moment. "Lady Lorelei?"

She would rather throw herself in front of a runaway buggy again then be subject to his company for any extended amount of time.

Thankfully, her mother saved her from responding. "Oh, I see that as very unlikely, Lord Chastain."

"Please, call me Benji," he said. "You are to be as a mother to me, after all."

"Very well, Benji," her mother tentatively tried the name. "Lore and I will be extremely busy preparing for her big day, and she may be indisposed until then."

"So it is settled." The comte stood and slapped Chastain upon the back. "We shall allow the women their time to prepare, and we will do what men do."

Lorelei had no notion of what her father referred to,

and truly, she didn't recognize the man before her. He smiled, he laughed, and he patted another man on the back. All actions her father, with his severe nature, had never allowed himself to do.

"Then I will be off." Chastain bowed to her once more before turning toward the door. "I will see myself out. I wish you a blessed evening, Camille and Lore."

The man dared use her shortened name.

If her mother's smile wasn't beaming so brightly, and her father wasn't pacing before the fire murmuring to himself about their good fortune, Lorelei would scream.

Alas, she knew it would do no good.

France was a country of unrest and revolution. And at the moment, Lorelei was the one sent to find the plans that could save them.

King Louis XV had hoped removal of the plans would stop attacks by their own countrymen, but when Lord Chastain's father had been gifted the title of duke and endowed with great lands and wealth by King George III, her country feared he'd sold the plans to England. Many suspected Chastain had been given the title by the English specifically to gain control of the plans, but the claim had never been substantiated, nor had any siege been successful. That simple fact was enough to keep King Louis XVI from storming England and taking back what belonged to him.

Finally, the comte spoke. "You have done us proud, my daughter."

"I will not marry that man, *Pere*!" she shouted. "There are other ways to gain what we seek."

Her father stopped before the hearth, his back to her, but his voice filled the room. "You will do as I say."

She flinched at the conviction in his words.

"Please," she begged. "Do not—"

"Lore, you will listen to your father." Camille spoke timidly from her chair. "Besides, he is a nice enough man."

"Nice enough?" she asked. They didn't know him as she did; they hadn't seen the ugly side of him that she had.

"He favors my tea." For all her mother's bravado, she did act the weeping woman on many occasions.

"Is the urgency so great that I must marry him so soon?" she asked. "I do not understand."

"Of course, I hope it does not actually come to be," her father scoffed.

"Then why even go along with the charade?"

"How else are we to gain entrance to his house?" her father asked. "You both can make a social visit to his London home without anyone thinking it improper. Mayhap with the excuse of selecting new draperies or some such nonsense. While there, you may search."

Her father rambled on and on about the new accessibility her sham of a betrothal would afford them, yet all she thought of was herself and her future. Any hope of staying in London, maybe pursuing the marquis, was gone. A woman was usually blamed when a betrothal was called off, no matter who had shied from the union.

Lorelei would be ruined, her reputation tarnished beyond repair, and the scandal would likely follow her back to France. De Pez, and most certainly Bonaparte, cared naught about that simple fact.

"When will you be able to call at Chastain's London home?" the comte asked.

"I do—"

"Oh, it will be a few days, at the least," her mother cut her off. "We must start preparations for a dress and the wedding: flowers, food and drink, the perfect place. Do you think Lord Chastain will allow us the use of his funds?"

"Wait." Lorelei held up her hand, and her father halted in mid-pace. "I thought you said the wedding would not *actually* happen."

"We must be prepared for any way this may proceed. What if he keeps the plans at his country estate…or, as our people fear, he's sold the plans to the English? It will be your responsibility to find them and return them to France."

"And what am I to do once we are married?" The idea of spending the rest of her life with him was a fate worse than death. "I cannot—"

Lorelei had much more to worry about than her reputation and suitability for a future marriage—now she feared actually having to marry the rakehell, Chastain…and sharing his wedding bed.

"*Ma fille.*" Her father hadn't used the term in many years. Now he stood before her, determined. "Once we have the plans, we will disappear back to France, and the Comte and Comtesse of Epernon will cease to exist."

And when the comte disappeared, so would Lorelei. Which would mean saying goodbye to Andrew for good.

Chapter Nine

Andrew stared, unseeing, at the papers spread across his desk: tenant disputes, repairs needed, and land acquisitions. Part of him was content to be back to some semblance of normalcy. He took great care in his day-to-day tasks, spending increasing time and energy on what used to be matters he insisted should be handled by his stewards and solicitor.

Anything to keep his hands and mind occupied. Otherwise, he would surely talk himself into taking action. He would seek Lady Lorelei out, persuade her to see him as an honorable match, and likely request an audience with the comte.

Why couldn't he do just that?

Simple: she'd given him no indication that she sought his attention, nor that of any man.

All the flowers, carriage rides, and dances would not stop her from rejecting him. The thought of confessing his tender feelings for her—feelings he hadn't had time to process, nor come to terms with—sent waves of unease through him. He'd never bothered himself with a woman in the long term, besides the few courtesans he'd favored enough to keep close for a fortnight or two, but this… This draw to Lorelei was unexplainable, and it took much to push thoughts of her away.

But every time he managed an hour without thinking about her, Andrew suddenly felt her in his arms, smelled her floral scent, and remembered her pounding fists on his torso, arms, and neck.

Something he didn't quite understand had come over her at that moment in the park—something she hadn't seen fit to explain. It was far more than the overwhelming sense of hysteria, or the aftershocks of realizing she was safe and unharmed.

As if on cue, female voices floated into his study where the door stood slightly ajar.

The words were spoken so hurriedly he could not understand what was being said, though if the matter needed his attention, Mrs. Bee or his butler would call for him.

Andrew departed his desk as the voices continued. He stepped lightly to his study door and peeked through the crack. Unfortunately, Mrs. Bee's sturdy frame blocked the guest from view, which stood to reason if the person was unwanted and uninvited.

"…I do not care if you contest your immediate relation to our good King George III." Mrs. Bee's voice rose in frustration. "I will ask once more, please leave your calling card, and I will give it to the marquis when he is not otherwise occupied."

His butler cowered against the wall to the left of the front door.

Andrew wanted to chuckle at the frightened look his longtime servant turned in his direction. He silently pleaded for Andrew to intervene, but knew he'd face Bee's wrath if he were to speak his request.

"I have told you, I do not possess calling cards."

The desperation in the girl's words made the voice all but unrecognizable to him, yet drew him across the foyer, closer to the commotion.

"Mrs. Bee," Andrew said. "Can I be of help?"

"Oh, my lord." Flustered, Bee turned to face him, bringing her hand to her chest. "I have everything under control. I was only—"

"Lady Lorelei?" He took in her slimming pale gown. "Do come in. Is everything as it should be?"

Not for the first time, Andrew had the nagging feeling that his thoughts had conjured her up to stand before him.

"I only wanted…" She let her words trail off and glanced nervously between Mrs. Bee and his butler as both listened to every word.

Andrew cleared his throat, bringing his servants' attention to him. "If you will excuse us." Stepping forward, he took Lorelei's elbow. "If you will be so kind as to join me in my drawing room, we may speak privately."

"My lord?" Mrs. Bee asked when he made to walk from the room, leaving both servants open-mouthed in his wake. Besides Benji and the occasional chit sent by Madame Sasha, Andrew rarely had guests. No respectable woman had crossed his threshold in recent memory. "Shall I prepare tea?"

"I will ring if tea is required." Truth be told, he had no clue what a lady required during a social call. Besides bringing her flowers, Andrew hadn't called on anyone socially—that didn't include intimate relations—in longer than he could remember.

With the door closed, he turned to her, drinking in the sight of her. "You look well."

Any other words eluded him. He'd wanted to be near her so much since she'd left him in the park. Nothing he said could fully capture everything he wanted to say and do.

Her eyes wide, she stared back at him, silent.

He hadn't any idea why she'd come, but she appeared ready to flee, much as she had after their near-miss at the park.

He expected her to apologize, maybe even give some semblance of an explanation.

"Andrew…" His name on her lips was so sweet to his ears, yet also the saddest thing he'd heard of late. "I am sorry if I disturbed you."

"Any time with you is never a disturbance. Please, sit."

"I do not have much time."

He wanted to tell her he'd take one minute or an hour, it mattered only that she was here with him now. But something troubled her.

"Tell me, Lorelei. Is something amiss?"

"Nothing, I swear." She sighed. "I only needed to see you, to tell you—"

"You owe me no explanation." At her confused expression, Andrew continued. "I know you were unnerved after the accident, shaking from the closeness of everything." He rattled off excuse after excuse, giving her a way out—letting her know he did not question nor judge her actions.

In the blink of an eye, she took the few steps forward and was in his arms. Every concern and question left him then, replaced by Lorelei's warmth as his arms surrounded her. It no longer matter what ailed her, or if she were upset; as long he held her close, he vowed that nothing would hurt her again.

For a brief moment, she was the girl he'd seen in the shadows outside that ball, whose shoulders had shaken as she'd cried silently. But she pulled back before he was ready to let her go and looked to him.

Andrew took in Lorelei's lovely face, and all he could think was how he'd worried about her. In fact, he'd had his horse readied on three separate occasions since the near-tragedy in the park. When she'd fled from him that day, he'd known she was still dazed from shock. He'd followed her at a distance to make sure she arrived safety home—which was a good thing because she'd never sent word to him.

And so he'd fretted over her.

"You are truly divine, my lady." Andrew let his fingers roam up and down the length of Lorelei's arm, pausing every few inches to caress the bare, heated skin. How he longed to touch his lips to the very spot he explored. The inner elbow was a most delicate, sensitive place. If one suckled just right, it was very possible to send a woman into a fit of passion.

"Your lordship," Lorelei whispered, but all he heard was, *More. I want more.*

"We have been over this, my sweet. My Christian name will do. Andrew."

"Andrew, I must—"

He could no longer contain himself. Fingers, once caressing her arm, now moved to her cheek, her neck, and pulled her face to his, stopping her words. Ever so gently, his hand moved into her dark hair, which hung in perfect English curls about her shoulders. So close he could taste her breath, he slowed to enjoy the feel of her silken strands running through his hands.

He ached to have her naked, her hair covering his chest—and her emerald eyes smoldering after a passionate bout of lovemaking. Their legs entwined as they rested, preparing themselves to sate their thirst once more.

"Andrew, truly, I must go," she pleaded, yet had never divulged why she'd come to him in the first place.

Her words brought him back to the present: his morning drawing room, not long past the cresting of the sun overhead, and him clad in his riding pants and boots.

And she, in the most pristine of pastel pinks, a walking dress completely at odds with her exotic looks. No woman with her amount of appeal should be covered in anything less than the finest silks of the richest hues. Deep red, green, and blue would befit her dark complexion and raven hair. If they married—no, when they married—he would outfit her in nothing less than the finest the Orient had to offer.

"No, you mustn't," he argued. "Stay here with me. For eternity." He had no idea what had come over him since he'd met Lady Lorelei. If he didn't know better, he'd say she was born of gypsy blood and had cast a spell upon his heart.

She pulled from his grasp, looking him in the eyes. "You know I cannot."

"No, I do not know that." He felt empty without her, and pulled her close once more. "I will call on your father this very afternoon, ask for your hand—and it will be done."

The draw to her had only increased since their time

in the park—possibly due to how close she'd come to losing her life.

"We have only met recently. That would be highly forward of you," she pleaded. "Please, I must go. My mother is waiting."

"Let her wait."

She laughed. One would expect a deep, sensual tone, but the sound was a sweet melody, light and refreshing. "I fear my mother is not a patient woman."

"Then allow me to call my carriage round to deliver you with all haste," he said. "I do not want to anger your mother before she has a chance to know my intentions."

"You will do well to stay on her good side. So I must go." She stood, smoothing her dress. "My maid awaits me in your stables."

"No, you will not walk." His protest was met with another of her coy smiles.

"Oh, but I will walk. Just as I arrived here, so shall I return."

"When will I see you again?" He had to know. "Will you be at the Sharden's ball this evening?"

"I do not believe so."

"The musicale tomorrow afternoon at Lady Turlington's?"

"I am not much for instruments."

"Then when?" He knew he sounded the petulant child, wanting his way and no other. "I will send word to them both to issue you and your family an invitation, if that is the problem."

"You mustn't." The fright in her voice told him not to push her further. London was a small town, and he would see her again, though it might not be today or tomorrow.

"Please, know I am very serious, and my affection for you—while sudden—is very pure."

"I can see that." She glanced over her shoulder at the closed door.

"No one can hear us. I assure you my servants are most discreet."

"I am not worried about gossip," she confided. "I care for you, too. Neither of us knows what the future holds. Just remember I do reciprocate your affection, though, it may be some time before we can see each other again."

His heart soared at her words, and plummeted just as quickly. "Your words sound like the sweetest of goodbyes."

"My family is leaving town for a holiday in the country soon. I am unsure of when we will return to town. So, I am not saying goodbye forever, but I am saying goodbye for now."

"Will you write?"

Again, she laughed. "I shan't be gone that long, your lordship."

"Tell me you will not forget about me."

"However can I forget about the most dashing Englishman I've had the pleasure of meeting?" she teased. "I fear I should be worried that your memories of me will fade as quickly as the setting sun."

"Then I shall move somewhere where the sun never sets."

But to him, her remembrance of their brief time together meant much, for it was just that: brief. He only hoped it was not forgettable, as well.

"I must go. Farewell, Andrew."

He was helpless to do anything more than watch her

walk through the door, hear her footsteps as she departed his house, and dream of a time when he would never, ever let her walk away from him again.

# # #

Lorelei swept the tears from her cheeks as she rounded the corner on to St. Martin Lane. She'd lied to Andrew, something she hadn't wanted to do. She'd left her carriage a few blocks away on Bond Street when she'd slipped out the back door of a bookstore and made her way to the marquis' home.

She'd gone on a whim, to say goodbye. To reassure herself that if things worked favorably for her in the future, then maybe, just maybe, she could return to him...and beg his forgiveness.

He looked at her as no one ever had before. Up until this meeting, she had doubted the depth of his feelings for her, hoping his words of love had sprung from a place of vulnerability and shock after they'd nearly been run down by that buggy, though her maid had told her later that Andrew had followed at a distance until he was assured she'd returned home safely.

Not once today did she pull away from him when he touched her, nor did she flinch when he set his lips upon her cheek. She'd wanted to give herself to him—washing away the filth that Chastain's touches had left on her skin—but he would not have it.

No matter what happened, she was certain honorable men existed.

The Marquis of Drake—Andrew—was proof of that.

Not all men were of her father's ilk. Not all men

took advantage of her as De Pez and Lord Chastain desired.

That knowledge comforted her. While the marquis was not meant to be hers, another would likely catch his attention and capture his heart, though he denied the possibility. A woman without secrets or motives. A woman without higher allegiances than to her husband and children. She wished for it to be so, as much as she feared one day a woman would come and claim his heart, erasing Lorelei from his memory.

Though not of her choice or making, Lorelei's allegiance belonged to the Comte and Comtesse of Epernon. Her parents, Mathis and Camille Parisot de La Valette, had sold her fidelity to the next man they suspected would have great wealth and influence, Napoleon Bonaparte.

She was Lady Lorelei Parisot de La Valette of French birth. Daughter to a pair of faithful spies granted a meaningless vanity title that had been given by her country, only to be stripped away after King Louis XVI's sudden demise. Since that day, her family had been virtual fugitives, moving from small town to even smaller village, never staying too long for fear someone would recognize them and alert the dictatorship of their location.

Lorelei kept her head down as she walked to hide her red, swollen eyes, and took solace in the fact that she'd told Andrew how she felt and knew he returned her ardor. They were fated to be as Romeo and Juliet, two lovers never meant to be, though the future did not turn out as hoped for those young lovers.

Andrew would find out about her betrothal soon, and she yearned for him to forgive her. To accept her future as she'd been forced to do.

He was a man like any other, and would move on; give his heart again to someone more worthy.

She turned into the alley behind the bookstore and hurried through the back door and into the warm shop. She hadn't noticed the chill outside until the heat from the store hit her, warming her numb fingers and nose. A looking glass sat close to the front counter of the store, allowing the owner to glimpse around a tall bookshelf. As she made her way to the front, she noticed the proprietor was not behind the counter, so she paused to assess her appearance. As she feared, her eyes were red and slightly puffy, but her hair was as it should be, hanging perfectly about her shoulders.

With focused calm, Lorelei departed the bookstore. A chime sounded above the door, signaling her departure. She heard a faint call of farewell from the store owner as the door closed behind her, leaving her alone on the most crowded street in London.

Blending into the flow of foot traffic, she moved across the street and a few shops down.

Another bell chimed as she entered a shop, but this time, the room was sparklingly clean, with not a trace of dust on any surface.

"Ah, you must be Lady Lorelei, Lord Chastain's intended." A lady, gowned in the most severe of dresses, greeted her. "Please, come this way. Your mother awaits you."

Lorelei allowed the woman to herd her through a narrow passage that opened into a large room covered in mirrors, with lace and other fabrics draped over every available surface. The mirrors reflected Lorelei's trim waist, long neck, and cascading dark hair. She knew she was deeply pleasing to the eyes, a trait of which her father was overly proud. She dreamed of her father showing pride in her intelligence or her skill at archery, but no, he was most gratified in his daughter's ability to turn a man's head with the coyest of smiles or a flip of her hair.

She'd come to loathe her appearance. If it had been up to her, she'd have cut her hair from her very scalp; she'd forgo applying the coal to her eyelids to enhance her green eyes. She would dress in the thickest of cottons or burlap and live a simple life, hiding her splendor and only shining for the man she loved. That would have been enough, and at the same time, more than she could ever wish for.

Yet, she'd gone along with what her parents and her crown demanded.

And that was a choice she would be made to live with.

"Lore!" her mother exclaimed. "Wherever have you been? I have selected several gowns for myself in my boredom."

Lorelei couldn't help smiling at her mother. She truly hadn't seen the woman this happy in a long time, if ever. Her mother was as vain as Lorelei hoped never to be. While she'd never been a great beauty, she had been enough to catch the eye of Lorelei's father...and some said the King himself. Camille had told her stories of her younger escapades, helping the crown find traitors amongst their own countrymen. She'd regaled Lorelei with tales of important men who'd tell all to a pretty face after a few drinks. At the time, Lorelei had idolized her mother, dreamed of doing the very same thing—all for her country.

"Oh, Mother. I am sure you quite enjoyed yourself without me."

But over the years, Lorelei had discovered the secrets her mother had worked hard to keep hidden. Not every mission had been a success—far from it. Camille walked with a bit of a limp that she—and Lorelei's father—tried to hide. When Lorelei was fifteen, she'd dared ask her mother about it, thinking it could have been a fall from a horse during a daring ride across an open field to evade capture.

It was with tears in her eyes that her mother had recounted the dark tale of a night spent in a tavern on the Scottish border, and a rowdy group of Frenchmen. She'd spent nigh on a month working as a bar wench and gaining the confidences of a group of men with ties to a rebel in France. They'd seen through her disguise—possibly from the very beginning—and decided to have a spot of fun with Camille before they fled. The night had ended with her mother being thrown from a second-story landing, breaking her legs in several places. She told Lorelei that she had feared she'd never walk again, but confided that the physical pain was nothing compared to the emotional pain she'd endured.

It was only a short year later, after she'd learned to walk again, that she'd met and married Mathis Parisot de La Valette at the insistence of her crown.

Lorelei stared at her mother as she relived the story told to her so many years ago.

An odd expression crossed her mother's face, as if she knew what Lorelei thought, and begged her to let the past be.

"Come, my daughter," Camille spoke, a hitch in her voice. "Mrs. Despond has the finest selection of marital fabrics in all of London."

Part of her wondered if her mother had had a

wedding, or if her bliss over the occasion was due to her lack of that special day. But she'd never ask, for the pain it caused.

Instead, she turned to the shop owner. "Thank you for accommodating us on such short notice, Mrs. Despond."

The short, rounded woman waved a hand in dismissal. "There is no bother, my dear. My family has dressed the previous four duchesses of Chastain. I'd begun to fret that young Benji would never select a wife."

"You dressed Benji's mother and grandmother?" She looked to Camille, whose interest had also been caught by the statement.

"Oh, no," the woman rushed to say. "I have outfitted Benji's distant cousins. As you most likely know, Lord Chastain, Benji's father, inherited the title and estates after his third cousin succumbed to a sudden illness. By that time, Lord Chastain's wife had already passed to the hereafter, God rest her soul."

The woman bowed her head in respect. "But that is enough gossip for today. Now, what have you in mind for your special day?"

While the dressmaker and her mother debated the merits of lace over brocade, Lorelei wondered if the previous Chastain's sudden illness had anything to do with her French counterparts. But no, her country could not have known Chastain's father's distant relation was a titled duke in England. It was absurd to think her crown had that much influence outside its own borders.

It made no sense to put an end to an English lord and send the keeper of the plans away from France, knowing he may very well flee the country to take up residence in the English countryside.

"What do you think?" her mother asked, holding up a bolt of the most delicate lace over a sturdy brocade. "Mrs. Despond made a very good point. Lord Chastain's country estate might well be very chilly this time of year, and if we insist on a wedding set in the gardens, it would be essential to have a dress made of something more substantial. I am sure Chastain would never forgive me if I allowed you to catch your death of a cold before your wedding night."

Lorelei's stomach lurched. In the last day, she'd pushed the thought of marital relations with Lord Chastain from her mind, instead focusing on a way to find the plans so this blasted farce of a wedding never took place. Her mother's idea to hold the ceremony at Lord Chastain's country home had been brilliant, to say the least, and had given her a thread of hope that she might yet avoid an unpleasant union with Chastain.

"You know I trust your judgment over all others, Mother." Lorelei moved to sit against a wall as the pair of ladies continued to argue, haggle, and toss bolts of fabric aside as they planned the perfect dress for a wedding that was anything but perfect.

Chapter Ten

"Ye look might pretty, m'lady," Isabelle whispered.

Lorelei looked up into the looking glass before her, making eye contact with her maid before smiling. "Thank you, Isabelle, but you must still call me Lorelei."

The girl nodded and moved out of sight.

Lorelei focused back on the mirror before her—and her exquisitely gowned body.

A heavy cream brocade clung to her every curve with a mesh overlay and beaded pearls swirling in patterns about the bust and trailing down into the skirt. When she'd first seen the dress, commissioned at her mother's behest, Lorelei had wanted to weep and tear the dress apart at the seams. She'd had to suppress her newly acquired aversion to pearls, for she would never tell the comtesse of Chastain's actions. They reminded her of that night in Covent Gardens, choking her as severely as Chastain had that eve. She'd longed all day to shed the offensive gown, now forever a reminder of her own servitude—to her parents, to De Pez and his chosen faction, and now to Chastain.

The bottom edge of the gown was caked in mud, now dried to dirt that fell to the floor. She and Chastain had married in the gardens only hours before, followed by a feast for the servants and local gentry—segregated, of course.

There were cheers all around as the duke's guests saluted the new Duchess Chastain. Her head still ached from the revelry of the day.

Now, she stood alone in her chambers, her maid sent to prepare her for Chastain and their wedding night. In the mirror, she stared at a woman she didn't recognize, preparing herself for a life of uncertainty and solitude.

The worst part was that she'd agreed to every condition; she had never fought her parents' demands that she help restore their name and status in France— and rightly so. She had been eager to help her family leave the shadows of fear and doubt, and regain a bit of the life they had known under Louis XVI…even if that meant putting their trust in a ruler who had yet to prove himself.

Lorelei may not trust De Pez, and certainly couldn't depend on Bonaparte's rise to power, but she'd always trusted the comte and his decisions for them.

"M'lady?" Lorelei looked over her shoulder to her maid. "Ye night shift be ready. Is there sum else ye be need'n?"

"Can you help undo my laces?"

"Oh, pardon me lapse." Isabelle rushed over, and Lorelei turned once more to the mirror as the maid hurriedly pulled at the laces. "It was right nice be'n yur maid."

"You say that as if you will no longer be my maid, Isabelle." Though she would not call the girl her friend, Lorelei felt a closeness to her that she hadn't found with another soul in London.

"I be leave'n with ye pa when he goes back to London."

Lorelei sucked in her breath.

The maid released the ties at her back. "Oh, I be sorry for hurt'n ye."

It wasn't Isabelle's hands that had cause Lorelei pain, but the maid's words. "I am not injured. I only expected you would stay with me. I am certain my husband will pay your wage."

"It not be that, m'lady," Isabelle said, returning to her task. "Me beau, Tomas, is in town, and I do be missing him."

"Oh, Isabelle." She turned to face her maid, embracing her. "I am so happy for you."

Lorelei had been so concerned with her own dreaded fate she hadn't stopped to think about anyone else around her.

"Thank ye." Isabelle pulled from Lorelei's embrace. "But right now, ye be need'n to be ready for ye beau. I hear men be right impatient on this night."

The moment was drawing closer, and Lorelei would soon not be able to avoid it or keep it from her mind. She hadn't been alone with Chastain since that one night at Covent Garden, and all she'd had to show for those brief moments was a ruined dress and the loss of her beautiful pearl necklace. In its place, a gaudy red garnet ring sat heavily upon her hand.

"I do be hoping Tomas asks ta marry me," her maid gushed. "He been working hard at his ferrier post, and saving all his coin."

So easily, Lorelei forgot that all believed this to be her blessed day, the day she'd dreamed of her whole life.

She'd married a duke, and a wealthy one at that. Yet, Lorelei had barely summoned a smile for the crowd who'd attended, and had fled the festivities shortly after their wedding feast was served—not that Chastain had noticed, for he hadn't pulled himself away to check on his new duchess.

"You may go, Isabelle," Lorelei said, dismissing her maid. "I can slip from my gown and don my shift. Thank you for all you have done."

The girl looked on the verge of tears as she nodded and fled the room.

One man was noticeably missing from their festivities, though Lorelei was thankful for his absence. Surely, Chastain would have sent word to his best friend about his impending nuptials, yet he hadn't come.

The Marquis of Drake.

She pushed the image of the marquis from her mind. Of course, he could not attend the marriage of a woman who had deceived him. Part of her had envisioned him riding into the gardens—effectively saving her from the horrid situation she'd been forced into.

But he hadn't come.

She stiffened when a light tap sounded at the door, her dress finally falling loose about her front.

"Lore?" her mother's voice called from across the room.

She breathed a sigh of relief at the sight of the comtesse, still wearing her exquisite gown from earlier. Chastain would have entered her suite via the door connecting their dressing room, not the one leading to the hall.

"Mother."

"My child." Camille closed the door behind her and

came to stand before her daughter. "You are so brave."

"I do not feel at all brave, but rather helpless." Her shoulders sagged and her dress slipped farther to the ground, leaving her in only her under-shift. "I do so hope this is all worth it."

Her mother gave her a reassuring smile. "Has your *pere* ever misled us before?"

"Of course not."

"Then let us trust him now." Her mother took both of Lorelei's hands in her own, looking down at the family ring Chastain had presented to her. "I promise you will not be long married, unless you choose to keep your new husband."

Lorelei could not imagine a world in which she'd choose to be forever linked to the duke, but she knew this marriage weighed heavily on her mother, as the woman had become more and more withdrawn as the days progressed. "Maybe you are right, Mother. One never knows what their future holds," Lorelei said to lighten the mood. "Besides, our family lives for adventure and the unknown."

"That we do, my child." Her mother embraced her quickly before stepping back. "But I mustn't keep you. There are many pleasurable things about marriage...even if the man is not whom you'd intended to wed."

Camille departed the room much as she moved through life, never disrupting anything, and with barely a sound.

For not the first time, Lorelei wished she could do the same: shed her physical form and drift on the breeze to another place—maybe even another time.

Instead, she removed her undergarments and slipped into her night shift to await the duke's arrival at their marriage bed.

#

Andrew entered the front door of his country estate, a spring in his step.

"Good morning," he called to his servant.

"Morning, my lord. *The London Post* arrived while you were out."

"I trust you put it in my study?" At his butler's nod, Andrew continued. "Very good. Please have my morning meal brought there."

Soon he would return to London—and Lorelei. The fortnight had been up for a few days, and he expected she had returned to town, and even now awaited his call. But with distance came a bit of clarity. No man wanted to be perceived as too eager in his efforts to woo a woman. It would behoove him to take his time, give her space, and wait for her to want him as much as he longed to rush back to London, make his intentions known to the comte, and make arrangements for their wedding. It would be a grand affair, a wedding the likes of which the *ton* hadn't beheld since the last royal wedding. People would come from far and wide to witness their union.

It would not happen as speedily as he'd like, for he knew Lorelei must have some family that would need to be notified, and then would require time to travel to England for the ceremony, though she claimed she had none. Hell, he'd hire a fleet of ships to get them here quicker if need be.

He settled behind his desk to review all last-minute missives from his tenants. He'd hired a crew to mend the stables, re-thatch the roof of the local parsonage, and see to the estate gardens. When he and his new bride traveled to his estate, he wanted it in perfect order, as she deserved. He'd also sent for more servants from the local village to tidy the manor, polish every wooden surface, and beat every rug. As a last-minute thought, he'd commissioned a prized artist to paint several new landscapes to adorn the walls of the morning salon and Lorelei's suite.

It had been many years since a woman had called Drake Abbey home, and he would do all in his power to make sure his home became theirs.

Aside from the light skirts he and Benji had kept company with over the years, he hadn't the faintest idea what a woman wanted. Would Lorelei be amicable to decorating her own rooms? Would she select bold, earthen colors or the pastel shades that were all the rage in London? He hoped she'd select deep shades befitting her exotic heritage.

Rightly, it mattered naught. His wife, the Marchioness of Drake, would have any and all she desired. If that meant knocking down his old manor and building a new estate to her personal liking, he would make that happen.

Ah, the life of a reformed rakehell.

The notion of one woman warming his bed for the rest of his existence sounded heavenly.

Setting aside the letters from his tenants and the recent correspondence from his London solicitor, Drake picked up the *Post*. Almost a fortnight old, he was sure the paper wouldn't hold any important news.

A page detailed the complexities of a new public waterway believed to one day improve the quality of life amongst Londoners. The next page was filled with all the latest gossip, including recent betrothal and marriages. Matches amongst London's elite were legendary and filled several pages.

He imagined his own wedding announcement. As if conjuring her name, he spotted Lady Lorelei Parisot de La Valette, daughter of the Comte and Comtesse of Epernon, visiting French nobility. He scanned the half-page announcement…and wanted to spit fire.

> *The Comte and Comtesse of Epernon*
> *are proud to announce the marriage of*
> *Lady Lorelei Parisot de La Valette to*
> *the Duke of Chastain, Benjamin Davis.*

As his rage receded, betrayal set in. The treachery of Chastain was expected—Andrew had also been an egocentric man. He sought his own pleasure at the expense of others; he took anything he wanted, and cared only for his own health. The fact that Benji had sat across from Andrew at White's and professed his willingness for a truce where Lorelei was concerned galled him to no end.

But Lorelei had been different.

His hands clenched, crinkling the paper he held. With unnecessary care, Andrew shredded the thin newspaper, tearing each piece smaller and smaller to make the story illegible.

She was a woman above all others. Most debutantes must be painted and dressed to look the prize, but Lorelei was exquisite without need for assistance from others. Many girls put forth an agreeable facade bordering on dull, while Lorelei was tame in her nature, but kept her spark of rebellion just below the surface. One only needed to look a bit deeper to discover her true qualities.

She'd returned his affection, or at least had led him to believe so.

Could he be so dim? Did the pair laugh at his expense?

No, she did care for him, just as he had a deep and abiding affection for her. No woman could deceive him so thoroughly as this, he was certain.

Andrew stood, knocking his heavy wooden chair over. He needed space—air. When the chair blocked his path, he reached under the lip of his desk, and with all his strength, hauled the massive piece of furniture off the floor and flipped it over. His papers, treasured letter opener, books, and inkwell scattered across the floor. Glass shattered when the miniature painting of his parents hit the oversized bookshelf that held his most valuable books and estate ledgers.

"My lord?" a servant asked with alarm from the now-open door.

"Out! Be gone!" he shouted.

Next he bent and grabbed his gilded chair by two legs, lifting it high, and swung, making contact with the hearth behind him. The ancient wood splintered, sending slivers to every corner of the room. Looking about the room—his sanctuary when in residence—he waited for his fury to ebb. Instead, everything he looked toward was tinted red. He moved to the large portrait of his family, commissioned when he was no more than three years of age.

The frame pulled easily from the wall. Drake held the finely crafted image before him, noting the similarities between his late father and himself: hair color, height, facial expression. He turned his gaze to his mother, a saint amongst women, captured looking to her only child with adoration in her eyes.

He studied the bond between his family, so strong that even a portrait artist had been able to capture it. He'd been alone for so many years, he'd forgotten how to genuinely care for another. People used others, and he'd fallen into the habit quickly after his father was gone and others came calling, only wanting something from him. Whether it was his coin or his favor mattered little because none of them—with the exception of Chastain—had stayed long. It had been a very long time since he'd felt anything remotely resembling affection for another person...until he'd met her.

His very own temptress.

A seductress in disguise.

She'd preyed on his insecurities, assessed his needs, and exploited his kindness.

He thought back to that fateful morning. He'd been so proud to present her with the most beautiful bouquet of flowers, the blossoms no rival to her splendor. The Comte and Comtesse had kindly accepted his call, though it veered from what was proper during courtship. Did they, too, seek to make him look the fool?

And what about their time in the park—and Lorelei's visit to him after that? He'd counted the days since then. She and Benji had had no time for a true courtship.

He could not believe that of his Lorelei. If anyone sought to harm him, it was Chastain. Another one of his games.

Andrew brought his knee up and threw the canvas painting. The wooden frame splintered as his chair had. No longer did his mother gaze on his youthful self in pride.

Throwing the ruined piece aside, he eyed the shelf that reached from floor to ceiling, packed with books, artifacts his father had collected, and years of ledgers. He took hold of one side and pulled, but the massive shelf held tight to the wall. Realizing it must be anchored, he looked to the objects adorning its shelves.

Trinkets his father had brought back to him and his mother when he'd journeyed to London for Parliament. How the previous marquis had loathed traveling and leaving behind his family, even for those brief sessions.

Andrew picked up a clay miniature of a country home and turned it over in his hands, studying the details: a holiday wreath hanging on the door, a roaring fire visible through the window, and snow covering the ground. He'd been apprehensive about touching the piece when he was young, fearful he'd drop it or damage it in some way.

Suddenly, preserving the delicate house seemed unimportant, for in his heart of hearts, he knew he'd have no son—or daughter—of his own to pass it on to, no one to cherish it after he passed. No one would ever await his return from London, counting down the days to be reunited again.

He squeezed the house between his hands and crushed it until nothing remained but dust, for that was exactly how he felt inside.

A heavy breeze would carry him far and wide, leaving pieces of him everywhere yet nowhere at the same time.

He rubbed his hands together to be rid of the powder still clinging to his skin, and small chunks bit into his soft palms. The discomfort was a welcome feeling, masking the hollowness that spread through him.

"Gunther!" he called.

"Yes, my lord?" His butler stepped into the room, most likely waiting just outside the door in case his master needed assistance.

"Ready my horse."

"Now?"

"Yes, now," he bellowed.

"Of course, my lord." The man bowed, but paused before departing the room. "Shall I send Mrs. Gladys in to tidy up this room?"

As if seeing the disaster he'd created for the first time, Andrew eyed the room. "I do not care if you set the whole manor on fire. I shan't be returning."

"Before the holidays?" Confusion clouded his face.

"Ever."

Chapter Eleven

"Just a few more days of searching. Please, *Pere*." Lorelei pleaded. "There must be somewhere we haven't looked."

"Lorelei, your mother and I have left no stone unturned. We must return to London," he said in French. They had been extremely cautious since their arrival. "It will give us time to search his townhouse while he is here. And I must send word to De Pez, letting him know that we still feel hopeful. I cannot risk sending the letter from here."

They'd acted the honored family since they had journeyed to the country for Lorelei's wedding. Every spare moment had been spent trying to avoid the dreaded day by intensively searching. Her mother had convinced Lord Chastain that a proper cleaning out and redecorating of the house was proper to prepare for a new duchess.

He'd given in to her requests, even helping his servants move furniture, but had quickly retired to his study for peace, taking the comte with him each day.

But now, they had a rare moment alone, Chastain having fled the house early and her mother being gods knew where on the estate.

"You are to leave me here? With him?"

"You are in no danger from your *husband*," her father sighed. "Please, hold yourself together and remember our cause. If I find the plans, I will come for you myself, and then you will have no cause to see him ever again, if that is what you wish."

The comte said the words as if he were giving her a choice: return to France with them, or continue on as Lady Chastain. She'd been committed to her family's goal in London these many months, but things had changed. Now, she was required to spend her nights in the arms of a man who cared little for her or her needs.

Chastain was cordial to her, and she suspected the lack of passion between them was not one-sided. She'd stopped herself on several occasions from asking why he'd married her. What had he sought to gain from their marriage? She had no great wealth or dowry to speak of, nor had he been captivated by her beauty or intellect. If an heir were what he was after, he hadn't shared that information, either.

Lorelei paced the library, flinging her arms wide. "What if we do not find them?"

"We will discuss that only when all other avenues have proven fruitless."

How her father kept his composure, she would never know. It seemed every path they tried left them as empty-handed as before.

"There is still the option of you asking Chastain where they are."

"Maybe Mother should ask," Lorelei hissed. "She

and Chastain seem to get on better than he and I."

"You will not speak of your mother thus." Her father stood abruptly, stopping her mid-pace. "She is not like you and I—she has been cursed with the ability to genuinely care about others."

"You think I am incapable of that?" The words cut her deeper than any knife.

"Do not be hurt, *ma fille*." He stepped before her, capturing her eyes with his own intent stare and placed his hand on her cheek. "You and I, we are much alike."

She wanted to be nothing like the comte. With him, there was always a hidden motive behind his actions and his words. He thought only of what would benefit his own goals. Up until recently, she had been thankful they'd also included her best interests, but with her marriage to Chastain had come the realization that her father viewed her as disposable. A pawn, much as her mother ultimately was. She was bartered and sold—for nothing.

She wondered if De Pez had offered more, whether her father would have given his only daughter to *him* in marriage.

"Do not look at me like that," he warned. "What we are doing is meant to save us all."

"And if we don't succeed? Answer me that question, *Pere*."

He sighed. "Then the plan is the same: we disappear, leave our lives and identities behind."

His plan was not well thought out and had little chance of keeping them safe for long. They'd been running for years now, living off the meager stash of coin her father had been able to hide over the years, but with their trip to London, they'd spent all they possessed— and for what? A chance to gain the favor of a man who may very well never amount to anything?

"So we will run from Chastain…and De Pez?" She almost thought it better to stay and take her chances with the duke.

The sound of an object hitting the wood floor had them both turning.

A maid stepped from the shadows, a duster in hand.

"What are you doing in here?" her father shouted at the girl in accented English. "Do you eavesdrop on our conversation?"

"Calm, *Pere*." Lorelei grasped her father's elbow to stop him from rushing across the room. "No one here knows French," she soothed him in her native tongue.

He didn't relax in the slightest.

"Be gone," he yelled at the frightened maid, who dropped her duster and fled the room, the door slamming behind her.

"*Pere*!" Lorelei shook her head. "You must be more respectful. What if she goes to Chastain and tells him of our private conversations?"

"That would a disaster." The comte returned to his chair. "But he is a lord, and will side with me. Servants should not eavesdrop on conversations, especially private ones. And as best I know, a man is entitled to a private word with his child."

His words held merit, as the titled stuck close to one another. Otherwise, anarchy and rebellion took over.

"Furthermore, your mother and I will leave immediately for London. Send word when you are to return. Now go."

"How long should I keep him here?" Her new husband had acted the caged animal as of late. "He tires of country life, and I know he would prefer to journey to town shortly."

"As long as you can." Crossing his legs from knee to ankle, the comte picked up his paper, signaling an end to their conversation. "We are done here."

Her shoulders dropped, and she fled the room. When would he learn that she had just as much at stake as he—more, since Chastain could become suspicious and discover her secret at any time?

The country was lonely, and about to get more desolate. Lorelei could think of only one place on the whole estate to go for solace.

Her mother reclined in the gardens with a heavy woolen blanket around her shoulders to ward off the chill. Camille had seldom left that very spot, except to sleep, since the wedding. Whether it was because she enjoyed the serenity of the place, or that she'd given up hope, Lorelei didn't know.

She hesitated to disturb her, for Camille had worked tirelessly preparing for Lorelei's sham wedding: coordinating flowers, selecting the perfect dress, arranging an exquisite meal consisting of Lorelei's favorite foods from home—all in ten days' time. It looked to have taken everything from her. Now she sat, speaking to no one and not lifting a finger to help in their search. Lorelei couldn't help thinking that her mother had earned this respite.

Under other circumstances, Lorelei would have agreed that the wedding had been a beautiful one, complete with striking bride and a dashing groom, married in a garden full of blooming flowers with the bright sun shining on her dark hair. Lacking had been laughter and smiles…though if the few longtime servants and country nobility had noticed, they'd said naught in front of Lorelei or her parents.

"Mother," Lorelei called as she stepped forward. "Can I ring for more tea?"

Camille balked and shrunk further into her chair, as if hoping whoever called her would go away if she hid well enough beneath her blanket.

"Are you cold?" Lorelei set her hand on her mother's shoulder, forcing the woman to acknowledge her. "I can also send for another blanket."

Camille looked up, her eyes filled with a sorrow Lorelei didn't understand. She'd aged ten years in the short time since they'd journeyed to London. Her hair was peppered with more grey then Lorelei remembered, with her mother not bothering to apply the powder used to keep it a shining black hue.

"No, thank you, my child."

"What troubles you?"

"Troubles me?" Confusion laced her words. "I am enjoying the fresh air, that is all."

"You have been doing such for many days now." Her father was agreeable to letting her while her time away here in the garden all day, but Lorelei worried for her. "Would you not be more comfortable inside, before the fire?"

If they were forced to disappear once more, leaving even their names behind, she feared her mother would be distraught. The precious little time they'd spent in London had cheered her mother greatly.

The comtesse watched a butterfly flit to and fro on the breezes, ignoring Lorelei once more.

"Father says you are to prepare to return to London." Lorelei tried another tactic to gain her full attention. "You are to leave very soon."

"You will come, too?" The sorrow fled from her face for the first time. "It will be nice to be back in London again, even if our garden is not as magnificent as this."

"No," Lorelei said, dashing the hope that had returned to her mother. "But I hope to follow as soon as I can."

"I worry about you."

Lorelei wondered if she'd heard her correctly. "Worry about me—whatever for? You taught me well, and I am prepared for any outcome." They'd spent many long days discussing what needed to be done to return them to the lives they once knew, though Lorelei had deviated from it at every turn—still, in no way was she prepared to accept failure and what that meant for their future.

"You are just a child."

"But I am wise for my years, *non*?"

"Or too naive to comprehend the severity of our situation," her mother said, pausing. "Or the…"

"What, Mother?" she asked when Camille didn't continue. "We will find the plans—I have not given up yet. Is there something you have not told me?"

"Your father…" Again, her mother could not, would not, say what was troubling her. "Never mind, my child. I must hurry inside and pack now. The comte will not tarry long if he is set on departing."

With a labored groan, Camille stood, keeping the blanket wrapped about her as she moved back to the double doors that led inside.

Her vacated chair, plush with lavender pillows, looked inviting. There was no reason for Lorelei to hurry back inside, for the dinner menu had been planned since

145

her arrival by the housekeeper. Lorelei had never been asked to inspect the silver or been made privy to any household disputes. The life of a duchess was one of languor.

They'd agreed she would do what was expected of a new duchess days after her wedding, leaving the comte to spend his days wandering the house and the property. He looked the idle man, enjoying the fruits of his daughter's advantageous marriage. He'd even accompanied Chastain to the local inn for a rousing night of drink and camaraderie, though the evening had been a waste when Chastain had imbibed so much that he'd fallen asleep before her father could probe him for any answers.

The servants and local gentry had been little help either, as none of them were overly familiar with the duke or his late father. Everything they learned pointed to Chastain being a man who enjoyed pleasure and leisure, entrusting his estate matters to his steward.

Not to leave any stone unturned, Lorelei had met with the steward and kept him busy with household questions while her father searched his small residence. He'd returned to the main house empty-handed and in a foul mood.

Lorelei felt something moist on her exposed hand.

The first raindrop that had fallen since their arrival in the country.

She remained sitting, letting drop after drop fall upon her skin. Soon, her face was wet, and her clothes soaked up the water that continued to fall as clouds pushed across the sky. Beyond the neatly trimmed hedge of the garden, two horses galloped toward the Chastain stable. One was surely her husband, his horse's hurried steps solid. Beside him rode a woman, her sable-blue skirt catching the breeze and whipping in the wind. Both their heads were lowered as they rode for cover before the full force of the storm hit.

Lorelei stood as they disappeared from view around the side of the stable, seeking her own shelter from the wrath of the coming storm.

Chapter Twelve

Lorelei entered the Chastain carriage, dreading even a short drive enclosed with her husband after they'd made the journey back to London only a few days prior. She took in the duke's dashing figure where he sat facing her across the carriage. To any woman who didn't know him, he appeared quite handsome, smartly dressed with a perfectly tied cravat, glistening boots, and a wickedly enticing grin.

Every inch the daring gentleman of the *ton*—and recently reformed rake since his marriage to Lorelei.

But she knew better.

After six weeks secluded in the country with no one for company but him—and his brigade of loyal servants—she was most agreeable to journeying back to town, even locked within the confines of a carriage for nigh on three full days. Thankfully, he'd chosen to sit astride his horse for most of the journey.

Added to her unhappiness was the absence of her parents, whom she hadn't seen since their departure several days after the ceremony. While she had been charged with keeping Chastain occupied so they could search his London townhouse, she'd heard nothing from either her father or mother since they'd left her. At the very least, she'd expected a letter from her father giving her their approval to travel back to London, but all she'd received was a hastily scribbled note from her mother declaring the new Duchess Chastain a success in the eyes of the *ton*.

Since the *happy* couple had arrived in London a few days before, she hadn't glimpsed hide nor hair of the man whose last name was now her own, and she was ever thankful for what kept him from her and her bed.

But this night he'd demanded her presence—and so they sat, across from one another, each avoiding eye contact.

Her weeks in the country had been occupied with her never-ending search of every nook and cranny on the large estate. She'd even gone so far as to visit the vicarage and search for hidden spaces within relics.

And she'd found nothing, amounting to hours of fruitless probing.

All she'd managed to do was collapse each evening out of total exhaustion. She awoke most mornings still clothed in her filthy gown from the previous day.

If her new husband noticed her lack of personal care or extreme fatigue, he did not so much as mention it, preferring instead to sate his lustful thirst elsewhere, quite possibly with the woman she'd seen him chasing on horseback at his country home. It was almost as if he'd taken what he wanted, namely Lorelei, and now that he was in possession of her, the duke was no longer interested.

This night, he was paying her as little attention as

she'd come to expect, which again, suited her fine. He hadn't looked at her since she'd entered the enclosed carriage—not even to ask if she'd like heated coals placed under the wool blanket covering her legs to ward off the cold. Nor had he waited outside the conveyance to help her inside. For all his years as a gentleman, he certainly had learned naught.

If she planned to spend any significant time with Chastain, she would have set to the task of bringing his manners up to snuff.

Lorelei only focused on the present undertaking, however: finding the plans and fleeing London for her home country.

Sadly, tonight wasn't about furthering that goal.

It was the first time the newly returned Lord and Lady Chastain were to appear in public—together.

She thought back to the first and only time she'd been in a ballroom with her new husband, but all she could picture was being in the marquis' strong, capable arms and twirling about the dance floor, their laughter calling attention to them both. It was just these thoughts that had kept her sane during her sojourn away from London.

Such a brief moment in her life. One song, five minutes in his arms, a room full to bursting, yet he was all she'd seen. His deep voice all she'd heard. She hesitated to think about what he thought of her now, particularly considering the afternoon she'd spent in his arms before her dress fitting. In her note, the comtesse had written that Lorelei's union was all anyone was talking about. Every afternoon tea, shopping excursion, and night at the playhouse had been filled with well-wishers. She suspected Camille was enjoying the attention bestowed her due to her daughter's marriage.

Lorelei brought the back of her palm to her mouth, her stomach suddenly lurching with unease. Her time in the country had not been good to her. She'd begun to dread eating because not a thing agreed with her, though hunger pains constantly plagued her. Unfortunately, her appetite had only increased with their return to polite society, and her stomach was still most disagreeable.

"Are you feeling ill?"

Her eyes snapped to her husband's in the dim light.

Chastain looked her up and down when she made no move to answer him. "Well?" he persisted.

Part of her refused to give him the satisfaction of responding. "My stomach is unsettled is all. I am sure once we depart this moving carriage I will recover."

He pulled the cloth aside that covered the window. "It is not far now. Please keep your midday meal where it belongs; it took my valet hours to achieve the shine on my Hessians."

Lorelei stuck her tongue out at him when he continued to stare into the twilight. She knew it was childish, and at odds with the decorum of a lady, especially one with the new title of duchess, but she feared letting any words slip past her lips—they would likely betray her true feelings for the man, who seemed oblivious to her discontent.

"I do not have to impress upon you enough how crucial this evening is for me."

For him? It was another ball, no different from the thousands he'd likely attended before.

"You see, I have taken a foreigner as my bride," he continued. "Many will turn their noses up at the thought of consorting with you, which will, in turn, cast a shadow upon me. It is something I should have given greater thought to before we wed."

His self-righteous attitude was maddening. "Do you not realize I have been the object of disdainful looks since my arrival in London?" Her tanned skin and exotic green eyes hadn't escaped her notice or anyone else's.

"You are married to a duke now, and that alone should open many doors as long as you set forth a proper appearance and demureness." He eyed her fashionable neckline. "Do remember in the future, you are no longer needing to attract male attention to procure a husband. Please, do not display your assets wantonly."

Did he seek to lay claim to her? Had he not already proven his dominance over her all those months ago, whether she agreed or not?

Instead of asking all the questions brimming just under the surface, she held her tongue and focused on making it through her evening. They hadn't discussed that frightful night at Covent Gardens. She preferred not to relive it, and feared what his response would be if she were to bring it up again. And he acted as if he'd never taken advantage of her.

"We have arrived." He let the material fall back into place before the window. "We shall make our way through the receiving line and greet our host and hostess. That will be followed by a quick turn about the dance floor. Afterward, I will procure you a drink, and then I will retire to the card room. When I am ready to depart, I will collect you for the return trip home."

"Of course, my lord." Lorelei kept her tone sickeningly sweet.

"Do call me Benji or Chastain," he said with a flip of his wrist. "We are intimately involved, after all."

#

Two months…two fucking months, and not a single word from her.

No 'I am sorry' letter scribbled on tear-stained paper.

No 'I made the largest mistake of my life. Please, come rescue me!' notes.

No knocks in the middle of the night on his townhouse door. Nothing. Not a word.

And he'd waited. Oh, how he'd waited. He'd waited while sipping bourbon. He'd waited while he read the morning *Post*. He'd waited each evening for word she'd arrived back in town.

He'd raved, he'd yelled, he'd bargained, he'd belittled himself and his servants.

Lately, he'd taken to sending his pleas skyward—anything that might bring her back to him.

He hadn't even a friend to go to, since Chastain had been the one to betray him.

Relief had not come to him. He had gotten no clarity—no matter how much he drank, or screamed, or cursed the heavens above.

Andrew had spent the morning sobering from the days and weeks before, eating bread and drinking water to flush the poison from his body. He'd bid his valet, Samuels, to ready his finest jacket and breeches. He had scrubbed his Hessians himself until they gleamed in the soft candlelight of his dressing room. Finally, he'd applied a bit of grease to his slightly long, limp hair and instructed his valet to tie his cravat in a rather daring knot.

And it was thus that he strolled into Lord and Lady Shawe's ballroom…and saw nothing else but Lorelei, dressed in an exquisite dress, being twirled about the dance floor by Chastain. They appeared to everyone within sight the new darling couple, freshly back to town after weeks spent alone together. He could not get a glimpse of their faces, but Andrew visualized Lorelei smiling and Chastain laughing at his own witty comment.

"Drink, my lord?" A passing servant paused beside him, offering a tray laden with flutes full of a bubbling liquid that in no quantity could erase the image of Lorelei from his mind.

Taking two, he decided to try regardless. If nothing else, he hoped the bubbles would cloud his vision of the *happy* couple.

He swiftly drained both flutes, replaced the empties on the servant's tray, and lifted two more. Before long, the tray held nothing but ten empty glasses—and Andrew still had a clear view of the dance floor.

He'd had enough—seen enough for a lifetime.

The idea of attending this ball, attracting the eye of another woman, and moving on, had been a preposterous plan, and now he knew it had no chance of working. If he'd been smart, he would have gone to Madame Sasha's country party and selected a new mistress instead of waiting about like a puppy.

The music finally came to a stop. Gentlemen hurried to return ladies to their chaperones and collect their next dance partner, or else disengage themselves from a senseless debutante and flee for the safety of the card room. It was then that Lorelei caught his eye.

Her face fell at the sight of him and her color drained, leaving her naturally olive skin a startling white.

Their eyes held. Andrew was unable to tear his gaze from hers, and she seemed incapable of the same.

In her gaze he saw something—a loneliness and despair that had never been there before.

With a hint of pity...

Dare he say regret?

But no, he'd been willing to give her everything. His title and wealth was hers to do with as she pleased—he'd wholeheartedly offered her something he hadn't given to another except his mother and Mrs. Bee, his housekeeper.

His fucking heart.

If she'd asked, he would have ripped it from his chest and presented it to her on a silver platter, if that would have changed anything.

Andrew cursed his irrational feelings for the woman. He'd had women more beautiful a thousand times over in his life. Her exotic heritage was not that special, as so many families had recently fled France to make England their home.

That only left one question—what was it about *this* woman, Lady Lorelei, that made her more captivating than so many other debutantes? If he knew, he'd be able to do something about it. Scrub her from his mind, wash her scent from his senses, and heal the scorch on his skin from her very touch.

Bits of conversation floated his way. "...dare he bring his French hussy here?"

Andrew's ears perked at the mention of France. Not far from him, two matronly women stood, their heads close together and glasses in hand. "To think Lord Chastain thought marrying the chit would make her respectable. He has not even seen fit to introduce her at Almacks."

"Oh, not that she will ever receive an invitation," the

other woman said with a laugh. "Look at her complexion, it is as if she spent the last ten years in the sun."

Both women shook their heads, as if anything but the palest skin tones were a curse.

"It is our duty to say something, is it not?"

"I do say so. She is, at present, forcing herself on dear old Lord and Lady Styliss. We mustn't allow her to inflict her revolutionary ideals on them."

Andrew watched as the two matrons headed in Lorelei's direction. Surrounded by a few elderly gentlemen and their wives, Lorelei hadn't the faintest idea what and who was headed her way—and Chastain was nowhere to be seen.

The last thing Andrew wanted to do was come face-to-face with her, actually have to speak, but it looked like he was her only hope of not being mortified before the whole *ton*.

Curse Chastain and his inability to stay at his wife's side in this den of wolves.

The matrons were a few paces ahead of him, but kept to the wall, while Andrew cut through the chattering crowd to head them off. No matter the duplicity he'd gone through at her hands, no woman deserved to be ostracized in public.

His stride was sure and fast, and within seconds, he stood at her elbow, inserting himself into the conversation.

"My dear Lady Chastain," Lady Styliss said. "I do believe that is the most inspiring thing I have heard all season."

The group looked engaged and hung on every word Lorelei spoke. She'd no doubt charmed the group of elderly men, though the women still held their reservations. She hadn't yet detected Andrew's presence at her side.

"Oh, my dear marquis!" Lady Styliss gushed upon noticing him. "Are you acquainted with the new Lady Chastain?"

"I am, my lady, for she is recently married to my lifelong friend."

Lorelei continued to gaze at the woman before her, allowing no opportunity for Andrew to make eye contact with her. "Good evening, your lordship."

"My lords. " Andrew issued a slight bow to all in the group. "My ladies. I do count myself fortunate to have made Lady Chastain's acquaintance before any knew she'd one day be Lord Chastain's wife. Furthermore, I will confirm that every word she utters is awe-inspiring. Would you not agree, my ladies?"

Andrew turned toward the two matrons who'd joined the group.

"I do not agree in the slightest," they huffed in unison.

The women looked to each other when the group greeted them with smiles all around.

"Lady Dickinson," Lady Styliss said. "Lady Chastain was just telling us of her adventure crossing the Channel. One Englishman, returning home from his grand tour, dared show her drawings he'd collected on his trip. And you will not believe it, but they were all nude men in women's hats. Can you believe it?"

"Why, yes," Lady Dickinson replied. When the group only stared at the old matron, she continued. "What I meant to say is that yes, I do believe it. Anything and anyone journeying from France should be watched carefully, as they are likely to be of no class whatsoever."

Andrew had had enough. "My lady, do you seek to insult Lady Chastain's home?" he asked. When she kept tight-lipped, he continued. "Why, look at her. She is the height of elegance and grace."

"That is the opinion of a man who thinks with parts I am too much the lady to name, and—" She took a breath, preparing to launch into her next tirade. Thankfully, the band hit a light note, signaling another round of dancing was to begin.

"My lady." Andrew took hold of Lorelei's elbow. "I do believe this dance is promised to me. Shall we?"

Finally, she took mercy on him and turned his way, a forced smile on her face. "Of course, your lordship. I could never refuse Lord Chastain's lifelong friend."

With her elbow stiffly in his grip, Andrew moved toward the dance floor. Unfortunately, it seemed Lorelei was not in the mood to be led about, and in turn, pulled him toward the open veranda doors.

"I find the warmth in this room disagrees with me."

As a breath of fresh air would suit him as well, he let her lead the way outside and away from the crowd, all of whom seemed too eager to listen to their conversation.

They weren't two steps outside the door when Lorelei stopped and ripped her elbow from his hand.

"What was that about?" she hissed, pressing the back of her hand to her mouth.

"I was saving you," Andrew said. "You should thank me."

"You rudely interrupted our conversation. Do you know how hard it has been for me to make friends since my arrival in London?"

"I fear I do not, for you had two very wealthy and titled men drooling over you the instant you stepped into that first ballroom," Andrew countered.

Flustered, she crossed her arm over her chest and walked further toward the veranda's ledge. "You know that does not count."

"Why ever not?" Andrew wondered if she knew the spectacle she created every time she entered a room. All eyes were drawn to her.

"That is neither here nor there. What do you want, Andrew?"

Mercifully, the veranda was almost empty, with only one other couple standing not far from the doors in the shadows, and a few people milling about the garden, out of hearing.

"I truly was saving you," Andrew continued.

"Why would I need saving?"

"Because, those two old matrons were on a war path—and you were their target."

"I can protect myself," she asserted. "I have been doing just that all my life."

Her comment struck him as odd, for she came from a solid family. "I do not doubt you could, but these two women are the final verdict at Almacks. They say who and when."

"Why should I care about Almacks? I am wed to a duke and have no such need for the marriage market or entertainments focused on that."

Andrew didn't understand why he cared either, yet he did not want to see her embarrassed.

"Plus, I will have you know that I have dealt with my fair share of ill-mannered *ton* since my arrival in England. Two old biddies cannot hamper my evening."

Andrew stepped forward…to embrace her…hold her hand…or just touch her—he knew not what. She took a step back.

He sighed.

"What do you want?" she asked.

"You." It was the simplest word, yet held emotion that far surpassed those three simple letters. Her betrayal hadn't changed his feelings for her, which had been obvious the second he'd laid eyes on her. If she were to confess her desires at this very moment, he'd have his carriage brought round and they would depart into the night, never to be seen again.

Instead, she said, "I am not to be had by you…or anyone."

"When did you arrive back in town?" He'd say anything to keep her talking and here with him.

"Not long ago."

"Can I call on you tomorrow?"

"No."

"The day after, mayhap?" His anger built as she continued to deny him. Anger at her for deceiving him— and anger at himself that he cared to see her at all.

"Andrew…" she let her words trail off in exasperation. "Please, do not make this any harder than it already is."

"There you are!"

Andrew's blood boiled.

They both turned toward the doors leading into the ballroom.

Chastain stepped out and motioned Lorelei to his side as if she were naught but a dog to be called to heel.

"Andrew, lovely to see you. Thank you for keeping Lady Chastain occupied." The words hit him like a slap in the face. "But I am ready to depart now. Come along."

Chastain reentered the ballroom, not checking to

see if Lorelei followed.

But there was no need.

Lorelei returned to the ballroom right behind Chastain, following him through the room and out the front door.

Chastain, his dearest friend since childhood, barely spared him a sideways glance. It was as though they were nothing more than mere acquaintances, two men whose past interactions had been limited to a quick word about the weather or what horse stock held the most promise for foals.

Worst of all, Lorelei now belonged to Chastain.

Chapter Thirteen

Drake lounged across the sofa in his private chamber. Before him, two women danced, slowly rubbing their scantily clothed bodies together. Their varying shades of blonde and red hair blended together, making it impossible to tell where one girl's ended and the other's began.

The intoxicating movement of their trim, slender forms enthralled him. How long he'd lain there watching them he couldn't say, but the floor around him was littered with empty decanters that had once housed his prized liquor collection. The amount he'd imbibed would have rendered any other man of his size useless or possibly dead, yet he was unable to even achieve a state of slumber, freeing his mind from the continuous barrage of images—of Lorelei, in the arms of Chastain. He'd hoped the papers had been wrong, that they'd made a mistake, but the ball he'd attended—last night...last week, he wasn't sure—had confirmed his fears.

"My lord?" Samuels stood in the doorway to his room, his upper lip curled in disgust. "May I bring your morning meal to you?"

Morning meal? He glanced over his shoulder to the bank of windows in his room. They were all covered tightly, allowing no light in, and blocking the scene taking place inside from the world beyond. Vaguely, he remembered ordering a servant to close the draperies and to keep them closed until further notice.

"I find I am not hungry, at least not for food." Andrew noticed his valet avert his glance from the two women still moving to an unheard song. "But please deliver a tray. These fine women must be famished." When the man left, he refocused on the ladies before him.

As soon as he'd returned to his townhouse after seeing Lorelei, Andrew had sent word to Madame Sasha, who quickly sent her best girls to him. The Madame likely sought to impress him after he'd neglected to attend her annual party. Though he and Chastain were not her most highly prized clients, nor her most frequent, she likely feared losing the coin she did gain from them at her establishment and card room.

Nothing about the two girls reminded him of Lorelei. With blonde and red hair, pale skin, and short stature, they should take his mind off her, yet he found himself unable to focus on their bouncing breasts and toned backsides.

The sight of naked female bodies usually did one of two things: bring him to arousal or lull him to sleep. This day it did neither, as his eyes remained open and his manhood flaccid within his unfastened breeches.

Before long, Samuels returned with a tray overflowing with bread, cheese, and hunks of meat.

"Is that not the housekeeper's duty?" Andrew asked.

"'Tis, my lord." He brushed a woman's

undergarment from the table and set the tray down. "But she requested I bring it in."

"Ha! She cannot be shocked. She has witnessed more vulgar acts within my home." Mrs. Bee had been in his employ since before his father had passed, and had cleaned up his messes more times than one could count. "Send her to me, now."

"Send her in, my lord?" His valet stepped back in alarm.

"Stop 'my lord'ing me, Samuels! You have known me since I was in knickers and used to sneak into my father's suite to try on his neck clothes." He paused and looked about. "This very room, to be precise. Now, fetch Mrs. Bee. Her sensibilities are not as delicate as you might think."

When Samuels departed, Andrew sat up and brushed the crumbs from his shirt. How they'd arrived there, he wasn't certain. Next, he fastened his breeches and pulled his boots back on, not bothering to lace them.

"Girls," he called. When both stopped to stare at him, he threw a wad of material he'd gathered off the floor at them. "Make yourselves decent with all due haste."

They scrambled to catch their clothes, bending right before him, sweeping lacy stockings up and moving toward his dressing room.

"Pity," he mumbled. It was a shame he could not call them back. The only pastime he enjoyed more than disrobing females was watching them dress before him.

"Now, what are you mumbling about?" Turning back to the doorway, his housekeeper, Mrs. Bee, stood with her hands on her hips and a very unpleasant expression on her face. "Look at you."

He looked down at himself: wrinkled shirt, loose cravat, and untied boots. "What's that supposed to mean?" He'd looked worse for wear on numerous occasions.

"That means your mother, God rest her kindhearted soul, must be turning in her grave."

Mrs. Bee was the only person who had the nerve to speak to him in that manner, and the only person he'd allow to get away with it. She had been the only woman to stand up and be the mother figure he'd needed in his youth after his own mother's passing. "I am sure she is quite comfortable where she rests, and I am certain that she has witnessed much worse from her only son than this." He chuckled.

"What has you in such high spirits?"

"Oh, the image of you opening my dressing room door and finding a pair of partially clothed *wanton* women."

"You are incorrigible, Andrew." She threw the items she'd collected at him, much as Samuels had done. "And rather deep in your cups I'd presume, as well."

He set his empty tumbler aside. He didn't know how long it had been empty or what liquor he'd recently drank from it, but at the moment, he'd do almost anything to keep on good terms with Mrs. Bee—otherwise, his liquor cabinet would certainly run dry.

"I am only having a bad day." He tried to explain away his behavior, as if he were once again a twelve-year-old boy being scolded for not completing his studies.

"A bad month, from what I have been told."

"And who deems it appropriate to discuss my personal matters?" He tried to stand, but lost his balance when his head began to spin, and came to rest back where he'd been. He kept his voice low so as not to be overheard—or have Mrs. Bee think he was being defensive. Once you were on the defensive with her, she prodded until she learned all your secrets.

"Your servants, that's who." She paused as Madame Sasha's girls exited his dressing room. One wore only his best shirt to cover her previously exposed body. After they'd departed the room, Mrs. Bee continued, "You know the ones I speak of. They are currently repairing the damage you did to your country estate."

Bother! He'd suspected his steward would write Mrs. Bee, but he hadn't expected it so soon.

"From the look on your face, I suspect you know exactly what I am speaking of," she said. She moved toward the door to leave, and he counted himself lucky that he hadn't experienced the full wrath of her displeasure. "You should be ashamed of yourself, *my lord*," she threw the words over her shoulder as she slammed the door behind herself.

Her use of 'my lord,' instead of calling him by his given name or Drake, told him he hadn't heard the last from her—and truly, he expected nothing less. Bee was his beacon, his touchstone in this hectic life—a life he'd created and reveled in since inheriting his title and, more importantly, his fortune.

The silence of the room invaded his mind, leaving space for him to ponder things he'd tried to push away. The point of keeping Madame Sasha's women within reach was to keep Lorelei at bay. Her actions spoke volumes: she did not want him, and had gone to extremes to show him how reckless she could be with her words—and his heart.

If she'd known he'd never before given his heart to

another, would she have thought differently—done differently?

# # #

Lorelei pressed close to the floor and slid under the massive four-poster bed, letting the thick quilt fall back into place, blocking her from sight. Unfortunately, it also blocked light from penetrating the darkness around her. She hadn't had the foresight to bring a candle, and would have likely set the whole room ablaze if she had.

With her visibility impaired, she pushed herself under the bed, her fingers prying at the floorboards in search of a hidden compartment. Her touch met with nothing but dust and mothballs…and tightly nailed boards.

If any servants loitered about, she'd likely be the subject of much gossip in their quarters by the noontime meal. She felt the filth cling to her, but she hadn't time to dwell on her appearance or the talk she likely caused in the house.

Chastain had departed for his morning fencing lesson over an hour ago and would return shortly.

She'd spent the last week learning his habits and routine while in town, which was far different from his activities while at his country estate. The power of observation was something she'd learned from her mother—and a skill she'd used many times before. Unimposing Camille Parisot de La Valette was the picture of demure. She moved about society with a quiet, unassuming grace that Lorelei knew she'd need more practice to achieve. Often, her mother could attend a party without a soul remembering she'd been there.

Many spoke freely in her presence and did not attempt to hide their activities when she was about. Which made her a valuable asset.

Over the years, Lorelei had emulated her mother in poise, disposition, and dress...and failed in every regard. Her father alleged Lorelei spoke too much, flaunted her intelligence, and dressed to catch the eye. Not long ago, she'd given up and embraced her own strengths.

At the moment, huddled beneath a large bed in a room she'd never wanted to visit, her hair no doubt covered in spider webs, she pondered what her strengths actually were. She was beautiful, but she didn't consider that an advantage for it brought too much attention to her. She'd completed her years in the schoolroom ahead for her age and would have liked the opportunity to study further, yet her father's commitment to his country took them too many places for her to settle into more learning.

The squeak of a door followed by female giggling stopped her.

Lorelei held her breath, waiting for more noise.

She hoped a pair of servants had stumbled into the room while doing their chores and would depart soon.

"Ah, my little delicate flower."

Her hopes were dashed with those words, said with a deep growl—a tone that brought back memories of damp ground beneath her and the tearing of fabric, the cold night air against her skin.

Another giggle followed, and soft feet could be heard crossing the room.

"A chase, then?" Lorelei's new husband called. "I fear you may outrun me. Is that what you seek, my little hellion?"

The bed above her dipped under the weight of a

body, knocking Lorelei's head into the wooden floor. She shifted to the side farthest from the door.

A larger weight pushed on the side of the bed and the quilt lifted from the floor, giving her a bit of light—enough to see her husband's boots as he bent to unlace them. He worked slowly at his task. Unlike the way he'd been with her that first time, he whispered to the maid. Promises were made about exactly what he'd do to her when he finished removing his shoes—and more still, what she should do to him.

Their talk went from sweet and exotic to vulgar, and Lorelei fought to keep from gagging at the places the girl said she'd like to stick her tongue. If Chastain was into that sort of sexual behavior, she was glad she would never have to satisfy him.

Lorelei pushed further away from the voices, thankful she didn't recognize the female's. She prayed the act would be quick and the pair would depart. The space below the bed was so tight she couldn't bring her hands up to block the sounds coming from above.

Unfortunately, the pair decidedly enjoyed each other, as the sounds that greeted her were of profound pleasure. Morosely, she wondered if this was their first time or possibly reflective of a longer relationship. Her mind drifted to the possibility that the pair were true loves, and that she had been the one to come between them—the duke and the housemaid did not make headlines as surely as the duke and the foreigner.

She should ask Chastain with whom his heart lay, for they both knew it wasn't and never would be with her. Another thing she was glad for.

"Oh, you are a filthy little wench," Chastain yelped. "You are quite adept at riding."

The bed had fallen into a rhythmic sway, like a boat rolling on the open seas on a breezy day.

Lorelei, with her limited knowledge of sexual matters, could not picture the act happening above her, but the heavy panting and grunting told her they both enjoyed themselves.

As the breathing became louder and shallower, and Chastain's groaning deeper, the sound of a smack reverberated through the room.

Skin to skin contact.

Lorelei was prepared to wiggle her way out of her hiding spot and stop Chastain. He'd hurt her once, but she would not stand by and let him hurt another. For months, she'd wished that someone had been there to step in before they had when Chastain had pushed her to the ground. But she was here now, and though the girl willingly participated in the sexual act knowing Chastain was an adulterous man, she could not blame her.

Moving toward the shallow light from where the bedcover had risen from the floor, Lorelei went through what she was going to say—to Chastain, and the girl.

She crawled out from beneath the bed and stood. Her happiness at being in the open light again was dimmed by the sight before her.

Situated on the bed, Chastain lay flat with the girl— a scullery maid she vaguely remembered seeing in both the country and here in London—riding him as one did a horse. The girl was completely unclothed, unless you counted the handprint on her derriere, which suspiciously matched the size of Chastain's hand.

Neither noticed her standing there, staring, her mouth open.

Their faces were contorted in ecstasy. That was the

only word to describe the looks upon both their faces: a mixture of pleasure so great it appeared painful. With one final thrust upward from Chastain, they both screamed out in satisfaction.

Lorelei realized her mistake too late to escape.

While Chastain had never given her pleasure of this magnitude, he was obviously quite capable with one deserving of his ministrations. He hadn't hurt the girl, but rather increased their mutual gratification.

The maid let out a giggle and rolled off Chastain toward where Lorelei stood.

When he shifted to his side to face his lady love, Chastain finally noticed Lorelei.

She must look a fright, her dress wrinkled with cobwebs likely clinging to her hair, and her face smudged with whatever covered the floor beneath the bed.

Strange what thoughts ran through one's head when faced with her new husband and his mistress naked within his own bed…in the middle of the day.

The girl hadn't noticed Lorelei, and Chastain didn't give her presence away when he leaned over and took the girl's mouth with his own, keeping his steely gaze on Lorelei the entire time. If he sought to teach her a lesson, he was doing a damn fine job at it. She stood there, refusing to move an inch, and watched as the pair kissed. Chastain's hand moved down the girl's back to cup her buttocks once more, squeezing it until the roundness bulged between his fingers.

Lorelei wanted to flee the room, to hide and never discuss this moment. It was nearly as embarrassing as the night at the Gardens. Again, she felt helpless, but she would not run as she had before. She would not give him the satisfaction of acting as if it had never happened when next they met.

Like it or not, they were bound together, at least for the foreseeable future.

Maybe, just maybe, she could teach him a lesson.

As he watched her, she also watched him, mirroring his look.

When he released the girl's mouth and a wicked grin crossed his lips, so did a grin cross hers, as if to goad him on.

It didn't take long for an alarmed expression to overtake him. He must have expected her to leave, to cower from the room in shame, but when she continued to stay, her gaze fixed on the scene before her, he fumbled...his confidence shaken. Possibly he found his game suddenly lacking in excitement.

Lorelei cocked an eyebrow and nodded. Hell would freeze over before she gave in to him and looked away. She'd learned to play these mind games at a young age, and was more adept at them than he could ever imagine. The days of her husband thinking she was a helpless, naïve girl were over.

Chastain trailed kisses down the girl's neck and continued to her shoulder, all the while keeping Lorelei in his sights.

Truly, she shouldn't be surprised at his outlandish behavior. They'd done their research on the current Lord Chastain before journeying to London. He was a confirmed rakehell who showed no signs of settling down, and no interest in repairing his damaged reputation. For all she knew, he didn't see himself as anything but the lord he was—above all who criticized his actions. Yet, she wondered for what seemed the hundredth time, why her? Why had he needed to have her?

She cleared her throat.

Chastain's eyes narrowed, and the girl whipped around at the sound, finally taking notice that they were not alone.

"I do hope you both are enjoying yourselves," Lorelei said coldly.

"My lady—"

"Do not 'my lady' me," she said. The girl shrank back in fear. "You will gather your belongings and leave this house. If I see you again, I will call the magistrate."

"You do not command my home," Chastain said.

"Ah, my beloved husband finally speaks." She wanted to laugh at the girl's terror, and Chastain's baffled expression. He most certainly hadn't realized his wife had a backbone. "This is my home, as well as yours, so please be a dear and put on your clothes. Upon completing that task, you will show your lady love out of this house."

"I am truly sorry," the girl mumbled as she scrambled to exit the bed. "I can't be being dismissed, m'lady."

"I have no doubt you are sorry I caught you in bed with my husband." She turned back to Chastain, who still lay on the bed. "As for you, set your mistress up with her own flat, as any respectable man of the *ton* would do."

Her confidence soared as the girl scrambled to collect her clothing and rushed from the room, leaving only her and Chastain. She plastered an innocent smile on her face, ready to do battle if it came to that.

When the door clicked closed behind the girl, her bravado dwindled as Chastain too climbed from the bed to stand before her, completely naked. His body still smelled of his exploits. His hands on his hips and his stance wide, Chastain was a daunting figure. Though he apparently hadn't been to his fencing club this morning, his body was lean and toned from another type of exercise.

She had no doubt that had they met under different circumstances, she might have been attracted to him, his cocky, self-assured attitude notwithstanding. Currently, all she saw was a man with no qualms about taking advantage of a young woman, and then embarrassing her in her new home.

"Now that you have said your part..." His eyes traveling the length of her as if she were the one sans clothing, "We both understand what this is."

For a fraction of a second, she feared he knew her purpose for marrying him. "Do we?"

"This"—he threw his arms wide—"is a marriage of convenience for me, and a gift for you and your family, seeing as how you are determined to make a place for yourself in society. A society, I might add, that does not take kindly to foreigners."

"You think I wanted this?" Lorelei suppressed her anger. "*You* approached my father, asked for *my* hand in marriage...giving me no chance to voice my opinion." She knew the argument was pointless, and didn't understand why she cared.

"Who would not seek to marry a duke?"

Her muscles quivered in anger and her pulse raced. "I can name at least one person who'd rather eat dirt than marry a selfish, egotistical buffoon of a duke."

Suddenly, Lorelei doubled over. Her stomach lurched more violently than ever before. Her knees buckled under her, and she pushed past Chastain to the bed.

"Are you all right?" Concern laced his voice and the fight left him. "Shall I send for the doctor?"

Lorelei concentrated on pulling air into her lungs and expelling it slowly to settle her stomach. Her head rested on the side of the bed where she knelt.

"I had heard word you were unwell lately. I will send for the doctor."

"No," she said through clenched teeth. "I will be fine, just send my maid to me and leave me be."

"Of course." He actually sounded contrite, though she knew better than to trust him.

"And *Benji…*"

His footfalls halted. "Yes?"

"Keep your dollymop from this house." When he didn't respond, she continued, "This may be a marriage of convenience for you, but I will not stand by quietly if you insist on making me look the fool."

Chastain continued out of the room, closing the door behind him.

Lorelei sat with her face against the cool bedcover, breathing in and out to calm herself.

It was then that the realization struck her, and she frantically counted backwards.

Seven weeks.

She'd been so focused on finding the plans and extricating herself from her sham of a marriage, that time had passed and she hadn't noticed. Her older dresses had become snug, which suited her fine because as long as she was forced to be wed to Chastain, she would not quibble about spending his coin to outfit herself.

But she hadn't dwelled on the reason behind her weight gain, overwhelming hunger, and extreme sickness.

Lord help her if it were true.

She carried Lord Chastain's baby, most likely a product of their wedding night, for he'd scarcely touched her since.

Her world tilted, and Lorelei collapsed on the bed as the nausea became too much.

Chapter Fourteen

Andrew had been forced from his own townhouse by Mrs. Bee and his valet. Logically, he'd sought refuge at White's Gentlemen's Club, where he paid handsomely for peace and quiet. One would think that having a title, funds, and your own home would entitle a man to a bit of harmony, but no. His servants were determined to drive him from the comforts of his own bedchambers.

White's held all the luxuries of his own home: fine meals and spirits, warm atmosphere, comfortable seating... Beyond that, he could also enjoy card games and the company of like-minded men, something lacking at his estate. Initially upon arrival, he'd escaped to a lesser-used corner of the room, not far from the warm fire, and spread the *Post* across his lap for some light afternoon reading. You'd think he would have learned his lesson with respect to current affairs, but his thirst for a diversion won out over his need to avoid any new information about a certain couple.

He'd barely settled into the paper with drink in hand before a gentleman approached him. Andrew could not remember the man's name, no less his title.

"Drake." The man offered his tumbler in salute. "Happy to hear about Lord Chastain's nuptials. Let him know I wish him good tidings." Blood hummed through Andrew's veins so loudly it nearly drowned out the man's words.

He didn't raise his own glass in salute to the new couple nor speak, preferring to stare quietly.

"I will leave you to your paper," the man wisely said before turning tail and returning to his seat across the room.

"Idiot." He returned to the paper, scanning the page for anything interesting to calm his nerves. To his vexation, not one headline caught his eye. It was all the same: levied taxes expected to rise, Bonaparte taking down Ottoman troops by the thousands, and the ongoing debate in the American colonies over slavery. None of these issues held his attention for long, though as a British lord, he knew he should be concerned about such goings-on.

Finally, he discarded the paper in favor of his drink.

He'd sobered since his confrontation with Mrs. Bee, and had actually turned away two lovely women sent by Madame Sasha to improve his spirits. His housekeeper was correct in assuming some time away from his townhouse would do him good, and further, would give his servants time to tidy the mess he'd made of the place. But he would not let her know that, so he had slipped from the house and hoped she didn't notice his absence.

Focusing on the fire, Andrew contemplated what was next for him. Attending social functions hadn't helped distract him. Unsavory women, while alluring, hadn't held his attention. And now, it seemed his club was not the sanctuary it had once been. He would retire to his country estate if Mrs. Bee hadn't impressed upon him how much he'd frightened the staff in residence, who still worked to repair the damage he'd done.

Maybe a trip abroad would soothe him, yet the thought only brought to mind images of dark-haired beauties with emerald eyes, their laughter floating across the room.

"Ah, there you are."

Andrew looked up from the fire as Benji plopped into the chair across from him.

"Why so glum?" he asked.

Andrew wondered if he were serious. The nerve of his *friend* waltzing into White's and daring to sit across from him as if the last two months hadn't happened.

"Chastain." He could only muster the one word.

"My good man." Chastain whistled through his pinched lips. "It looks as if you haven't had a proper shave in over a month. Has Samuels finally decided to seek employment from a man who more adequately appreciates his efforts?"

Andrew set his drink aside and faced his friend. "What do you want?" If Benji insisted on having this conversation here, in public, then Andrew would give him that. "Have you come to gloat?"

"Gloat about what?" Benji asked. "Hell, no. I have come to avoid my new wife. I find married life highly disagreeable."

Startled by the turn of the conversation, he pondered what man in his right mind would find Lady Lorelei disagreeable. Chastain had won the ultimate prize and didn't seem to realize it.

"The woman is incorrigible," Chastain went on

before signaling a passing servant for a drink. "Just today she turned up—out of thin air, I might add—in my bedchambers."

Andrew wanted to chuckle. He dreamed night and day of just that occurrence. "Ah, yes, do expound on the horrors of marital life."

"I knew you would understand, my friend. It appears you are the smarter of us." Chastain sat back in his seat and stretched his legs toward the fire. "It has been most dreadful."

"How so?"

"Well, I am so deep in despair I do not know where to begin—and I am certain she must feel the same."

"How about starting with what currently has you so upset." Andrew didn't recognize the man before him, for Benji actually looked to be unhappy and incapable of fixing whatever ailed him. And the thought that Lorelei suffered as well was unacceptable. "You said you found her in your bedchambers."

Benji kept his silence while a servant brought him his drink. After taking a small sip, he continued, "The whole mess was quite inappropriate. Sally and I had slipped into my chambers for a late-morning romp—"

"Just a moment, who is Sally?"

"Oh, she is of no concern. Only a comely maid I happened upon at my country estate while I was exiled after my wedding. Fine little filly, I might add. But that is not the important part," Benji said, and waved his hand in dismissal. "We—Sally and I—had barely reached our end when I looked up, and you will never guess who stood there…just watching."

Andrew could guess exactly who stood there—and what she must have been thinking.

Anger. Hurt. Betrayal. Devastation.

He wanted to feel empathy for her. He searched deep for a feeling of sorrow on her behalf.

Yet, all he could muster was a smirk and the satisfaction that she'd reaped what she'd sown. The fact that his friend was suffering as well was another feather in his cap.

"That must have shocked you greatly," Andrew said, realizing Benji waited for a response. "What did you do?"

"What did I do?" he said with a sigh. "She did not give me a second to *do* anything."

Andrew visualized Lorelei, fuming with anger.

"She had the nerve to dismiss Sally."

"Truly?"

"Yes, told the girl to gather her things and never return to my house."

"The nerve…" Andrew was enjoying his day more and more as the moments passed. "And once you were alone?"

"She told me to set my mistress up in her own townhouse like every other *respectable* man of the *ton* does."

"She did not!" Andrew worked hard to suppress his mirth.

"She most certainly did. The gall of the woman to infer I do not know how to properly outfit my mistresses."

"I do hope you put her in her place."

Benji remained silent.

Oh, Andrew knew well his lovely Lady Lorelei had a spark to her. He stilled at the thought. She wasn't his, and never would be. No matter if either man liked it or not, she belonged to Chastain. Andrew's claim on her was not real. Though she had deceived him, brushed off all he'd offered her for a future, he did not wish harm or unhappiness upon her.

"Well, what is your plan now for gaining back your dear wife's favor?"

Benji only stared into the fire. "I have no plan for that. I will avoid her as much as possible, and hope she is agreeable to living in some semblance of a truce."

"Until when?" he asked.

"Until we both perish, I suppose."

"That sounds horrid." Yet, sparked hope in Andrew.

"Horrid?" Benji asked. "Most of London lives thus, and it seems to work to their advantage."

Andrew thought on the concept—one he expected to live himself one day. It was absurd to him now. A life filled with obligated lovemaking to produce an heir, and then years of living side by side without any affection. His own parents had flouted society's conventions and married for love—he'd grown up knowing his parent's misery when spending even one afternoon without each other. He'd seen the agony in his mother's eyes when his father left for town and was unable to bring his family.

To each their own.

Andrew held his glass aloft. "I wish a happy future for the both of you."

And he did, even if that future did not consist of the couple finding said happiness together, but in the arms of another.

"Thank you, my friend."

"But it would likely be in your best interest to set your mistress up in her own home, as Lady Lore—Chastain suggested."

#

She'd paced his chamber long after he'd left the room…naked.

Lorelei could not believe the nerve of the man.

No—she had known exactly what she'd agreed to when her father told her of his acceptance of Chastain's marriage offer.

No screams of shock sounded from the hall, so his servants must be accustomed to their master walking about with nothing to conceal himself.

He'd barked at his butler to have his horse brought round immediately.

As her rage dissipated, so did the discomfort in her middle.

She had much to do and think about, without dwelling on her advancing condition and what that meant for her future—especially her intention of fleeing London after finding the plans.

While Chastain was not an attentive husband, that did not mean he would be a bad father. He was distant, but had never physically hurt her after that one night in the gardens. She would be smart to remember that her intentions with respect to their marriage were not more honorable than his. Lorelei had entered into holy matrimony with deceit in mind.

Plus, after she produced an heir, she would be free to spend her time doing whatever she pleased—and whomever she pleased. A life in London, away from the calculating De Pez and whomever he pledged his allegiance to, may well suit her.

The very thought of being free thrilled her, unrestricted and able to do what pleased her—and her child. A small cottage with a white fence, maybe a small garden where she could till the earth to feed them both.

Once Chastain found out she carried his heir, he would never let her go, and she feared she would never be able to abandon her own child, even if she knew he'd be well cared for and raised by one of the wealthiest men in all of England.

And if she stayed, her child would not be made to endure the life she had thus far. He would owe no allegiance to anyone, beyond himself and England. It was possible that fatherhood would change Chastain for the better, as well.

She wondered for only a brief second if she could forsake the comte and comtesse for another life—one that didn't include espionage and the threat of death around every corner. But there was only one way that could ever come to be.

With her stomach settled and her husband away, she needed to find those plans, deliver them to De Pez, and hopefully be strong enough to stand her ground and forge her own way in the world.

Maybe, just maybe, if the baby were a boy, Chastain would be satisfied with his heir and Andrew could forgive her.

Lorelei had no clue where to continue her search. Chastain's bedchamber had always been the least-likely place she suspected to find the plans, but she'd had the chance to look, and Lorelei hadn't wanted to squander it. Nothing about Chastain and his movements led her to believe he knew what his family had been charged with or that he understood the gravity of the situation. He'd not made so much as a mention of his own French heritage. Was it possible he'd been too young to even remember a time he hadn't lived in England?

When a person didn't know the import of something, they usually did not hold it as closely as another might, one that understood the consequences of losing that item. Take her father, for example: Lorelei knew of at least four objects he kept on his person at all times. She did not know the significance of these items, but she knew they meant something to him, and that he feared losing them. Her father was an intelligent man, and, therefore, knew the least-likely way for them to be stolen was if they were with him at all times.

With that in mind, Lorelei knelt to Chastain's discarded and forgotten clothes. Riffling through them, she searched for anything that did not belong or was out of place. Finding a key would be too much to hope for. Sure enough, there was nothing.

She suppressed her frustration at her continued failure.

Perhaps she was looking in all the wrong places, but where the right place could be eluded her.

"My lady?"

Lorelei quickly stood, dropping Lord Chastain's garments back to the floor, and turned to the door where the butler stood. "Yes."

"A Monsieur De Pez awaits you below." At her silence, he continued. "He says he is a friend of your father's, but I will turn him away if that is what you desire."

"Oh, no," Lorelei said. "I do know him. I only was unaware of his presence in town. I will see him shortly in the drawing room."

For the second time, De Pez had journeyed to London without her knowing… If he'd ever left in the first place.

He'd obviously been keeping a close eye on her and her family's whereabouts, or he'd been to see the comte recently. A shiver ran through her. Her parents were very capable of taking care of themselves, yet, she did not want them punished or harassed due to her.

Lorelei moved to the looking glass above the washstand. She was a dreadful sight: dust clung to the front of her dress, her hair sat haphazardly upon her head and threatened to tumble into her eyes at any moment, and her skin was pale. She brushed as much of the filth from her dress as she could, and gave her hair a little nudge to reassure herself it wouldn't come loose as she descended the stairs. There was nothing she could do about her complexion but pinch her cheeks, which didn't help overly. She'd blame it on the constantly overcast skies in England…and her preoccupation with her search.

She hesitated to stall another moment. The last thing she wanted was for De Pez to meet Chastain, or to give the Frenchman time to wander about the house.

When she entered the drawing room, De Pez reclined in a chair with a cup of tea, a plate of sandwiches at his side.

"I have always adored the hospitality of the English." He raised his cup and took a sip. "Earl Grey! My favorite. Do sit, *Lady Chastain*."

She complied with little thought.

"It has been many years since I sat in this very chair."

"Someone may recognize you."

"I hardly think so." De Pez took in the room. "Not a thing has changed, and I find that very fortunate."

"Why is that?"

"Because I may very well be able to help you in your quest. I—we—are losing valuable time to establish ourselves as loyal allies of Bonaparte."

Lorelei stayed on guard. She did not trust the man. "How?"

"I may be convinced to let slip where I have searched in this very home, and if there are a few hiding spots that the plans may have been moved to after the previous Lord Chastain's unfortunate death."

"I would not trust your words, regardless."

"Ah, you are such a wise little kitten," he purred. "It would behoove you to keep your claws hidden, though."

"I am 'my lady' or 'Lady Chastain' to you. You will address me with respect." Her stomach began to churn again.

"For now, I will." He stared at her pointedly. "But soon, the tables will turn, and you may very well beg me to call you my little kitten."

"I would rather die."

"Oh, that would be most agreeable, too."

Lorelei had no idea what the man meant, but knew his penchant for eliminating people he saw as a threat. "My father would not be very happy to hear you call into question my life, De Pez."

The man set his drink aside and sat up straight, a mischievous glint in his eye. "I would never seek to irk the comte."

The statement was comical. The two men had completed many missions side by side, and when on assignment, trusted one another with their very lives. That had never stopped the competitive nature of their relationship, however.

"I am relieved you say that." Lorelei stood, signaling the end of yet another unplanned meeting with De Pez. "I will have the butler show you out. It is always lovely visiting with you. Can I send you with a basket of cheese and bread for your return trip?"

Chapter Fifteen

Andrew's foot tapped a fast rhythm on the floor and he gripped the head of his cane in his hands, his knuckles white. No sooner had he sent Benji on the hunt for suitable accommodations for his mistress than Andrew had fled White's. His carriage sped through the busy early-morning streets toward Chastain's townhouse. Where had all these people, horses, and coaches come from? Never had he cursed the heavily populated thoroughfare of his beloved city.

"Go around them," he shouted out the window to his coachman.

"I will try, my lord," came the muffled yell of the man holding the reins.

He sat back again and let the cloth fall back into place, blocking his view of their slow progress through town, wishing he'd driven his open phaeton, instead of being trapped in his enclosed carriage.

Andrew had tried to put Lorelei and her deception from his mind. He'd attempted to reconcile his thoughts of never seeing the woman again but in chance meetings at social functions.

Keeping his distance from her was not an option, however, especially after hearing the shock she'd faced earlier in the day. While she'd made a fool of him, it was possible Chastain had lied to gain her hand in marriage— and Andrew needed to find out if that were true. And, if so, why.

Lorelei needed his help.

With Chastain duly occupied, Andrew would have the time to speak with her.

Finally, the carriage slowed to a stop.

Departing, Andrew halted as a man walked down the front steps of Lorelei's townhouse.

"Good day, my lord." The man nodded and continued on his way.

Andrew paused at the accent before hurrying up the steps to catch the door still wide open.

"Hello, my lord," the servant said in greeting. "Lord Chastain is not at home at the moment."

"Ah, that is a shame." He tried his best to look downcast at his friend's absence. "It would be the height of bad manners if I did not give my best to Lady Chastain. Does she happen to be at home?"

"She is. I believe she is still in the drawing room." Lavendis, Chastain's butler, stepped back and admitted him entrance. "Right this way. I will announce your presence."

"No need." Andrew clapped the man on his back. "I will just slip in and say a quick hello then be on my way."

He knew the house as well as his own, and without waiting for a response, Andrew headed toward the drawing room. Having both inherited their titles and estates at a young age, he and Benji had bounced between homes frequently, and spent weeks and sometimes months in each other's presence. No part of him missed this, however.

The door stood ajar and Lorelei could be seen standing before the fire, slightly bent and cradling her midsection.

He was by her side in an instant, his arm around her shoulders as he guided her to a chair.

"Are you unwell?" he asked. "Shall I send for a doctor?"

She looked to him, clearly confused. "It is the second time today someone has offered to send for a doctor."

"You look very pale." They were not the flowery words he'd planned on the drive here, and from the look on her face, would not endear him to her. "I mean, I am only…worried about you."

She laughed, a wicked, almost insane cackle that filled the room.

She most definitely was not well, and he blamed himself. Had he come to her sooner, or perhaps forced her to flee with him that day she'd come to his townhouse, this would all be different. It was only now he realized she'd come that day to say goodbye.

Her laughter receded and she looked to him with seriousness. "I am as well as can be expected, your lordship."

"I have a most trying time believing those words."

Her eyes betrayed her, penetrating his as if pleading for his aid even as her lips remained silent. Andrew could lose himself in those green depths, content to languish in that happy place for eternity.

He massaged her shoulder as he stood next to her, determining his next move. "Can I assist you with anything? Perhaps call for a fresh pot of tea?" She was averse to his fetching a doctor, but mayhap a hot beverage would return the color to her cheeks.

She only shook her head.

"A blanket to warm you?"

"Andrew…"

"Yes?"

"I am with child."

"With child? What?" His blood ran through his veins colder than ice. "But, but—isn't it too early to tell? You must be mistaken."

"I wish I were, but I am not." Her words lacked all emotion; they were as cold as he felt. "Growing in my womb is the next Lord Chastain. God willing, it is a male."

"Does he know?" he questioned. "He did not say—"

Lorelei pulled away from him. "You saw him recently?"

"Just now, at White's." He wouldn't lie to her.

"So, you are no doubt aware what transpired this morning?" He didn't respond. "You do know! And what? You thought you'd swoop in here and comfort me? In my devastated state I would seek solace in your arms? Is that it?"

"No. I could never think to take advantage of your state of discontent." It was then he realized he had hoped for exactly that. Andrew had expected her to be either so filled with grief over her husband's deception or so violently angry that she *would* run to him.

"That is good. Because despite my youthful years, I

am no more the child than you, your lordship."

He despised her return to formalities—and wanted to dispense with Chastain for the change he'd wrought in Lorelei.

"I will endure the life I created for myself."

There was more to this woman than he knew, far more than she'd allowed him to see. He was suddenly certain of it.

"Lorelei," he breathed, hoping to return to the moment she'd called him by his given name—and before she'd announced she was carrying his best friend's child. A spark of hope ignited when she looked at him, her eyes softening. "We can leave now—I have estates all over England, and one in Scotland. No one will find us. We will raise the child as our own." He could not believe the words were his. Not only had Lorelei changed, but she'd changed him—in ways he did not even want to contemplate.

"Are you telling me to run away with you?" She paused. "Again?"

"I am not telling, Lorelei. I am asking—begging you to come with me!" She only stared at him, her eyes empty. "Allow me to take care of you, cherish you the way you deserve. You will never want for a thing…neither my affection nor material possessions. All I have will be yours."

Lorelei lifted her chin, tears streaking her face, and the cold, callous expression was gone. "You think I do not know what I gave up when I refused you the last time?"

He kept silent, wishing her to go on, knowing she needed to say her piece.

"You think I do not dwell every waking moment on

what we could have had together?" Her questions continued without pause. "Do you think I do not know the future I have created for myself, and now my child?"

"We can change that course," he said. "Today. Now, this very minute."

"Do not be obtuse."

"What?"

"I will not live on the run, in hiding, forcing my child to live under an assumed name. I want him—or her—to live in the sun without secrets and fears." Her words were desperate, catching in her throat as they left her as if she had more to say, an actual reason she could not accept his offer.

He could imagine the pain it took her to refuse his offer because the agony threatened to also tear him apart.

"You must go, before someone finds you here."

He stood there, when all he ached to do was offer her comfort.

"Please, just go," she begged. "I will send for you if I ever require your assistance."

Regardless of all the answers he wanted, he heeded her wishes.

He took one last long look at her, burning her imagine into his memory, not knowing when he'd next see her. He would remember her mischievous, captivating emerald eyes, the dark expanse of her near-ebony hair, and her skin—so tanned one would assume she spent every day in the sun.

Without thinking, he leaned down and set his lips upon hers. Yes, he wanted—needed—to memorize their contours and feel them, as well.

Their kiss wasn't demanding, neither forcing to control, simply a light brushing of lips. He reveled in the moment. Her fingers didn't rise to run through his hair, and his arms didn't wrap around her tightly to bring her body closer to his.

He stood.

She sat.

Neither moved to the other's level.

As if in two different worlds—destined to be on separate paths for all time.

# # #

Lorelei sat frozen in her seat before the fire, long after it had burned down to mere embers and gave off no warmth. No one had intruded. No one fetched her a cloth to wipe away her tears. No one brought her food or drink.

She was glad for it, too. The hopelessness drained from her with her spent tears, cleansing her of negative thoughts and the bleak outlook on her life.

She would give herself this time to mourn what could have been, to say goodbye to Andrew; she didn't know if she loved him, but with a bit of time, she was certain she would have. Perhaps even as much as he appeared to adore her. She couldn't allow herself to love anyone, not Chastain or the marquis or even her parents, for they could be gone from her life in an instant.

That fact hurt more than all others combined, for she would shortly give birth to a child—a child deserving of her love and devotion, yet she knew the importance of distancing herself even from her young. One day, someone would use that very love against her.

And she would not be able to bear it. Without even knowing the child, she realized she would give anything for that tiny being; offer up all her country's secrets, her parent's true identities, and take her own life to make sure her young survived—and flourished, beating the odds she'd put it up against.

Lorelei said a prayer to a God she didn't believe existed that her child would escape this life. Perhaps she could convince Chastain to give up the plans in order to save his child, for she knew he would not do so for her. Then he could disappear with the baby, live a quiet life somewhere and leave her and her deception behind.

Would she be strong enough to let them go?

Thankfully, she had many months to contemplate that—and the possibility of finding what she sought.

A thought struck her and she sat up straight, wiping the last remnants of tears from her face, and with it her hopelessness.

She could use the plans to gain her—and her child's—freedom.

Lorelei could offer them in trade for independence, the opportunity to be a wife and mother, no longer a servant to her country.

As the idea took hold, possibilities for her future began to swirl. She would still be cursed with a man who didn't love and respect her, but she would have a child and a true home. Maybe one day she and Chastain would form a truce, a peaceful and agreeable way of living together.

But before that could happen, she must get her sickness under control and find those damned plans.

With their delivery, she would be rid of De Pez, not beholden to her parents, and could insist she'd fulfilled her obligations. And then, she would beg for her life back—as if it had ever truly been her own.

For her freedom, she would defy all the comte had

entrusted her with. For a chance at the life many were fortunate to lead, she would forsake all she'd been raised to embrace.

Lorelei would choose herself—and her child.

The promise of a future without the fear of being discovered took hold.

She glanced around the luxurious room, decorated in jade and gold. In the past, she hadn't remained in a single residence for more than a year, in places that never felt remotely like a home, filled as they were with furniture provided by her government or belonging to the previous tenants.

But this—this room, this whole estate, could be exactly as she wanted it to be. Perhaps she would strip the old, heavy draperies and replace them with a soft peach twill with hints of yellow. The chairs and sofas would be easily re-covered to match. And she'd seen the most divine rug shop on Bond Street where one could order a floor covering woven to one's personal preference. The servants were forever asking her if she needed anything, if they could assist her in any way. She would request their aid in moving the furniture to better suit her.

And the nursery. She'd been searching the house, but had yet to find where her child would sleep, take its first steps, learn arithmetic.

She smiled, a genuine smile, for the first time in weeks. Now that she had Andrew behind her and had accepted her future—slightly altered from the one of which she'd dreamed—she realized she could be content. She could live the simple, stable life she'd envisioned in her youth. Though she knew Andrew would always be in her thoughts, she couldn't allow herself to hope for more. Even if the *more* she longed for would make her happy for a lifetime.

Her husband would never love her, but he had given her a child, someone she could love unconditionally, without strings or obligations. From this moment on, her happiness depended solely on herself and what she brought about.

Lorelei was married to a duke of unimaginable wealth. Surely she could indulge herself in making this house her home.

Yes, she needed to plan for her child's future. Make a home he would see as a sanctuary, his refuge from the cruel world. Her son would one day be Lord Chastain, a duke. One of England's most privileged elite, and Lorelei, as his mother, could also live such a life.

"M'lady?" The whispered question pulled her back from her daydreams. She looked over to see a rotund maid at the door.

"Yes?" Lorelei responded.

"I be new here, and want'd ask if ye be needing anything."

New? Sally's post must have already been filled after her unexpected departure. "What is your name?"

"I be Alexandra Dutton, m'lady," she said hesitantly, her gaze on the ground.

"And you did not work for the duke before today?" Lorelei inquired.

"No, m'lady. I was sent for from the agency. I be right happy to have this position."

"We are most pleased to have you, Alexa—"

"'Scuse the interruption, but it be just plain ol' Mrs. Dutton."

"That will do fine, and I will strive to remember that. Tell me, Mrs. Dutton, do you have experience with children?" Lorelei needed someone she could trust, besides herself, with the care of her child should her plan not work. "I find myself in need of a nursemaid." Lorelei set her hand against her stomach, the slight bulge unnoticed by all.

The maid finally looked up at Lorelei, and she was surprised to discover the woman was not as young as she'd first appeared. "Not meself, m'lady. Me late husband, God rest him, passed before we had the time ta have a young'un of our own, but me sister had a whole horde of the wee ones."

"I think that will do, Mrs. Dutton," Lorelei confided in a whisper. "Our first chore will be to find the nursery in this oversized house."

Chapter Sixteen

Lorelei was finding it hard to hide her condition from those around her. Her clothing was increasingly snug, she was unsuccessful keeping anything but stale bread and tea down, and her body craved sleep more and more each day. The servants treated her like a child, rushing to her side every time she left her bedchamber—likely thanks to news of Mrs. Dutton's position as nursemaid spreading through the staff. Chastain had kept his distance, never entering her chambers nor demanding her presence in his own. Now that she'd searched his room entirely for the plans and knew they were not there, she hoped never to cross the threshold again.

This morning, she sat in the drawing room visiting with her mother, and desperately tried to cover the bulge at her middle with her needlepoint. Heaven only knew why she bothered at all. Chastain had noticed—though he hadn't spoken to her about it—and had agreed to her decision to retire to the country for a few months. She—as well as her father—had searched every square inch in his townhouse with no success, and she knew another visit from De Pez would signal the end of her assignment. When he did not gain what he sought, drastic measures were taken—though that did not always get De Pez what he wanted, either.

De Pez's previous mission had been labeled a disgrace. He'd been remanded back to his home country, and had spent years sorting old reports. Then Louis XVI's untimely departure from this world caused an uproar the likes of which Lorelei and her family had never seen before. Suddenly, De Pez—and Lorelei's family— were seen as liabilities, and their faithfulness to their country was called into question. They'd been forced from their home and driven into hiding by the Directory. De Pez resented Lorelei and her family for their ability to survive. But when he'd approached Lorelei's father with his idea to bring them back into their country's good graces, the comte did not pass up the opportunity—even though they all knew everything rested on the ability of one man to seize control of the country. If Bonaparte failed, their futures looked grim indeed.

"Lore?" her mother asked.

She shook off the dread of what her future might entail and forced a smile. "Yes? I do apologize. I have much on my mind, Mother."

Camille set her tea aside and shifted closer to Lorelei. "We all have much on our minds at the moment, but do not fear. Your father and I have taught you well. We do not expect you to disappoint."

A crushing weight settled on her shoulders. Her success or failure would determine the future for not only her, but also her parents. "Thank you for your confidence."

"Tell me what you've discovered in the last few

weeks."

"I wish there was something to report." And she did. Lorelei had spent every spare moment—when servants weren't keeping such a close eye on her—scouring the house. "I have not located the plans anywhere in this house."

"Did you check for hidden areas behind paintings?"

"Of course, and also a trap door in the floor of the stable, the kitchen for a false wall at the back of the pantry, and the housekeeper thought I was a bit off when she found me rummaging through the bin of filthy laundry."

"Have you broached the subject with Lord Chastain?"

"Heavens, no." Lorelei was lucky—or unlucky—to be in the man's presence for only a few minutes a day. As her sickness increased, he'd stopped asking her to join him in the evenings for *ton* activities. "We seem to be the norm for *ton* marriages. Furthermore, he is a duke, and must be very busy."

Lorelei didn't know why she justified her husband's lack of interest to her mother. His inattentiveness to her was advantageous to her goal, yet still made little sense. Perhaps she'd at first looked the prize of the season, he and Andrew both seeking to court her. And by a stroke of luck—he most likely thought it was his charm and debonair air—she'd chosen him over a very wealthy marquis. With her won, married, and bedded, there was nothing left to hold his attention, especially since Lorelei was not the meek and agreeable wife he'd hoped for. While throwing out the maid he'd taken liberties with had seemed the right thing—the satisfying thing—to do at the time, now it seemed the worst thing she could have done.

"You know you must fix this." Camille gestured to the room around her. "This rift that separates you from Chastain. It is the only way he will confide in you. How else do you expect to get information about that which we seek?"

"I know that, Mother," she sighed. "But I am at a loss as to how to get him to trust me, let alone spend any time with me."

"Have you tried?"

"Of course, I have." It was a lie, yet she was reluctant to show her mother her weakness at something that happened to be one of her mother's greatest strengths. If it had been about getting access, searching and returning with an item, then she would have excelled. But this required a more intimate form of manipulation. "Tell me, Mother, how do you get others to do exactly as you want without them knowing you're guiding their every move?"

Camille smiled. "Oh, I believe that is a natural gift...and one I passed on to you, if you will only look deep enough."

"I do not know what you mean." The power of persuasion was not one she excelled at. "If I can charm with my beauty, I do."

"Oh, no. You must learn to use your brain a bit more because you cannot always rely on your physical assets. One day they may be taken from you."

"You are speaking in riddles."

"Then let me explain." A sadness filled her mother. Her shoulders sagged and her eyes were unfocused when she gazed at Lorelei. "Do you remember how I told you never to trust any man?"

"Yes—except my father, of course."

"I believe you added the bit about your father," her mother said, "but you were always an idealistic child. I have taught you not to trust any man. And do you know the reason for that?"

Lorelei thought back to that long-ago conversation.

"Do you remember the story about how your father and I met and married?"

Of course, she did. "You met after you were injured."

"Do you think your father loved me at first sight?" she asked. "I was beaten and destroyed, inside and out. One could barely tell my eye color due to the swelling of my face. I couldn't walk, and was relegated to a chair."

It was hard to envision her mother in that condition. Lorelei's eyes began to water for the injustices her mother had faced at such a young age—about the age Lorelei was now.

"Do not shed a tear for me, my child," her mother soothed her ache. "My country was prepared to send me away, to wash their hands of me and the damage they were responsible for. Your father wanted nothing to do with me, but I changed that. It was I who showed him my usefulness, gained my legs again, and healed—if not on the inside, at least outside.

"Within a short time, your father and I married, and he thought he was the one in control. He spoke with the powers that be and regained my position—and a second chance."

"But you love him, do you not?" She'd always wondered about that exact thing, and finally summoned the courage to ask.

"Love is an odd concept," her mother sighed. "I loved what he could do for me. I loved what I would gain by having him on my side, and I loved his sense of loyalty to me—sometimes even over his country. I would not want another partner at my side."

Camille had called her husband a partner. While Lorelei understood that was true, it seemed not to fit nor encompass all that their long marriage was. She and Chastain had no chance at anything resembling the closeness and balance that the comte and comtesse shared.

"So, in many ways I do love him, yet I know the time may come when we have to give each other up. I think every person must always be willing to love another, yet reserve enough of themselves to go on after it is over."

An emptiness, vaster than the deserts in Africa, filled her. She and Andrew would never be given a chance to love one another this much.

The sorrow in her mother's words made little sense. "I do not understand. You and Father have a tie that seems unbreakable."

"It may be for me and my well-being that he gives up what we have. You see, I have no doubt that he loves me with all his heart, and may very well do something foolish for me. But this is all talk for another day." Her mother fussed and reached forward for Lorelei.

Without thinking, she set her needlepoint aside in order to grasp her mother's hands—a rare physical gesture for Camille.

"My child—" Her voice cut so abruptly that Lorelei's gaze snapped from where she looked at their entwined hands to her mother's face. Camille looked past their hands to Lorelei's dress. "Oh, my heavens."

She looked down, worried she'd ruined the moment with a social misdeed. "Have I spilt on my dress?" As the words left her mouth, she realized what her mother was staring at. No crumbs from the small sandwiches they'd had or drips from their lemon tea, but the small bump poking out beneath the peach-colored sash tied high above her waist in today's current fashion.

"Oh."

"Might I say this changes things," Camille said as she placed her hand against Lorelei's growing belly. "Does the child belong to Chastain?"

"Yes." She looked down in shame. "I was going to tell you—"

Camille looked to her with a new level of respect, nodding her chin in approval. "Yes, you are no longer only a foreigner who married an English duke, but now the soon-to-be mother of a future duke, and heir to the Chastain legacy—future keeper of the plans. That is well-done, my child."

The words struck a blade to her heart that her own mother would see her child as only a means to an end. Lorelei would love her child, not use it.

"It is only well-done if I'm able to locate the plans. For all I know, Chastain's father died before telling him about them." She'd fretted that exact outcome since first meeting Chastain. "What if he knows naught of the plans—mayhap threw them out with the rubbish, or burned them to keep warm during the cold months, not knowing their significance?"

"Then that would be very bad—or could be extremely fortunate… In that case, at least they would have been destroyed."

"But that would leave us with nothing to present to De Pez. I fear our time is running out," Lorelei confided.

"Time is always of the essence, my child." Her

mother sat back, a sad smile on her face. "Yet, the situation is never so dire."

"Mother, what is wrong?"

Her mother looked to where her hand still caressed Lorelei's stomach. "Lore, as a parent, I should be overjoyed at the news of my first grandchild. I should, in my jubilation, jump up and down and embrace you at the glad tidings—already mentally writing my friends with the news. Instead, I am already pondering the life this child will lead, much the same as the one you have led. Will he or she be forced into answering our country's call to duty when the time comes? Live in fear of losing you?"

"I have thought long and hard about this." Lorelei knew she could change things, make a better way for herself and her child. "I think this child will be the key to my freedom."

"How so?"

"I will find the plans and use them...as a bargaining chip of sorts." Lorelei was proud of what she'd mapped out, thinking once again of the possibility of earning her parents' freedom, as well.

"Lore, you must understand, our government will take what they want, regardless of what conditions you may seek to put upon the transaction. They will not only take the plans, they will make sure you have nothing left and nowhere else to go besides back to your rightful place."

Lorelei couldn't help but wonder where her rightful place might be. "I think you overestimate their interest in me. I am a weak female, used only for my beauty, to gain them something they desire."

"We both know you are more than the sum of your outside," her mother chided.

"But they do not," Lorelei argued. "Be forthcoming, Mother. I was selected for my perceived powers of seduction, correct?"

"Yes, but they would not have agreed to it unless they had faith that you would fulfill the task."

Lorelei suspected they'd only agreed because the comte and comtesse would be there to assist her if she discovered she was unable to handle things. It was her parents De Pez trusted, not her. Hadn't he said as much?

"No matter their reasoning, Mother," Lorelei continued. "Mrs. Dutton and I will be retiring to Chastain manor soon for the duration of my pregnancy. This will afford me ample time to figure out what is next—for me and my child."

"I do not relish being so far from you, my child." Her mother worried needlessly. "What if your labor is difficult? Do promise me you will have a nursemaid nearby."

Lorelei hadn't given much thought to the actual birth of her child, nor the primitiveness of Chastain manor. "Do not fret, Mrs. Dutton has delivered many babies, and town is only a short ride from the manor if a doctor is needed." She hadn't a clue if Mrs. Dutton had even seen a birthing, but she couldn't admit that to her mother. "I will do well, you shall see."

Chapter Seventeen

Andrew thrust and counter-thrust, jabbed and parried, matching his partner lunge for lunge. The man was years his junior, and many would say newly in his prime, yet Andrew's body coursed with rage—a red-hot fury, boiling barely under the surface. His fencing arm was steady before him, his other hand clenched behind his back in standard form. Focusing his negative energy, he pushed his opponent farther toward the opposite end of the room and the crowd who'd gathered at some point during the heated match.

He trained his eyes on the man before him, his mind blocking the jeering of the gentlemen lining the room. Sweat gathered on his brow and crept lower, threatening to blur his vision. Andrew couldn't risk the split second it would take to swipe it away—even an instant of broken concentration would be all it took for the younger man to overtake him and no doubt end the match with the point of his lance at Andrew's throat.

A growl echoed off the walls and only grew louder.

Andrew wanted to shout for silence, demanding a

stillness to befit the match he currently fought.

Only then did he realize it was he who'd issued the animalistic sound.

He advanced.

His opponent executed a superb beat parry to deflect his incoming attack.

They were evenly matched, likely trained by the same fencing master, and Andrew feared they would be at this bout for some time.

His only hope was that he'd mastered the art of endurance while his opponent favored a swift, unrelenting assault that would quickly exhaust his stamina.

It was time he challenged the man's skill. With a feint to one side, Andrew tried for a compound attack to the opposite side. The action threw the man off guard and he stumbled slightly. Andrew took the opportunity and nicked his opponent's cheek, opening a thin line that reached from the corner of his mouth and ended nearly at his earlobe.

The sight of the crimson blood nearly cost Andrew his advantage in the match when the man surprised him with a circular parry with his point, slashing a mirrored thin line across Andrew's upper arm. He could not spare the moment to look at the flesh wound, but knew by the sting of the cut as warmth spread down his arm.

Next, his opponent tried for a direct riposte, which Andrew easily anticipated and blocked with an arc of his blade, their metal hitting with a resounding *ting* and sliding apart. Both men took the opportunity to move apart, much like their weapons, to regroup and assess the other.

Andrew held his foil out in a perfectly executed

extension and quickly flicked his blade, whipping past his opponent's next parry.

He was unsure how much longer he could hold off the man's expert sword work.

His hilt was slick with perspiration.

A sound issued from the crowd, and the man raised the tip of his foil, signaling the end of the round.

He delivered a curt bow in Andrew's direction, followed by a mumbled, "Excellent bout, Marquis."

Andrew could do naught but watch as the man left the fencing area. Happily, another gentleman took his place immediately.

Breathing deeply, he prepared himself for another round. Another chance to direct his pent-up aggression toward another. Mrs. Bee would be happy for the respite—and the decrease in damaged household items.

"En garde."

Andrew's eyes snapped from his opponent's fencing arm to the man's face at the familiar tone. Of all the men who could have cut in on this match, Chastain was the unlucky fool who would gain the brunt of Andrew's anger—fitting, as he was at the root of his ire.

Andrew echoed Chastain's words and took a defensive position, but he didn't hold the position long before he executed a fast step and lunge—a *speed patinando*. Andrew knew from many years of training with Chastain that the man hadn't the skill to parry. Sure enough, Chastain issued a *passe*, which missed its target and enabled Andrew to move swiftly into a *raddoppio*.

"Always the superior partner where rapiers are concerned," Chastain drawled as he regained his footing. "Too bad that skill does not extend to women."

Andrew knew his friend only sought to raise his

hackles, eliciting some type of outburst that would lead to Andrew's downfall, and ultimately, his defeat.

"What are you doing here, Chastain?" Andrew parried while Chastain easily moved to avoid his attack.

"So formal, Andrew." His opponent emphasized his Christian name. "I am here, as I am every week at this time."

It was difficult to admit that Andrew hadn't even known what day of the week it was before this very moment. Of course, Benji would keep their longstanding appointment at Gentlemen Jackson's—and it was likely his friend was completely oblivious to Andrew's foul mood. All the better, for he would be unprepared for the sound beating coming his way.

"Tell me, Andrew, what might we have planned for this evening?" Chastain said. He feinted halfheartedly and then retreated, keeping his point aimed squarely at Andrew. "I find myself with much free time on my hands of late."

The man was truly clueless to the days—no, months—of agony he'd caused. The total amount of hours Andrew had spent drinking and carousing likely added up to weeks of misspent time. Time he could never regain.

"I had not thought past this very match, *my friend*."

If Chastain noticed the animosity in the words, Andrew could not tell. "In the moment—I have always enjoyed that about you."

That was the only way Andrew knew to make it through the endless days. Minutes and hours he spent thinking only of Lorelei, dreaming of the day they would be together, the many ways he'd make her happy—all to no end. She'd chosen Chastain as the more worthy companion.

Andrew sidestepped when Chastain lunged toward him, his foil making a circular pattern with little power behind it.

How many hours had he and Chastain whiled away in this very room? Neither sought to best the other, only using fencing as a means for exercise as both loathed the habit of brisk walks about the park, and neither would be caught dead rowing down the River Thames in a misguided attempt to keep a lean physique. Neither was desperate enough to resort to fisticuffs, either.

"Well?"

"Well, what?" Andrew asked.

"Tell me you have something daringly scandalous in mind for this evening." Chastain feinted and moved to the edge of the room in an attempt to lure Andrew in his direction. "Come now, I need a distraction… Some jolly good fun, if you will."

"What about Lady Chastain?"

"What about her?"

"Will she be accompanying us?" He wanted to ask so much more about her. Was she well? Had she settled in at Chastain's London townhouse? Did she go out? Was there anything she needed—or wanted?

"Gawd, no. That would be the exact opposite of a jolly time." Chastain hopped from foot to foot.

The man looked a fool, and, in fact, even though the crowd had dispensed, a few men still watched, chuckling at the sight of him.

"Pay attention, or my tip will be to your throat before you realize it." Andrew parried and thrust his foil, trying to make good on his promise, but Chastain easily blocked it with his own. "Lady Chastain is agreeable to your nightly escapades without her? I understood she was very concerned with your activities."

Chastain spun a little circle, his foil connecting with Andrew's from behind his back. "She will shortly no longer be my concern."

Andrew made the mistake of letting his tip fall. With a swiftness and skill Andrew hadn't thought Chastain possessed, his friend's blade made a quick pass across his chest. Without looking down, he knew the sharp point had cut through the outer layer of his jacket. With his foil once again at the ready, he would not let Chastain have the upper hand again.

"Not your concern… How so?" he asked. "You are married."

"Yes," Andrew heaved, his stamina waning. "But she will be traveling to my country estate until our child arrives—and if I am a smart man, I will convince her to stay on there for the duration of her life."

"Then congratulations are in order, my man," Andrew said with as much good cheer as he could muster. "You must be very proud…and so soon after the wedding."

Andrew must have sounded convincing, for Chastain stood a bit taller. "It is a blessed occasion, indeed."

It baffled him Chastain wanted nothing to do with his wife, while Andrew longed for just a glimpse of her, the chance to run his fingers through her silken hair, mayhap share a whispered secret or two.

"And you truly think she will go meekly to the country?"

"Heavens, no." Chastain lunged once more, and Andrew countered with his own thrust, throwing

Chastain off his feet. Stumbling forward, his friend lifted his foil so as not to drive the point into the polished floor as he sought to regain his balance. "Very good show, old sport."

Chastain dropped his foil and turned back toward Andrew, a good-natured smile on his face, only to find the sharp tip of Andrew's foil at his exposed throat.

"Come now, Drake." Chastain must have noted the seriousness in Andrew's eyes. "Let us dress and head to White's to celebrate my coming freedom."

"Was it not only a few months ago you celebrated your nuptials?"

Chastain thought for a moment. "I suppose so, though it feels like a lifetime ago. I do wish someone had warned me against tying myself to a dreaded female. And then I had to make it worse by leaving my seed within her. Now I am free of her nagging, but find I hear her body's discord with the pregnancy every time I am home. It is truly depressing when a man's home can no longer be his castle and sanctuary."

Andrew was hard-pressed not to let the man drone on. Though Benji spoke ill of Lorelei, at least Andrew was hearing something of how she fared. "Why not send for her mother to be with her?"

"Oh, her mother visits on occasion, but is very busy with the comte's political duties. Will you drop that damned point?"

Andrew hadn't realized he still held his foil aloft, nor that they'd drawn a crowd larger than before. "My apologies." He dropped his arm and, with it, his foil. "I could use a night out. When does she leave?"

"She was packing as I left, or doing as much as possible considering how sick she has been. It is truly irritating." Chastain turned toward the men's retiring room and signaled Andrew to follow. "She has even turned me away in my own bedchambers. Can you believe the nerve of the woman?"

"No." Andrew infused a measure of shock into his words.

"Yes. Says the motion makes her sick, as if she's again crossing the Channel on a boat. The last time she nearly vomited upon me."

Exactly what the man deserved.

"She has my mistress removed from my house, and then dares to withhold her wifely duties." Chastain removed his sporting shirt, pulled a clean one over his head, and then tied his cravat and tucked his shirttails into his trousers. "I will not stand for it, I tell you. She must go…and to where, I do not care."

Andrew would cherish the chance to call Lorelei his wife, the Marchioness of Drake, yet Chastain seemed impervious to his good fortune. "Your estate is several days' hard travel. Why did they not leave first thing this morning?"

"Lorelei is too sick to travel until after the noon meal." Chastain paused as he sat and pulled on his Hessians. "She and her nursemaid, Mrs. Dutton, plan to depart any moment now—and then I will no longer have need to look over my shoulder, fearing she will be there watching my every move."

Alarm coursed through Andrew. It was obvious she shouldn't be traveling at all, let alone without the assistance of her husband. "Are the roads safe for two lone women to travel? Especially one in Lorelei's delicate condition?"

"Safe? I pity the highwayman who would dare stop

my wife's carriage, for she would surely tear him limb from limb with only her tongue as a weapon. Plus, my fortune has never been that good… To have my wife permanently indisposed."

Andrew was appalled. "You cannot mean that."

"Of course not, Andrew." Chastain chuckled. "I need my heir first."

Within minutes, after promising to meet Chastain at White's within the hour, Andrew leapt into his carriage and bid his driver get him to Chastain's townhouse with all due haste. It was as though his life was constantly repeating itself—yet again she fled from him; yet again, he rushed to her side.

His reclining pose belied the tense, rigid feel of his own body. The thought of arriving on her doorstep alone seemed foolhardy. Lorelei could easily turn him away.

As the idea struck, Andrew gave a loud rap on the roof of his enclosed carriage and leaned out the window to shout to his coachman.

"Yes, yur lordship?" his driver shouted over his shoulder as he navigated the early-afternoon traffic surrounding Hyde Park on his way to Chastain's residence.

"Is the apothecary still located off Bond Street?" Andrew rubbed his shoulder where the point had broken the skin.

"I believe so, yur lordship. Can I get ye anything therein?"

The driver's answer pleased him, and a sense of rightness settled.

Businesses changed locations, closed, or moved on to other cities with little warning or fanfare, and Andrew could not waste additional time gallivanting about

London if he was going to stop Lorelei before she left town.

"No," Andrew called over the clipping of horse hooves. "I can collect it myself."

There were only so many subjects one was comfortable discussing with one's servants—and a female's delicate condition, especially a female not belonging to him, was not one of them.

What he would say or do to change Lorelei's mind he hadn't the faintest idea, but he needed to try. Thus, arriving empty-handed was not an option.

As the carriage rolled to a stop before the shop, Andrew realized he may not have to discuss what ailed Lorelei with his driver, but he would have to explain a bit of the situation to the clerk within. Luckily, the woman inside was kind and understanding, asking only pertinent questions without prying into the situation.

Within minutes, Andrew was once again ensconced in his carriage, a bag of peppermint leaves in his coat pocket, his driver maneuvering expertly around other carriages. Andrew pulled the curtain from the window and glanced out to gauge the sun's progress across the sky. It had reached its pinnacle and had started its descent not long ago in the clear blue sky.

He fingered the paper sack in his pocket.

It was a small gesture of his feelings for her, yet so much more than anything Chastain had ever done.

Surely she would understand, truly see, how much he cared for her—that he was more than capable of providing for her, especially in her delicate condition. If it were his child she carried, he would never leave her side. Every moment of every day would be spent focused on her comfort.

And it would not likely stop after the birth of the child.

No. Andrew swore he'd make it his life's mission to care for her, make her feel cherished, loved. She would want for nothing if he had his way.

But a simple sack of peppermint leaves?

It would have to do for now, as time was not on his side.

Pulling the curtain aside once more, Andrew saw they'd moved past the congested business district and moved freely past London townhouses, now only a few blocks from Chastain's house.

At long last, the house came into view, just as a traveling carriage started away from the drive.

"Stop that carriage!"

"Right, yur lordship." Quick to action, his driver flicked his whip, and the coach pulled forward, throwing Andrew back against the velvet seat. The curtain fell back into place, obscuring his view of the fleeing carriage. "Halt!" his driver shouted.

When his coach slowed, Andrew leapt from it and rushed to stop the loaded carriage before him. Lorelei was prepared for a long stay in the country if the amount of luggage strapped to the carriage were any indication.

"Lady Chastain," Andrew called when he was within hearing distance. "It is the Marquis of Drake." Before the Chastain coachman could dismount, Andrew reached for the door of the carriage, but it swung open before he could pull it, revealing a servant.

"Excuse ye', why did ye stop me coach?" the woman asked. "Me lady be right heated if'n I'm not directly 'hind her."

Andrew looked past the woman and into the dim

interior of the carriage, hoping his fears would not be confirmed, but he knew from the first sight of the servant that he would not find Lorelei within.

"Where is Lady Lore—Chastain?" He focused on the woman before him. He'd never seen her in Chastain's residence before. "Is she still at the townhouse?"

When the woman only stared, giving him no answers, Andrew realized that while she was a complete stranger to him, so was he to her. And he would dismiss any servant that spoke out of turn to a stranger about his whereabouts. The servant was agreeably tight-lipped.

"My apologies," Andrew said. "I am the Marquis of Drake, a friend of Lord and Lady Chastain's. I was hoping to have a moment with your ladyship before she retired to the country."

"Ah." The woman finally started to understand. "Ye be miss'n her by a bit. She was feel'n quite the thing and departed afore the noon-day meal."

Andrew's shoulders sagged at the news.

"I be meet'n her in a few hours to take rest for the night." The woman must have felt a measure of compassion for him. "I be Mrs. Dutton. Soon-ta-be nursemaid to the new lord. I can bring her word from ye."

The woman was a kindred spirit if Andrew had ever met one. If Lorelei had chosen Mrs. Dutton to assist with her child, then surely she was worthy of his trust, as well. If he had pen and paper, he would have scribbled a note. Instead, he pulled the paper sack from his pocket and handed it to the nursemaid.

"Would you give her this?" When Mrs. Dutton only eyed the sack, he continued. "It is peppermint leaves. They can be soaked in tea. I have been told it will relieve the severe sickness."

He felt like a schoolboy, calling on a girl who'd caught his eye, only to be told she wasn't at home. He wracked his brain for any justification he could find for his concern over her condition. He knew gentlemen normally ignored this time as if it didn't exist.

A small smile lit the woman's face. "I do think she be happy for this." Mrs. Dutton accepted the bag and slipped it into her pocket. "I will add them ta her tea this very night. She has been so very ill. I worry about the poor babe."

"Ah, well," Andrew stuttered. The conversation had become uncomfortably intimate. "Please, give her the leaves. I have been told that sickness is a sure sign of a healthy, strong youngster. You will tell her I said so? And send word to me if Lady Chastain needs anything."

Frowning, Mrs. Dutton nodded and returned to her carriage.

Andrew watched as the carriage made its way down the street and rounded the corner out of view.

Lorelei was gone.

If Chastain had his way, his wife would remain in the country for the foreseeable future—out of Andrew's reach.

An aching in his chest threatened to bring him to his knees.

He rubbed the spot, vaguely recognizing it as the place where his heart beat just behind his ribcage. He would learn well from those ribs, and keep his heart under lock and key. For when his heart sought something, it only led to this very ache.

Chapter Eighteen

"I said send in another woman!" The words ripped through the room, bounced off the silk-covered walls, and echoed in Andrew's head.

Madame Sasha only stood in the doorway, hands on her hips, her blonde curls bouncing as she shook her head in denial of his request.

"You cannot refuse me," Andrew called from his position on the bed. A breeze entered the room from the hall and sent a chill across his naked, exposed flesh. Pulling a thin blanket to cover his manhood—it would be of little use when the next girl arrived if it was frozen to the point of shriveling—he tried again, "Sasha, I would hate to think of the massive amounts of coin I have sent to your coffers due to my patronage of Craven House."

"Be that as it may—" she started before Andrew cut her short.

"You will send another woman to me!" his voice thundered once more. "Do not make me summon one myself."

"You are drunk, my lord."

"That is nothing new to you."

"I understand that, but…" her words trailed off.

"But…" Andrew prodded.

"In all your many nights here, you have never been unkind to my girls."

"I have not laid a hand on your girls." Andrew may have been drinking as fast as he could pour, but he knew—to his very soul—that he hadn't harmed any woman. Never in his life would he dishonor his own mother by laying a hurtful hand on a woman.

"The sword is not the only means of hurting a woman. Words can wound deeper than any rod."

His words were not as clear as his actions, and in his hazy state, it was quite possible he had said something that might offend. He vaguely remembered a girl whose looks had displeased him greatly.

"Just send me another girl."

"I most certainly will not." Madame Sasha surprisingly held her ground, even though the loss of revenue would hurt her business. "Please leave, or I will have you thrown out."

Andrew chuckled. "I have no plans for leaving."

The woman huffed and fled the room, closing the door soundly behind her.

He took the opportunity to scan the room for his decanter of spirits.

Ah! There it sat, on the table closest to the door.

Wrapping the blanket around himself, Andrew crawled from the bed and made his way across the frigid room. When Sasha returned with another girl, he would instruct her to stoke the fire, which had turned to nothing but a few amber coals sometime during the previous few hours.

The decanter lifted easily in his hand as he brought it to his lips, not bothering to track down his tumbler, and he drained the remaining liquid. After seeing to his warmth, he would have another decanter brought round. Normally, Craven House prided itself on catering to London's elite gentlemen, seeing that their every need was fulfilled.

Andrew felt highly unfulfilled at the moment.

Returning to the bed, he decided to lie down once more and await Sasha's return.

Within moments, his eyelids became heavy.

What was taking so bloody long, he wondered?

He really must work on cutting down his drinking. It would be the height of embarrassment if he gained the reputation of one unable to perform behind closed doors. That sort of gossip made its way through the rumor mills more quickly than sand through an hourglass.

Maybe a small nap would do him good, clear his system—and return his lust.

Andrew allowed his eyes to close and breathed deeply—in and out.

It had been so long since he'd willingly released himself to sleep. For when he did, the dreams started—dreams of what could have been: always happy, light, and full of a love he'd never know.

He surrendered to sleep. Before long, he found himself spinning across the dance floor of a crowded ballroom, Lorelei secure in his arms. He loosened his grip ever so slightly, and she took a small step back, allowing him to take in her entire form. Her body was clad in a color he'd never seen before…not quite crimson, yet not pink either. The silk clung to her body and cascaded over her hips, swirling outward around her feet as they moved across the floor. He could not see her feet, but knew she wore kid shoes of the softest leather, the color matching the pearls hanging about her neck and from her ears.

The sounds of a waltz continued to hypnotize Andrew as they glided through the crowd. If he were able to look around, he'd most likely see every face in the room following their progress. Thankfully, he was unable to take his gaze from hers. Her moss-green eyes stared at him with as much intensity as he knew his own eyes held.

How had they ever denied this connection between them? Ever agreed to even a moment without the other?

Suddenly, Lorelei pulled from his arms. Her hand laid flat against his chest, she pushed, freeing herself.

Gracefully, she moved away from him, still swaying to the music as if she were still held tightly in her partner's embrace.

He could do nothing to coax her back to him.

He tried.

He shouted to her, but she appeared to not hear his calls over the music.

He pushed through the crowd, but more and more couples stood in his path.

Until he no longer saw her swaying to the notes.

It was then that he felt the pressure on his shoulder. If someone had been holding him back this entire time, the man might find himself without an appendage very soon.

Andrew turned to confront whoever kept nudging his shoulder.

No one stood there, yet the prodding continued.

He shook his head, trying to make sense of the situation.

Lorelei would never leave his side.

Andrew's eyes sprung open.

His entire body ached, not only the place where his heart had once dwelled.

The sound of carriages and pushcarts rang in his head, and the early-morning light burned his eyes.

And the offensive smell. Was that his own unwashed body?

No. He cracked his lids once more, just enough to search the area around him without letting in the dreaded light.

Bringing his hand up to block the blinding sun, he searched his immediate environs. He recognized nothing—not the cobblestones beneath his prone body or the walls close on each side. Rubbish lined the brick building behind him, adding to the stench that settled heavily around him.

He brought his fingers up to probe his head, feeling through his matted hair for any signs of a busted skull. When his touch found no lumps or blood, Andrew made to sit up.

Nausea overtook him before he'd made it to his elbows.

What in the blazes had happened to him?

Last he remembered, he was having a rousing time at Craven House, sampling Madame Sasha's latest crop of girls. Then...his mind would not grasp what came next.

Suddenly the past—how long had he spent at Craven House?—came crashing down on him. Lorelei had left him. He'd drowned his sorrows in liquor and women of questionable morals. Andrew had fought with Madame Sasha...and now he lay in the filthy street much like the rubbish he felt like, suffering from not only the aftereffects of his debauchery, but a case of wounded pride.

He needed to get himself together.

Being thrown from a house of ill repute during a drunken fit was a new low, even for him.

He pondered his circumstances as he brushed the filth from his wrinkled clothes. He pined for a woman who clearly did not want him…or didn't know she would be happier with him. Didn't understand how he could take better care of her, give her all she desired—and much she didn't.

Andrew stood, pushing down his upset stomach and calming his spinning mind, and ran his hands down his coat to remove any last clinging debris. A slip of folded paper was sticking from his pocket.

The crisp, embossed paper had only his name written in flowing ink on the outside. The sand used to dry it still clung to its surface. With hands shaky from his sudden withdrawal from liquor, he unfolded the note.

In handwriting as crisp as the paper, Andrew read Madame Sasha's words:

Andrew,

Though I have greatly enjoyed your patronage of Craven House, I believe it is time we part ways. In the future, if you find you have need of another establishment such as Craven House, do remember your manners and good breeding. As many men of your status boast of their lineage and class, it does behoove them to act with a certain decorum at all times.

The letter was signed with a simple 'S.'

Modest and elegantly stated, just as he would expect from a woman of Sasha's ilk.

The delicate, perfumed paper ripped easily in his hands. How dare she treat a marquis as she had? He was a man to be shown respect, not tossed aside like garbage.

His feet hit the ground hard as he fled the alley, hoping no one noticed his sudden appearance upon the walkway. It was with luck that Sasha's goons had dumped him only several blocks from his townhouse. She'd most likely wanted to teach him a lesson, but unfortunately the old saying was true: you cannot teach an old dog new tricks.

And at the moment, Andrew felt very, very old—and worn out.

Furthermore, he was the one to teach lessons, not some upstart brothel owner.

Once home, he detoured from the usual path to his study—and his well-stocked liquor cabinet—and instructed his butler, Alfred, to have water sent up for a bath. It was time he decided what was next for him. Mayhap a new hobby or such.

What did a man of his *status* and *class* do during the daylight hours when he was determined to neglect his rightful duties? Surely they did not sit around waiting for a drink—or, heaven forbid, a woman who did not want them. It was an aimless daily existence he'd worked hard to forget by managing his estates, communicating with his stewards, and securing his father's seat in Parliament. But now, it all seemed too much for him, his heart in none of it.

As he lounged in his claw-footed tub, filled to the brim with warm water, he realized that all great men had one thing in common. They did not wait around for things to come to them—oh no, they went out and got what they wanted. Men like Alexander the Great did not allow circumstances or other people to dissuade them from their goal.

But he'd tried calling on Lorelei…sending flowers…and lastly, those damned peppermint leaves. And still no word from her. Could one make another fall in love with them? Maybe his love for her didn't require her mutual feelings—simply having her to himself would be enough.

Yes, maybe it was the game that drew him to Lorelei and set off his anger toward Chastain.

It was not how the taking came about, but the endgame that mattered.

A knock at the door pulled him from his thoughts.

"Enter," he called.

The door swung open revealing Mrs. Bee, her arms laden with freshly laundered shirts.

"Good heavens! I am bathing."

"Nothing I haven't seen since your birth." Mrs. Bee continued her chores, exiting his main room for his dressing closet. "I am sure the sight of you will not scorch me eyes."

The woman took far more liberties than most men would allow. "Is that not the task of my valet?" he asked when she continued to work. From the sound of things, she was hanging his shirts and tidying up his boots.

"I suppose so," she finally answered. "But I needed to see you for myself. You'd disappeared for several days—I was worried."

"You know better than to worry yourself with my whereabouts."

"Oh, you know I do know better, yet," she chuckled, "when word was sent round to expect you home sometime this day I was a bit curious."

"Who sent word?" he asked, knowing the answer.

"Note wasn't signed, but the writing looked to be

female." She returned to the room and tended the fire. "So I assumed another mistress had kicked you from her home."

"You know I do not favor or frequent a mistress."

"I do."

"One woman just is not enough for me," he said under his breath, hoping Mrs. Bee's ears were trained on something else. "Do you mind giving me a bit of privacy? My bath is complete, and the water is getting a might frigid."

"Privacy?" she asked. "You awoke in a dirty, trash-filled walkway in a drunken stupor…"

"How do you know that?"

"I am not ignorant, Andrew," she said. "I sent a footman to follow the man who dropped off the notes. They passed back by where they'd dumped you."

"What did he look like?" He may not be willing to take out his anger on Sasha, but the man who'd dropped him in an alley—ripe to be robbed or, worse yet, killed—had some answering to do. "Tall? Dark hair? Broad shoulders?"

Mrs. Bee straightened from where she stooped to stoke the fire and turned to face him. "Oh, that does sound like a handsome man."

Andrew immediately moved his hands to cover his manhood where it lay flaccid below the water—water that was now truly as frigid as he'd said it was. "I am not jesting in this matter!"

"And neither am I, your lordship." Mrs. Bee left the room without another word, slamming the door behind her. The solid sound and the force of the action caused the windowpanes to quiver in her wake.

It was best not to cross his housekeeper, yet he

couldn't help yelling after her, "Why did my servants not collect me?"

With effort, he dragged his sore and tired body from the water, ready for a few hours of rest.

Chapter Nineteen

Lorelei gently bounced the precious baby, swaddled in a thick wool blanket to ward off the evening chill. Her fears of childbirth, and subsequent care for a newborn, had proven unfounded as the days had passed since little Peter's birth. Between Mrs. Dutton and a local midwife, her baby had come into the chaotic world an unmitigated joy.

As she walked to and fro in the nursery, he made cooing sounds in his attempt to fight sleep. Which suited Lorelei just fine. These scarce moments of true peace were hard to come by and she feared nearing their end. It was time her responsibility to her country resumed priority in her life. She'd relished the week of recovery after Peter's birth when Mrs. Dutton had insisted, quite adamantly, that she remain abed and let her and the other household staff handle things. The thought of endless days and nights spent sequestered in her room with only little Peter for company would have caused her insanity only months before, but the time had passed with a speed to which she was unaccustomed.

While she'd lain about, nursing, caring for, and bonding with Peter, Lorelei had expected her husband's arrival—dreaded it, actually. Word had been sent immediately to Lord Chastain when she'd taken to her birthing bed and the midwife had been called.

Yet, he hadn't come.

Lorelei was happy to put off their reunion for a while longer.

The day would soon be upon them when she and Peter would journey to London for his christening at St. George's Church, when Lord Chastain would present his heir to society.

For now, she was content to have her dear boy all to herself. Lorelei blocked out the future, did not want to dwell upon what would come to be after she'd completed her assignment. The questions had circulated in her mind since she'd realized she was pregnant. Would she be allowed to stay in England? Would she be lucky enough to raise her child herself? Would the day come when she would have to give him up or—even worse—give him away?

No, she would not allow it.

She could not allow it.

She would rather give her child up to another—or perish—than allow him to come to any harm.

Chastain's suitability as a parent nagged at her still.

The man couldn't even be bothered to come meet his child and heir.

But she'd found solace and security in Mrs. Dutton's presence, knowing the woman cared for Peter as much as she did. If anything happened to Lorelei, Mrs. Dutton would be there to care for her child.

Finally, Peter stopped his fussing and relaxed in her

arms... Sleep was not far now.

Lorelei sat in a rocking chair Mrs. Dutton had found in the attic of the old manor. The lovely woman had had it cleaned and polished, ready for Peter's arrival. Now it stood before the hearth in her room, perfect for these quiet moments.

Gently, she rocked back and forth as Peter looked up at her. Her love for him grew daily, if not hourly. She wondered how her parents had allowed themselves to raise her in the dangerous life they lived. Lorelei could think of nothing but keeping her child safe and protected, even if that meant shutting the comte and comtesse out of their lives.

Peter put up his last great resistance before falling asleep, grabbing the paper sack that had been close at hand since Lorelei's arrival in the country.

Scribbled on the outside was only, '*Peppermint leaves—to be used for increasing females.*' She smiled every time she saw the bag, a part of her wishing the last year of her life could have been different, but she knew that leaving Andrew behind had been the wisest decision—even if it wasn't one she'd made by choice.

When Mrs. Dutton had presented her with the gift from the marquis, Lorelei was hesitant to even use the leaves, wanting to keep them, treasure them, but the nursemaid had gone on and on about their usefulness. Reluctantly, Lorelei had begun having her morning tea with the peppermint and, as surely as the woman had said, her sickness receded, to be replaced by a healthy glow and increased appetite.

Lorelei fought the urge every day to write to Andrew and thank him for his kindness, but she could not bring herself to involve him once more. She didn't deserve the thoughtfulness he'd shown her. With distance and time, she would forget about him, and her feelings would diminish just as surely as her sickness had. She would remember him as a kind soul…and always cherish the memory of their first—and only—dance, and the kiss that would never be forgotten.

Life, while neither easy nor fair, could be manageable if she didn't allow herself to dwell on what could have been.

She sighed. It was all lies, for she knew she would never be able to forget him.

"Ah, my lady." Mrs. Dutton's whisper startled her and she jostled Peter. Thankfully, he remained asleep, still clutching the bag. "He be such a good sleeper. Ye be very lucky."

"Yes, he is." Lorelei stood and moved toward the crib that had been moved next to her bed. It was difficult for her to be away from her boy for any amount of time. "Have you seen any child as peaceful as he?"

Mrs. Dutton leaned over the railing of the crib and ran her fingers down the newborn's cheek. "Not a one, m'lady. Me sister's brood be all criers, each and e'ery one of 'em."

"What can I help you with?" Lorelei asked. She'd sent the woman on her way an hour ago, her duties for the day complete.

"Ye have a visitor. I came ta tell ye, I can tell him ta go away, or take care o' the wee one until ye return."

Dread filled her. Had Chastain finally come to meet his son? But no, the lord of the manor would have come straight to her room without needing announcing.

Seeing her panic turn to confusion, Mrs. Dutton continued. "He didna give his name, but his accent be odd. Shall I bid him leave, maybe tell him ta return on the morrow?"

De Pez—she was sure of it. "No, I will see him. Please, show him to the drawing room."

"Ye be sure, m'lady?" she asked nervously.

"Of course," Lorelei soothed the woman's apprehension. "He is likely my father's friend." Yet, she was very unsure why he'd journeyed all this way when her parents resided in London.

Had they been harmed? Maybe that was why they had neither written nor visited. She tamped down her sense of trepidation over the unexpected arrival. They were on the same side, after all.

Mrs. Dutton hurried from the room, leaving the door open behind her.

Lorelei took one last look at Peter before slipping her arms into her heavy robe.

De Pez would not like being kept waiting, especially after journeying for days.

When she reached the drawing room, she found De Pez standing before the fire, soaking up the warmth after his long journey. From this angle, the Frenchman appeared almost harmless—just another gentleman, completely at ease. But she was not foolish enough to buy into that nonsense. De Pez was a cruel man, incapable of compassion and lacking decency on his good days. His tranquil posture was anything but what it appeared, as well. His well-tailored coat hid a body toned from years of athletic pursuits.

Her slippered feet made no sounds when she entered the room and moved toward the fire before the chill of the evening penetrated her dressing gown.

Though she was silent as a mouse, her movement

not even stirring a breeze, she knew the instant De Pez became aware of her presence. His relaxed stance disappeared and his shoulders stiffened. He assumed the posture of a warrior—ready to do battle.

That did not bode well for her.

"Another unexpected visit." Lorelei attempted to gain the upper hand. "I hope your travels delivered you safely here."

"Lady Chastain." He didn't turn from the fire when he spoke. "I heard of the arrival of your son and wanted to offer my congratulations—and those of our new leader—on the blissful event."

Happy event for whom, she wondered? "That is kind of you, but you could have sent a note." Besides which, as far as she knew, Chastain hadn't announced Peter's birth. Truly, most hadn't realized the current Duchess Chastain was carrying.

"Come now, you know my preferences, I am not much for quill and parchment, but prefer a more personal touch." He let his words sink in before continuing. "Much more impact in a hand-delivered message as opposed to black on white."

Again with his thinly veiled threats. "I am sure the comte and comtesse would have conveyed the import of your message without you troubling yourself with the tedious journey here."

Finally the man turned to face her, a snide smile covering his face. "Oh, but I wanted to greet our new Lord Chastain personally."

The man was getting ahead of himself, and that troubled Lorelei. "The current Lord Chastain is very much alive, and I fear my son is sleeping soundly in his crib at the moment."

"Mayhap next visit." De Pez took in her appearance from head to toe and then met her eyes in the dim light of the room. "You are looking exquisite as ever. Childbirth and motherhood certainly agree with you."

Lorelei sensed he was taking stock of her continued usefulness to the crown and not the changes she'd so recently experienced. "It is what we lowly women are destined for, am I not correct?" she asked.

"If you say it is so, then it must be true."

Lorelei inclined her head and gestured to the chairs set a few feet from the fire. "Would you care to sit? The tasks of motherhood are exhausting, and I find myself almost dead upon my feet at this hour of the night."

She hoped he'd turn down the offer in favor of giving his message and being on his way, but the man was full of surprises this evening. Too late, Lorelei realized she was alone in the room, Mrs. Dutton having stayed on the floor above and out of hearing distance.

"Thank you, Lady Chastain." He took the seat closest to him and also nearest the fire.

Under his scrutiny, Lorelei wondered about her own appearance. Dressed in a simple robe thrown over an old dress not even fit for a maid mopping the floors, she looked anything but the duchess she now was—or the spy she'd always been. She hadn't donned a proper gown since her arrival in the country, and certainly doubted her old ones would fit after Peter's birth.

"Please, tell me what you are here to say and be on your way." With her parents and husband not in residence, that allowed Lorelei to get to the point without fear of someone overhearing their conversation. Chastain hadn't sent a full staff to attend her and the baby; it was only Mrs. Dutton and a few servants to cook and clean for them. "I do not have all night, and I am sure you are in a hurry to find your way back to London proper."

"I have already taken residence at an inn not far away," he said. "You may glow with motherhood, but your manners are certainly lacking. I will get to the point of my *visit*."

"Please do."

"The comte and comtesse have been avoiding my calls to their townhouse."

"And what does that have to do with me?" She knew exactly what it had to do with her, but perhaps she could play ignorant long enough to get him out of her home—and far from her child. "I have not heard from them since my arrival here."

"Bonaparte has overthrown the Directory and made his stake as the new leader to France—but he awaits the plans, should something go amiss. Have you all forgotten your responsibilities?"

"Of course, not," she hissed. Besides Peter, there was not another thing she thought about. "I have searched this home high and low—twice now, and have found naught. The plans are not here."

He steepled his fingers before him. "Then why are you still here?"

Avoiding you, she wanted to scream, but instead, she kept her voice calm. "My son is too young to travel, but shortly we will have the approval of the midwife to journey back to London, where I will resume my search."

"Do you not have a nursemaid?"

"Of course."

"Then you can leave with me now." He stood, as if all were settled. "We can tell the duke that your kind *uncle* came to meet the newest lord and requested your company back to town. Your servant can follow with the child as soon as he is able."

"Peter."

"Pardon me?"

"Peter—his name is Peter." For some reason, De Pez referring to her son as 'the child' annoyed her greatly. Peter was not an asset to be used in any fashion he deemed. He was a baby—her baby. And she most certainly would not leave him behind, her responsibilities be damned.

"That is of little consequence or import to me. Now, please rest. I will return for you in the morning."

Lorelei squirmed under his intense glare. The nerve of the man. "My husband sent word that he will collect Peter and me within the week and return to London for the announcement of our child's birth." It was a lie she feared De Pez would see through. "I will await his arrival and journey with him."

"I would not want him to become suspicious of either of us." She knew she had him when he sighed. "Of course. Your beauty is not your only attribute to be admired."

"Then you must go." Lorelei stood to usher him to the door. "Before any of the other servants see you."

With great reluctance, he allowed Lorelei to show him to the door. Outside, his steed wandered unattended, munching on the hedges lining the drive. The man swung into his saddle with the ease of a man half his size and age. Even before his feet gained purchase in the stirrups, he set the animal into action and headed down the drive to the lane beyond—and out of Lorelei's life, for the time being.

Lorelei watched until his retreating form was out of

sight before leaping into action herself.

"Mrs. Dutton," she called to the empty foyer. "Mrs. Dutton!"

She ran toward the staircase, knowing the woman would be unable to hear her if she were by Peter's side. Taking the stairs two at a time and holding the front of her robe closed, Lorelei's footsteps echoed in the deserted halls.

The nursemaid appeared down the hall when she exited Lorelei's chambers.

"Heavens, m'lady." Mrs. Dutton stopped in front of Lorelei, her breath coming in a rush. "What be all the commotion about?"

Lorelei was as winded as Mrs. Dutton from her run up the stairs. "Ready Peter's things for departure."

The nursemaid stared as if her mistress had gone crazy. "Beg'n yur pardon?"

"Now," Lorelei said. "…and hurry. We must leave for London posthaste." Without waiting for a response, she returned downstairs to summon the carriage. They must reach Chastain's townhouse under cover of night or word would spread of their arrival. She needed to stay one step ahead of De Pez.

She only needed one last look around the townhouse before she made several important decisions for her and her child. The consequences for failing to complete her mission would be steep, and would likely include her life—and that of her child.

If she didn't locate the plans, then it would be necessary for them to go somewhere no one would find them.

Not De Pez.

Not even her parents.

Her hand faltered on the balustrade and she slipped down a few steps before regaining her balance.

If her search continued to yield no results, she'd be forced to explain everything to her husband. Tell him of her motives behind the marriage.

And beg for his mercy—and protection.

Chastain would seek to keep his son safe, even if he denied her his forgiveness. But she would cross that bridge when the time came.

It would take an hour to ready the carriage for the journey. She would do well to use the time wisely. With Peter's preparations in Mrs. Dutton's hands, Lorelei rushed to Chastain's study for one last search. The likelihood of her returning to his country manor was slim, so she pulled books from shelves, emptied drawers in search of a random key, and lifted pictures from where they hung. There were no hidden areas to be found, nor any key or papers pertaining to the whereabouts of the plans to Carcassonne. Just as every time she'd riffled previously. Either Chastain was a damn good hider or he was oblivious to his family's sordid past in France. Her gut told her it was the latter.

Why had her parents been avoiding De Pez? They knew she needed time—time to search, as well as time to heal. It made no sense. It was as if the comte was working against her. It was possible they'd decided to distance themselves in case she failed, in order to minimize the repercussions for themselves—though it was difficult, bordering on impossible—for Lorelei to believe her mother would allow the comte to behave in such a way.

She took one final cursory look around her husband's chambers, already knowing it would prove fruitless, before Mrs. Dutton summoned her.

In the hall, Mrs. Dutton cradled a sleeping Peter, still swaddled in thick wool, against her oversized bosom. "You said to call when all was ready."

"Thank you." Lorelei took Peter from the woman, surprised he'd slept so soundly through the hurried packing and then his nursemaid's shouting. "Let us be on our way."

The long carriage ride would give Lorelei time to speak with Mrs. Dutton, confide in the woman. For the first time that she could remember, Lorelei needed a friend. The stark reality that Lorelei quite possibly had no allies awaiting her arrival in London scared her beyond words. She'd never felt truly alone and without support, though the career her family had forced her into was a solitary profession at its core.

Lorelei would accept neither the loss of Peter nor her life, though as long as Peter was safe, her own life ranked lower on her list of priorities.

And she feared the only hope for her son's continued security and happiness lay in a woman she hadn't known long at all.

After they'd settled and Peter was nursing at her bosom, Lorelei started her story: one of faraway lands, late-night dealings, and ill-fated lives torn to shreds…and her plans for rectifying everything.

Chapter Twenty

The incessant banging had started nearly an hour ago. Relentless, continuous hammering on his townhouse door.

At first, Andrew wondered why no servant answered and sent whomever it was on their way. But then he remembered he'd given his entire staff the evening off so they would not witness his grief, which frequently turned violent as the night progressed.

Today, nearly five months after he'd seen her last, he'd read in the paper that Lady Chastain had welcomed a bouncing, healthy baby boy into the world only a week prior. The young had been christened Peter Davis, soon to be the next Lord Chastain. He read of the planned elaborate ceremony to be held at St. George's Church to introduce the child to members of the *ton*.

Chastain had his heir.

Since that time, Andrew had only succeeded in living in a perpetual state of drunkenness, unable to shake off the melancholy.

Mrs. Bee hadn't even tried to talk sense into him in

weeks, instead following behind him tidying up the havoc he wrought. She was a resourceful woman, and had most likely discovered the cause of his moods. This night, she'd gladly helped usher the servants from the house when he'd thundered through the main hall yelling for everyone to leave, immediately.

Now, he sat by a pathetic fire he'd tried to stoke himself—failing miserably—and listened to the beating upon the front door that echoed through his empty house.

"Fuck!" He slammed his tumbler on the table, amber liquid spilling over the side and onto his hand. "I am coming."

His boots pounded on the polished floor.

The knocking did not recede as he grew closer, yet the thundering in his head did. He awoke each morning still feeling the effects of his drink from the night before. He'd stopped leaving his townhouse after the first month, as he was no longer welcome at White's or Gentleman Jack's. He'd become a recluse—not even daring to attend social gatherings for fear of seeing Lorelei and breaking down…or worse, encountering Chastain and beating the man to his death.

Andrew took a deep breath before grasping the handle.

Pulling the heavy door open he faced a young girl, slightly familiar, yet he couldn't place her. Had she worked as a servant in his home? Surely not, or she would know never to knock on the lord's front door. Perhaps she was of gentle birth and they'd danced at a ball or shared a drink at a house party.

"May I help you?" The irony was apparent even to the girl when she flinched back and remained quiet.

"Well? I haven't all evening…"

He took in her look: comely face, neat red hair hidden under an ugly cap, and a full-length cape. In her hands she clutched a small valise, her knuckles white.

"I do not have all night."

"I am sorry for disturbing you, my lord." She paused, squaring her shoulders. "I am from Madame Sasha's."

"Yes…?" He hadn't visited Craven House since Sasha's henchmen had dumped him in that alleyway.

"She sent me to inform you of my condition." Her words were little more than a whisper.

"And how is your condition of any import to me?" He couldn't fathom the ploy Sasha was playing at. She was likely trying to regain his coin. "Say your piece and be on your way. What message has Sasha for me? She made it crystal clear I am unwelcome at Craven House."

The girl set down her satchel and began to unbutton her cloak.

It had been some time since he'd looked upon the naked form of a woman, and never on his front stoop. "If you plan to seduce me, you may want to come inside where it is far warmer."

Terror overtook the girl's face and her eyes widened in shock as she pushed aside the folds of her cape to reveal her rounded belly, the cause unmistakable. "No…"

"This cannot be." He was unsure if he'd said it aloud or only in his head.

"It can," she assured him. "At first I did not think it possible, either. During my time here, you were dangerously drunk and barely able to stand."

"When?"

"Over eight months ago now."

The dates matched. Those days he spent locked in his bedchamber, Sasha sending a flood of women to sate his need, dispel his sense of loss at the news of Lorelei's marriage to Chastain.

"I fear I will not live through this birth. Tell me you will take care of our child," she pleaded. "Madame Sasha has bid me not return until after the child is born."

"And what?" he asked. "You expect me—a fucking marquis—to welcome you into my home? Perhaps set you up in my adjoining suite all because you—a whore—claim to carry my child?"

"No, I—"

"Well, you have severely underestimated my compassion for other beings."

"I just thought—"

"No, you were obviously not thinking at all," he seethed, "when you came to my house, banged on my door, and expected to find sanctuary in my home."

"What do you expect me to do?" she asked. "Have your child on the streets? We will likely both perish in these conditions."

"Do you think you are the first to arrive on my doorstep professing your love, and claiming that you are carrying my child? You are not."

"I never said I love you," the girl said.

"Be that as it may, you will leave and never return." Just as another woman, Pearl, had all those years ago. "You will forget about me, and name your child for the bastard it will be."

"You are a heartless, cruel man," she cried.

"I have never presented myself as anything but." Except to Lorelei… For Lorelei, he would have given everything. He would have given her child his title and all

252

that came with it: a name, estates, and wealth beyond anything one could wish for. "Now be gone."

She hurriedly re-buttoned her cloak and took her valise in hand. "If I do not survive, I will send the child to you." She threw the words over her shoulder as she walked down the steps.

"No, you will not. I will cast it out with the trash if you do." He slammed the door to add threat to his words.

He needed a drink—a stiff, endless drink.

He set his forehead against the cool door as he heard the girl's soft cries outside. As they receded, he knew she'd taken her things and left.

Andrew longed to open the door and shout to her that he'd make a dreadful father; that he'd shirk his responsibilities over time—mostly that she, and her baby, deserved better than he could give them. Children should be raised in happy homes, and Andrew knew beyond a doubt that his home was not a happy one. Her child would be better off with one parent who loved it than a father prone to drinking and fits of rage.

Truly, it was he who didn't deserve the child, not the other way around.

Turning from the door, he spotted Mrs. Bee in the shadows. "What are you doing here?"

She stepped from her post into the pool of light from the candles burning above the foyer. "You know I haven't anywhere else to go. This is my home." She shrugged and let her arms fall to her sides. "Which is why I worry about you so."

"Worry about me?" Her words made no sense to him. He was a marquis, and arguably a very powerful man—if he chose to assert that power. He'd never wanted for anything in his life.

She smiled, the sweet upturned lips he remembered so fondly from his youth. "Yes. You were always such a sensitive boy, and after your parents—God rest their souls—left this world, I worried you'd fallen in with the wrong crowd."

"Benji?" he asked. "We have been friends since we were in knickers."

"I know that." She moved toward him, as if to make him understand. "You two have been getting into quite a bit of trouble since then, too. But now I see he was a distraction and perhaps a good one. I wish I knew what has had you so distraught as of late. And now this? A child, very possibly yours? I recognized the girl, if you must know." Bee laid her hand on his arm, where he had it crossed tightly across his chest. "She was one I threw out that day."

"That has no bearing on whether the child belongs to me," he said defensively.

"Can I confide something to you?"

"What? You once bore a child out of wedlock—maybe gave the child away and you regret it even to this day? I am not so easily guilted into taking responsibility, especially when the woman is a trollop."

Mrs. Bee shook her head, and Andrew felt an overwhelming need not to disappoint the woman before him. "I wish my dear, departed Eugene had lived long enough for us to have a child—"

"I am sorry for my outburst." And he was. She'd done nothing but care for him since he was young, continuing long into his adulthood, and now he repaid her with harsh words. "My remark was callous and uncalled for."

"Do not be sorry, not in the least. That was a

lifetime ago." She squeezed his arm in reassurance. "You see, what I have to say is not about me, but you."

Andrew wanted to walk away from the conversation; his gut told him what she would impart would change something—possibly his whole existence.

"Do not fret, for it was never that much of a secret, nor did it gain momentum as a scandal." She smiled, as if remembering a long ago time. "You mother became pregnant—with you—before she and your father had wed."

"But my mother did not gain employment selling her body."

"No, that is very true, she did not."

"And my father was clearly already in love with her."

"Possibly."

"There is no possibly about it!" His anger returned. How dare anyone—even Bee—call into question the love his parents shared? "I grew up on nothing but stories of their early relationship. How they'd known one another since before they left the schoolroom."

"Come sit down, Andrew." She walked into his study and sat before the fire. She kept her eyes off the disaster he'd created in the room, and he was thankful for that. "You see, your parents may have known each other—maybe even had a bit of tenderness for one another—but they were never intended to be together. It was up to them to take matters into their own hands."

"Why could they not be together?" He felt like a babe returned to the nursery, listening to fairytales of heroic knights and women of great beauty.

She sat back in her seat. "You see, your mother was a woman of great wealth, while your father's family—though being titled—had empty coffers. Your grandfather, after discovering his daughter was pregnant with the Marquis of Drake's child, agreed to the marriage on one condition."

Andrew tried to temper his interest in his parents' sordid tale, but failed miserably. "What?" He racked his brain, trying to remember any talk of conditions between his parents.

"Your grandfather would only allow them to wed if your mother controlled the coffers."

"No—that is simply not done, particularly in their time."

"But your father agreed to that condition...and more."

"Why?"

"For love...and self-preservation."

"That is preposterous."

"That it may be," she sighed. "But the marquis was faced with losing not only the woman he cared deeply for and his own flesh and blood, but he also faced a future that may have included debtor's prison. I think, in the end, the choice was an easy one."

He had to know. "To what else did he agree?"

"Ha, that is a funny thing." A satisfied smile crossed her face. "I am sure your solicitor can attest to this, but it is written that if no male heir presents itself, then a female may take over the marquis-ship. Thankfully, that never came to be, but your grandfather made certain it was set before King George III for approval and the heir or heiress clause was instated."

"I had no idea," he said, dumbfounded.

"There was no reason you should have," she chided. "Your mother was an only child, much like you. Since the clause never came to pass in their lifetime, I am sure they rarely thought of it. But now, you must be aware. If no surviving relation for the title exists, then a child—even one born out of wedlock—may petition the crown for inheritance."

"That is not all too uncommon, for men to seek a title with flimsy proof they are of noble birth." Andrew had never planned to have children. Now, he regretted his momentary lapse of judgment when he was delusional enough to think that Lorelei was the woman for him. She wasn't, and he would never make a good father, regardless. He was self-centered and highly disdainful of anything that even remotely appeared pleasurable to those around him.

Between him and Benji, they'd proven that fact over and over. If they wanted something, then they took it—regardless of the consequences. They'd done just that for years, with every debutante, married, or wanton woman they'd desired. When he at last realized his mistake and tried for something different—better—he failed. They'd done it for longer than he could recall, using a woman's feelings against them. Lorelei had accepted his words and then had thrown him by the wayside in favor of Benji.

It only proved that change was not always good, and one should never stray from who they were—and had always been. He was a man who used people when necessary to get exactly what he wanted, though he'd always been open and direct about it, never misleading anyone.

So, why hadn't he fought, lied, cheated, and stolen for the thing he most recently sought?

Mrs. Bee had been quiet, letting him digest the information she'd imparted.

Looking up, he realized she hadn't been silent, but

had departed her seat by the fire. The room around him was empty, save for him, reinforcing what he'd always believed: he could only rely on himself.

Chapter Twenty-One

"…and this is all the paperwork you have that was approved and signed by the King?"

"Certainly, your lordship," Andrew's solicitor, James Adams, said from behind his modest desk. "I assure you that all is in order. I was under the impression your father had spoken to you of this matter."

The man smiled proudly, as if this were the news Andrew had wanted to hear, when that could not be further from the truth. He'd met with the man routinely, and Adams had never seen fit to inform him of this.

"Never," Andrew mumbled.

"My uncle was very thorough and diligent in everything he did," Adams explained. When Andrew sat, Adams followed suit. "You see, this type of arrangement has not been successfully accomplished during my lifetime, and only once during my uncle's."

The scheme was preposterous and completely outlandish…and he could not believe his father and maternal grandfather had worked with a solicitor to see the deed done. The thought of a bastard being about to inherit the title of marquis—and the possibility that it extended to females, as well—had his head spinning, and not because he was still recovering from his latest bout of drinking.

"May I explain any of the documents to you?" Adams asked.

"No, thank you." Andrew tried to sound courteous, but was finding it difficult to appear calm while he was boiling inside.

He flipped page after page as the man stayed silent. Seeing his father's signature and seal at the bottom of each page brought him pride, while simultaneously heightening his unease.

"Am I correct in saying," he said, "if a child is proven to be mine, even though no marriage has taken place, the offspring could petition the courts to inherit the title of marquis?"

"That is exactly what your father wanted." James closed the file before him. "And the process is much simpler if you agree to consider the person your heir."

If word of this spread through London, Andrew would have numerous women coming forward claiming their bastards were of Drake blood.

"And this extends to female offspring?"

"Your father—and grandfather—wanted to cover any and all contingencies."

"Then why not only make a portion of funds available to illegitimate offspring?" He was thinking out loud, but hoped the man could offer any insight. "Rather than the title and all that it encompasses?"

"Your father, God rest his soul, was a man in love—and headstrong to the extreme. I heard many stories, though he passed before I finished my education."

Adams clasped his hands on the desk in front of him and leaned slightly forward. "Yes, I do agree the changes to his estate are out of the norm—radically so—but yes, if you had been a female, you would had been able to inherit even if your parents hadn't wed. A definite coup, I would say."

More like a travesty that could ultimately jeopardize his whole future.

If the woman who'd come to him last night pressed this issue and sought legal counsel in the matter, then not much digging would be required to find these amendments. Though the likelihood of a mere strumpet seeking financial gain from an illegitimate child was rare, he did not want to take the chance of this news spreading.

"But if I contest the bid for legitimacy then I will be heard by the courts?"

The solicitor's forehead furrowed in question. "You? You seek to contest your own right to the title?"

Andrew realized the man hadn't the faintest idea he was actually worried about another claiming to be *his* child—or a money-hungry mother stepping forward. He had the sudden urge to thank Mrs. Bee for her forthright confession, seeing as how she should have told him years ago... Or his own father could have warned him.

"Oh, no. I ask for myself and my offspring," he said, trying to put the man at ease.

"Very well, your lordship." The solicitor stood. "I have another appointment shortly. If you will please take those papers with you, review them, and we can schedule another meeting if you have anything else to discuss. Again, I am deeply sorry you were not notified of this upon your inheritance of the title."

The man bowed over his desk.

Suddenly, Andrew felt the weight of his station—the Marquis of Drake. The room closed in around him.

He needed air.

Space to breathe.

And...Andrew hadn't any idea what he should do next.

For the first time in months, he wished he could call on Chastain and talk through his issues. The man could always be counted upon to suggest a good plan—or at least offer a distraction.

Andrew made his way outside and looked up and down the busy street.

Within seconds, his driver was at the curb, ready to deliver him wherever he demanded.

But he wasn't in the mood to be ushered about town, dropped at his club or townhouse.

"My lord?" his servant asked when he didn't immediately move toward the waiting coach.

"I will walk," he called over his shoulder as he started down the street toward the busier shopping district. "Wait for me here. I shall return." The weather was calm, with nary a cloud in the sky. A brisk walk would do him good.

Before long, he was whistling an unknown tune, and already several blocks from his solicitor's office. It had been months since he'd entertained himself by venturing out during daylight hours. Free of the headaches caused by over-imbibing, he welcomed the sunlight against his skin and listened to bits of conversation that floated his way from passersby.

Andrew nodded to those who acknowledged him, but kept his pace steady to avoid idle chitchat. He'd sought companionship during his last stroll in the park, but today was different. Yes, he was in a pleasant enough mood despite the conversation with his solicitor, but he was a long way from finding pleasure in idle conversation outside a lady's dress shop.

The sun started its long descent, and the crowds thinned on the street as many sought their midday meal. When his stomach lurched at the thought of food, he decided to head back in the direction of his coach.

He paused to gauge how far he'd actually wandered. He recognized a small bookseller a few doors down, bordered by a narrow alley and a strip of park on the other side. If he'd anticipated his desire for a walk, he could have requested his servant prepare a lunch for him to enjoy in the park.

It was then that he heard her voice—a voice he dreamed of every night and listened for all hours of the day.

# # #

"…that cannot be!" Lorelei yelled, not caring who heard. "You cannot and will not do this."

Her father had resorted to following her—tracking her like she was prey.

With her arm twisted behind her back, and her father's face so close to her own, she couldn't escape. "Unhand me."

"I will release you when you give me answers."

"I have told you all I know."

"We both know that is a lie, Lore." The conviction in his eyes frightened her. It was almost as if he'd lost complete control of himself.

She'd failed, time and time again. "I have searched

his estate, his townhouse, and even his stables—to no avail. What will you have me do next?" She winced as he tightened his grip on her arm.

"It is time I take this over." He released her arm and shoved her away from him. "You lack the fortitude to do what needs to be done."

"How have I not done everything in my power to find those plans?" Her father was acting erratic, unpredictable, which was in complete contrast to his usual ways.

"My plans are no longer your concern," he said as he paced the narrow alley. "Return to Chastain's townhouse and pack your things. We will leave by nightfall."

"I cannot just leave." Lorelei searched for any excuse to change her father's plan. "I cannot make off in the night with Peter. Lord Chastain will not let him go."

"Then leave him," the comte said with a shrug. "You will have the opportunity for another child."

The words threatened to rip her heart from her chest. They were words that a grandfather should never speak about their grandchild.

"That is not an option for me."

"Have you forsaken your own family?" he accused. "If so, then stay—play the lovely duchess, but know that nothing in your life will be easy from this moment on."

"You cannot mean that, *Pere*," she pled, stepping toward him. She reached out for his sleeve and looked into his eyes. He couldn't mean the hurtful things he said.

"I will do what is required of me," he shouted back. "As will you, or suffer the consequences." Sidestepping her hands, he reentered the bookstore he'd followed her from and was gone.

She didn't know what to do, where to go. Nowhere was safe, though she knew as long as Mrs. Dutton had Peter he would be fine. But Mrs. Dutton couldn't protect her, too. Nor was it right to ask that of the woman.

Rounding the corner, she ran directly into someone—or something.

Arms flew out to steady her.

"Pardon—" Her words cut off abruptly when her eyes met his. "Andrew?"

Quickly, she swiped the tears from her face and straightened her shoulders.

"Lorelei." He held her at arm's length, taking in the sight of her.

She must look a mess, her face pale and thinner than it had ever been.

She cleared the emotions lodged in her throat before speaking. "Andrew, what are you doing here?"

"With whom were you speaking?"

He looked over her shoulder as she turned, but her father was gone, the alley deserted.

"I wasn't speaking with anyone," she denied, hoping he hadn't heard more of her argument with the comte. "I was…I was just…leaving my dressmaker's shop."

"You have a habit of returning to town without sending word." The sudden change of topic took her by surprise.

"I have only recently returned, your lordship." With one last glance behind her, she put her arm through his and turned toward the busier part of town. "Though, I must confess I wanted to send word to you," she said, distracting him from his inquiries.

The smile she turned his way worked, though inside she wasn't smiling at all. If she could just keep her lips turned in a smile, then perhaps the crumbling she felt within would stop.

"I am wounded your modiste had occasion to see you before I."

"Well, it would be the height of impropriety for me to call on a marquis when not suitably attired," she responded. She kept her eyes on the street and her voice light. "But I am certain Lord Chastain and I would much delight in having you to supper soon." Though would it only be Peter and Chastain in residence?

Before long, the trite back and forth between them—as if they were nothing more than acquaintances meeting for the second time—stopped.

They walked in silence.

She was unwilling to disturb the precarious balance they'd established.

Perhaps she feared that if their conversation strayed from the mundane, it would approach a deeper level than she was prepared to explore.

He leaned close and whispered, "Come with me. My coach is not far."

"I mustn't." The words came on a breathy sigh. "Please, Andrew, just go."

She longed to accept his offer, to climb into his coach and drive off, even if it were only for an afternoon. That may be all the time left to her before she'd need to make the biggest decision of her life.

She could flee with her parents, leaving Peter in Mrs. Dutton's care, or go against her father's wishes and face the wrath of De Pez and the French government. She knew for certain she could not risk taking Peter with her, because it would only jeopardize his life.

That left one option: she and Peter must disappear

together. Leave London, Chastain, the marquis, her parents, and her country behind.

Andrew grasped her arm when she pulled away, his fingers biting into the skin above her wrist. His grip tightened for a brief second then he released her.

"Please."

No one would have heard the pain in his simple, heartfelt plea. Nor would they know the depth to which that plea resonated through her… At least, she hoped they would not.

They walked side by side in silence once more, not touching. She felt his pent-up response beside her.

He must feel her presence as strongly as she did his.

She wanted to give in—give in to everything he wanted from her.

Their connection was something she'd long tried to deny, or at least tamp down to a manageable ache. She'd thought of him, but it was too much to hope that he'd done the same. She was his best friend's wife. That she'd met him first mattered naught.

And so they walked, with no destination in mind.

For the first time since she'd returned to London, Lorelei was unconcerned who saw her. A dozen French government officials could be trailing her now and she didn't care. They could all go on about their business and leave her alone.

She was an English duchess…and, therefore, untouchable.

Though she knew well what had happened to the last Lord Chastain.

He was no more.

For now, she had this time, these few hours before she must make the decision that would change so many lives—though in truth, she wondered if the decision had already been made.

She would consider the thought once more when she and Peter were safely out of harm's way. If that ever occurred.

For the moment, she was protected when she walked side by side with Andrew. Not because he was a marquis…or influential…or wealthy, but because he would allow nothing to happen to her.

"May I call on you?" he asked, breaking the silence.

"You know that would be improper."

"I want to give my good tidings on the birth of your son."

"Chastain's son?" she asked.

"Your son, Lorelei."

"You will have ample time for that when he is presented to society." He didn't need to know that that day would not likely come, and if it did, Lorelei would not be present.

"Do you need anything?"

"You sent the peppermint leaves." She looked out the side of her eye to gauge his reaction. "That was very kind of you."

"You left town so quickly I hadn't the time to wish you farewell." The sadness in his words took root in her.

"I wish I hadn't had cause to leave so suddenly, either." She wanted to give him peace, but feared she would only lead him to believe there was something— could ever be something—more between them. "But we both know that even if I'd stayed in London there would be needless gossip if you continued to show favor to me."

"So instead you fled?"

Lorelei didn't want to answer the question. It would

be easy to blame her exile to the country on Chastain, make him appear the cruel and heartless man he actually was, but that was untrue.

She'd chosen to leave.

She'd needed to go.

If not to gain distance from a future she'd been hard-pressed to deny herself, then to have space to clear her mind, search for the plans...and try desperately to forget the man she could never have.

And where had that gotten her?

Ordered to a seamstress to have proper evening attire fitted, that's where. She'd expected her clothes to be tight, yet she'd found they hung off her frame. Presently, her coat was the only thing covering the dreadful mess that was her walking gown.

Andrew stopped mid-step. "Lorelei, answer me."

"What do you want me to say?"

"Anything." His eyes searched hers.

"I am sorry!"

"Not that," he yelled, taking her shoulders in his hands. "Never that."

"I am sorry," she continued. People watched their exchange, but she was helpless to stop the flow of her words. "I am sorry I ever locked eyes with you in that ballroom. I am sorry I allowed you to lead me onto the dance floor. But most of all, I am sorry I married your best friend."

"Why?" he asked, as if he hoped it was because she loved him instead.

"Because we are now forever entwined." She watched the light dissipate from his eyes with her every word. She would not give him the faith she lacked. "You are now cursed to see me with another for as long as your friendship lasts with Chastain."

Her words were cruel and meant to cut him to the quick.

"And I," she said, prepared to drive her point home, "now must live with my own mistakes and the life I created. I truly wish it were just mourning a love I pushed away. But know this—you shall forget me as I will forget you, in time."

Too late, Lorelei realized that Andrew hadn't been walking aimlessly as she had. He'd been herding her, in a way, exactly where he wanted her.

His carriage stood beside them, his manservant holding the door wide.

"I must get home to Peter." Though she said the words, she wanted the complete opposite. This might well be her final chance to be with Andrew, to know the touch of his skin against her own, to feel his lips upon her body. She craved the kind of passion she'd never known with another.

"Tell me it is not what you want, and I will walk away now," he said into her ear. "I will walk away and leave you with use of my coach to be taken wherever you desire."

She flinched when he said the word desire, her body stiffening next to him.

They both certainly craved the same thing.

"I must go…"

"And you will. It is only a few moments of privacy that I am asking for." She didn't need that much urging to continue toward his carriage. "I believe you owe me this small favor…" He let his voice trail off.

Her sense of right would push her the last remaining steps.

"If Benji finds us together—"

"He will not."

"One time about the block and you will drop me off here?" she asked.

"You have my word."

Lorelei took his coachman's offered hand and stepped up into his coach.

"Where to, your lordship?"

Chapter Twenty-Two

He couldn't keep his hands off her for long. He wanted all of her with all haste—now and forever. But he'd agreed to a simple carriage ride around the block, ten minutes at best. He took in the sight of her, sitting ever so prim and proper on the opposite seat facing him. He wanted to be next to her, to feel the heat of her desire for him, and she would feel his, as well.

It was like no time had passed—she hadn't run off with Chastain. She hadn't lied to him, though he should be angry with her. Yet, he could muster no emotion but need.

Moving next to her was also an impossibility at the moment, for he would never be done drinking in the sight of her. It puzzled Andrew that never did she look anything but perfect—to him, for him, and with him.

"Well," she whispered. "Are you going to say anything?"

"Words could never be enough or express everything I have to say."

She pulled her lower lip between her teeth before

speaking. "Will you at least try? We have but a few moments."

Andrew was at a loss for words. There were so many questions, but he feared every answer he'd receive. Could he handle it if she genuinely loved Chastain? Would he be capable of keeping his distance if she asked? If all hope were lost, would he be able to cope with a life without any chance of possessing her?

For the first time in his existence, Andrew was terrified of his future and what it held.

He'd inherited his vast estate and title at the tender age of seventeen... He'd basked in the glory of wealth beyond most people's wildest dreams. Never once had he worried over the immense responsibility of managing his properties or his duties to Parliament.

Not ten years ago, he'd come face-to-face with one of his most horrible deeds, and not once had he been frightened of the consequences of his incorrigible actions. The woman—and his child—could still be seen here and there about London...the child claimed by another.

But losing this woman—a woman who was never his to begin with—petrified him.

And yet, he sat there in silence. No words could make her understand his need for her. He'd once thought it only a physical need, but now he knew he wouldn't be happy or complete without all of her. Her body, her thoughts, her very being belonging only to him.

"I—"

"Andrew," she said at the same time. "I think I owe you an explanation before you speak."

"You owe me nothing," he breathed. He was off his seat and kneeling before her. Her knees spread, and he moved between them to get closer to her. "I want to give you everything, but I understand if you truly have an affection for Chastain."

He'd said it, the one thing that frightened him most. If it was a marriage of convenience, he could live with that, but once a woman's heart belonged to another there was no changing that, even if the man were undeserving of her heart and did not return her feelings.

She set her hands on his shoulders and he looked to her face, waiting for the response that would crush him at his core.

"You do not understand, and I fear that is my fault."

"Understand what?" he said, more harshly than he'd intended. "You married my best friend…knowing *my* affection for you. Knowing I intended to make you my Marchioness."

"Andrew," she started, but then stopped, as if she couldn't bring herself to tell him she was in love with Chastain and there was no hope for them.

"Just tell me, Lorelei."

"I have told no one."

"But you can tell me," he pleaded. "I will be here regardless of what you say."

"You will look at me differently."

"Never…"

"He accosted me…threw me to the ground…ripped my dress."

Andrew pulled back from her in disbelief, but he knew his mistake the second he saw the hurt on her face, her arms crossed over her chest, closing herself off from him.

"That cannot be…" Andrew tried to make sense of her words. "Chastain may be without genuine care for others and selfish to the core, but to harm a woman?"

She lowered her gaze, breaking their eye contact.

If she were to trust him, he needed to bring that barrier down.

"I did not mean to say he did not take advantage of you," he said, returning to kneel before her. "When did he do this? Your wedding night? If he hurt you—"

"No," she whispered. "It was long before our wedding."

"Before?" He wracked his brain, trying to think of a time they'd been together. Things had happened so quickly he could not pinpoint Chastain's opportunity. "When he took you from the ballroom that first night? The son of a bit—"

"Not then, but a few days later."

The next day, Chastain had been on his way to Madame Sasha's country party. Andrew remembered that morning as clear as day: he'd returned from delivering Lorelei's flowers and Chastain had been waiting for him to depart for the country, yet Andrew had called off in favor of pursuing Lorelei. But had Chastain not continued on to the party?

They had barely spoken since, for the distance Andrew put between them was also encouraged by Chastain. No more had they dined together or attended the theater.

"It was my fault," Lorelei whispered. "I sent him an invitation to meet me at Covent Gardens."

"An invite to a play does not constitute an invite to your body, Lorelei." He tried lessening her guilt. If the blame lay anywhere, it was on his shoulders. If he'd gotten into his carriage and left London that morning with Chastain as planned, his old friend likely wouldn't have been in town to receive her invitation. He reached up and took her chin in hand, bringing her eyes back to his. "You are not to blame for his crude behavior. You understand that, do you not?"

"But I called him to meet me there, unchaperoned." A single tear burned a trail down her cheek. "What else was he to think?"

Andrew leaned forward to kiss a trail down her face from where the drop had escaped her eye to her chin still in his grasp. She was utterly breathtaking, even in her sorrow.

"Never think you caused it," he said.

In his mind, he played back the events from that time, remembering the night Chastain returned from the country and sent word to meet him at White's. Benji had been drunk, so deep in his cups—and his shirt had been stained with dirt. Could his friend have done this and then met him for dinner?

She searched his face, as if judging the validity of his words. He waited for her to speak, still fearing what would come next.

"Can you show me what it feels like to be with someone you love?"

He sat there breathless, unsure how to respond...what she expected of him. And most of all, whether he deserved the chance to show his love for her at all.

"I have wanted that since the moment I laid eyes on you." She stayed silent, and he sensed she could not admit she'd wanted the same...with him. "You needn't say or do a thing. I can show you love."

He leaned forward and took her mouth then, his lips pressed to hers; seeking her, claiming her—but most of all, showing her.

#

The room around her was everything, yet nothing she expected. Masculine to the extreme with its heavy, immense furniture, high-backed chairs crafted to handle the size and weight of a man, and dark-blue draperies and bedclothes. It appeared the room had been cleaned recently, or else no one had used the area as of late, for not an item was out of place. The heavy chairs sat in the best position to gain the most warmth from the hearth. Another fireplace was situated on the far side of the room, closest to the bed.

She craved nothing more than to be in that bed, sheltered from the outside world, and safe from those who threatened her and her son. But mostly, to be wrapped in his arms. How many nights had she dreamed of just that?

Lorelei knew she shouldn't be here. She belonged with her son, making plans for their future. A future far from London, De Pez, Chastain—and unfortunately, outside Andrew's reach. But she found that possibility difficult to accept.

"May I take your coat?" he whispered in her ear.

The material slid from her arms when she shrugged. She didn't hear it hit the floor, and assumed Andrew must have caught it. In that moment, she didn't worry about her ill-fitting gown, for Andrew would never judge her or send a harmful word her way.

Trust was something she'd rarely given another.

But Lorelei trusted him. Believed that if things had been different, Andrew would have been a marvelous husband and doting father.

Unfortunately, things were not different.

They had this one afternoon, and if all went according to her plan, she and Peter would disappear, never to be seen again.

She would allow herself this one afternoon, a brief few hours of pleasure and happiness, for after she left him, Lorelei had the hardest decision of her life to make. Though that decision was already solidified in her mind, the execution of it was something with which she hoped she could follow through. From this point on, she would forever be looking over her shoulder, trusting no one, and always questioning their intentions.

For now, then, she would not question anything—not Andrew nor his intentions.

Lorelei would take all he had to offer her, though she knew she would be unable to give anything in return.

"Are you cold?" he asked.

"No." A chill ran through her, not because the room lacked warmth, but from her own anticipation. She'd lived this very moment a thousand times over in her mind. The room was different, but this man was the same.

"Then why do you shudder?" His fingers traced a slow path up and down her bare arms.

"Because I want you," she breathed.

She was startled by the depth of her own emotions. After Chastain's misuse, she'd never thought to truly want another man in this most primal sense. Though she found she wanted more than just his body, but also his mind, his passion.

He moved to the buttons lining the back of her dress and deftly began to unclasp them. The fire before her warmed her front while the opening of her dress allowed air to cool her heated skin.

She stared into the fire as her dress slid from her body. There was no turning back now.

Which met her needs, for she didn't want him—or this—to stop.

"Please," she pleaded.

"Tell me all you desire, my Lorelei." He kissed the tender spot behind her ear as his hands continued to move across her back, lightly trailing the delicate fabric of her shift. "I am yours to command."

Lorelei took orders. She executed well-thought-out plans created by others... Never had she taken the lead to get exactly what she wanted, though it seemed that time was upon her. If she could take control now with this man, then she most assuredly could handle whatever her future held.

"I want to see you...touch you." That was all she wanted for the time being, and more than she could ever hope for.

She turned in his arms, covered only in her shift, stockings and shoes, yet she did not feel at a disadvantage while he stood before her fully clothed.

Lorelei felt a measure of power.

"I should like to remove your cravat." She didn't wait to finish the words before lifting her hands to the task. Gently, she took one corner in her fingers and tugged, but the intricate knot did not give. She stared at it, knowing her forehead bunched pensively.

She'd never undressed a man, and did not foresee a simple cravat to be her undoing.

With more force, she pulled at the cloth, and it at last came loose. She threaded the silk between her fingers, enjoying the smooth caress of the material, much like the way her favorite emerald gown hugged her form—or *had* hugged her form before she'd had to throw the exquisite dress away to hide the dirt stains and torn pieces from her ladies maid.

Andrew lifted her chin, searching her eyes. "Why do you stop?"

With a faint smile, she pushed all thought of that night in the gardens from her mind, and once again began to pull the cloth from around his collar. Next, she let it drop to the floor between them and moved to his buttons.

"I find this shirt not to my liking." She made the mistake of looking up at him then, and her fingers stilled. She didn't know what raw, unabashed desired looked like, but she was positive that was exactly what she saw in Andrew's eyes. Her fingers fumbled back into action. "I much prefer the touch of skin."

"I find I do, as well." Andrew bent slightly and pulled her shift up and over her head, leaving her completely exposed to him, with only her stockings for cover. "Now, if you will finish your task, our skin shall finally meet."

Lorelei brought her hands back down to his buttons, making fast work removing the garment. The fine material pooled at their feet, joining his neck cloth and her shift.

When her hands came to rest on his solidly muscular chest, she wondered at the warmth she found there. She'd pictured a man's rock-hard chest to feel cold to the touch, ungiving with no compromise. Yet, she'd been gravely mistaken for over his muscles his skin was smooth and pleasing to her touch.

She only wished she had hours—no, days—to explore his body. She felt certain a lifetime would not be enough.

Alas, she only had this time, this moment, to last for eternity.

Trailing her hands down his chest and over his flat stomach, she reached for the clasp on his belt. Her hands shook as she pulled it loose and dropped it to the floor, adding to the mixed pile of their clothing.

"Let me look at you," Andrew mumbled, pushing her to arm's length. His sharp intake of breath told her the fire behind her highlighted her tall frame. "You are heaven sent, my Lorelei."

She glanced down at herself. The dim light accentuated her curves and didn't touch the hollows of her body. She feared her body had been marred by her recent pregnancy.

"Come here, I will show you how divine you look." He spun her away from him and they stepped across the room to a door not far from the fireplace. Andrew reached over her shoulder and pulled the door open, revealing a mirror hung on the inside of the wood, his dressing closet well organized behind it. "Look…"

And she did.

The fire, now at their side, made her hair look ablaze where it framed her face in loose waves down her back. Her slender neck held all the poise and grace of a true lady. And her breasts, still tender, stood high and ample with her darkened nipples hardened in the heat from the fire. Her stomach, while no longer tight and flush with her hips, held a suppleness that was still pleasing to her eyes. Her rounded hips flowed into her legs just as they should with her thighs pressed close. Her stockings covered the shapeliness of her calves and ended in her kid boots.

Her gaze moved back up her body to her face where her expression was one of amazement, her mouth shaped in a round 'o' that accentuated her high cheek bones.

"As I said—beautiful." He swept her hair from her shoulder and trailed kisses over the spot and down her arm.

She was mesmerized by the sight of him worshiping her body. His hands moved down to hold her hips securely against him while his mouth continued to explore, coming to slightly kiss and nip the side of her breast. As if he didn't trust his mouth to do the job properly, one hand left her hip and came to settle under her other breast, kneading slightly.

The sight was erotic in a way she'd never expected. Watching one's own seduction in a looking glass.

His hand and mouth released her breasts as he knelt behind her.

Andrew held her steady—facing the mirror—when she made to turn in his direction.

Kissing his way down her back, his hands next came to massage her rounded derriere, moving her fleshy posterior with the incessant pressure of his attentive hands.

With him out of sight, Lorelei could only bring her eyes back to her face in the mirror as she moaned. Her eyes—always a deep green—seemed conflicted, as if adrift in a storm. The last time she'd truly taken measure of herself, she'd seemed hollow, her eyes almost lifeless, but now they sizzled with restrained passion.

She gasped when he started to push her stocking lower on her thigh, his lips following the path of her sheer undergarment.

Her legs buckled when he ran his tongue along the back of her knee, the spot almost as sensitive as the place behind her ear.

"Just wait," he muttered as he started on the other stocking.

She'd never dreamed that the touch of a man's mouth—or his fingers—upon her leg could elicit such yearning.

Andrew gently tapped her inner thigh and, as if she knew what came next, she spread her legs slightly and his hand came to rest between them, cupping her core as he placed kiss after kiss upon her hip from his kneeling position behind her.

A sudden warmth between her thighs had her squeezing them together, trapping his hand where it rested.

"Open for me, my sweet Lorelei," he coaxed her. "Do not be afraid."

"I am not afraid." And she wasn't. If she were unsure about anything, it was how she could ever walk away from this—and him. "Please, do not stop."

The words came out on a moan when he stopped his delicate kisses.

She parted her legs once more in hopes his fingers would explore the tender area.

To her displeasure, she watched in the mirror as he dropped his hand.

For the first time since she'd stepped into his coach—was it only an hour ago or days?—she felt alone.

Andrew slid across the polished floor to kneel in front of her, instead of behind. In the looking glass, she saw his head of hair, his broad shoulders, and tightly corded back that disappeared into his pants below.

Instinctively, Lorelei brought her hands to his hair and ran her fingers through the silky length, as he leaned forward slightly and continued the course his mouth had started on her back. His lips burned a path from under her breasts, down her stomach. His tongue flicked her navel and then moved lower.

She itched to grasp his face and bring his lips to her own. Yet, her body sensed there was much more pleasure to come before that happened.

"Andrew," she again pleaded.

He paused long enough to say, "Tell me what you want."

"I do not know what I want, but I need..." Lorelei's voice trailed off when the right words escaped her. "I know that I want more."

He chuckled, though she knew it was not at her inability to find the words or to tease her.

"I will show you what you need." Sitting back, he took her booted feet in his hands one by one and removed her shoes, then pulled her bunched stocking off, as well. He tossed both stockings and shoes over his shoulder.

Chapter Twenty-Three

Andrew looked up at Lorelei, her innocence in passion and matters of the flesh belying her very nature. Was it possible that Chastain, the educated seducer, hadn't applied his many talents to his own wife?

"Yes, show me." Lorelei closed her eyes, her head tilting back.

She was truly exquisite, every curve of her body from the delicate slope of her clavicle to the arch of her back. She was made for passion.

Made for *him*.

Andrew returned his attention to her stomach, trailing kisses ever lower until he reached the nest of curls that hid her most sensitive place. With steady fingers, he reached forward to find her core, slick with need. When he touched her, she pushed her hips toward him.

"You know exactly what you want," he purred. He would have her writhing before he gave her what she wanted. He'd had to move quickly when she'd started to remove his pants, for he knew his will would have given itself to her if the barrier of his clothes hadn't been there.

"I swear, I do not." Her hips pushed into his cupped hand.

"Then your body betrays you." Her body moved a fraction of an inch away from him. "No, never move away from me."

Finally he stood, towering over her though she stood a head above most women.

"Andrew?" She looked to him, puzzled. "I did not mean to offend—"

"You did not." He took her hand and walked toward his bed, his boots sounding loud in the quiet room. "But I tire of the hard floor and I am sure you are cold."

From the flush of her skin, the last thing she felt at the moment was cold.

Lorelei remained silent.

Though she didn't hesitate, a flicker of fear crossed her face when he stopped her before his bed.

"If you do not want this, I can take you home." Even though the words came from him, Andrew was far beyond stopping. He would have Lorelei—this very afternoon, and every day that followed.

Thankfully, she shook her head. Pushing to her tiptoes she laid her lips against his; her mouth molded to his perfectly. Andrew parted his, his tongue running across her lower lip. Instinctively, she let him in, deepening the kiss.

It was far more than any kiss they'd shared. Her lips were asking for a promise, and his gave the answer she sought.

He could no longer keep his hands from her.

Andrew grasped her waist and lifted her, her bare feet a few inches off the floor, and set her on the bed.

Taking a step back, Andrew undid the clasp that

held his pants. When the flap opened, his member jutted forth. Andrew bent hastily, unlaced his Hessians and pulled them off. Finally, he stepped out of his pants.

He never took his eyes from her as he worked. It wasn't that he expected her to have a change of heart, but that he'd been forced to be without her for so long he feared she might disappear right before his eyes—and that she would never come back to him.

It might be the desperation in her gaze or the way she reached for him every time he took a step away.

He stood before her, naked and vulnerable to her stare, much as she'd stood before him only moments before.

But unlike him, she kept her eyes focused on his, never straying to take in the sight of his body.

It took everything in him not to give in to her unspoken plea and go to her, show her great pleasure and…love.

The force of the word—only a thought—had him staggering back a step.

It couldn't be, it was only his obsession getting the best of him once more. She was married to his best friend, had forsaken him for Chastain all those months ago. He hadn't any claim to her then, and now her heart was still not his for the taking.

Could he change that?

He took in the sight of her, naked before him and spread across his bed, waiting…

Andrew would show her how she should be treated…that she should have chosen him—that there was still time for her to be with him.

"My Lorelei," he whispered, approaching the bed once more. "I have waited too long for this moment."

Finally, she looked at his body, her eyes lingering below his waist before snapping to meet his face, embarrassment clouding her expression.

"Do not be ashamed to look." He set his hands on the bed on either side of her and leaned in close, "—or touch."

And how he longed for her delicate hands to touch him—run down his chest and sink even lower. Or pull at his hair while her head was thrown back in ecstasy.

Andrew lowered himself onto her, supporting his weight on his elbows, and kissed her. His lips pressed into hers, and within seconds, they melded and moved in unison, his tongue darting to explore her mouth. The very taste of her was almost his undoing. Not to be outdone, Lorelei also sought to explore, not only with her mouth but also her hands, which now grasped his shoulders in a grip he thought was beyond her strength.

When he released her mouth and moved to her earlobe, nipping and then gently suckling, her back arched off the bed. He reluctantly let go of her earlobe and focused his ministrations on her slender neck, directly under her chin.

"Andrew," she sighed. "I need you."

"You have me."

"No. Inside me—I need you there, now."

Her words were his command. Lifting from her slightly, he looked into her eyes as he situated himself between her legs, his manhood rested against her opening. His skin was now aflame, though he was unsure if it was the heat coming from her center and traveling through him or if he was the source. Either way, he would soon be alight if he weren't inside her.

"Open for me." He pushed into her when her legs

parted farther. It took all his restraint to hold steady as his size stretched her. He looked between them as he entered her, memorizing this moment. "Are you well?" he asked.

She hadn't moved beneath him, and he worried he'd hurt her.

"Yes," she whispered. "I am more than well."

Andrew took his eyes from their joined bodies to take in her smile. At her reassurance, he thrust the remaining few inches and embedded himself to the hilt. He stilled and waited for her to respond and set their pace.

When she rocked her hips, taking him deeper than he ever imagined possible, he almost lost all control.

"Andrew."

His restraint snapped and he gave himself up to the passion flowing between them—no reservations, he held back nothing.

Lorelei writhed beneath him each time he withdrew and thrust deep once more, her moans as sweet as the songs of the angels.

Her hips met his every surge, the pace of their joining increased to a frenzied speed.

When Lorelei called out her release, he plunged deeply once more, letting his own seed spill inside her at the same time he kissed her lips.

# # #

Lorelei stared at Andrew, who'd slipped into a deep slumber after he'd brought her to completion once more. He slept so soundly she didn't want to wake him, but she had to leave before any of his household staff knew of her presence, or her own servants questioned her absence. She had much to attend to this night.

Yet, she could not bring herself to crawl from his bed.

Lifting her hand, Lorelei lightly traced his strong jaw to his perfect lips. She took in every aspect of his face and stored it in the special place of her memory reserved for things she'd likely never see again—the place she kept fond memories of her father when he was the doting parent or remembrances of her childhood home in France. Those times had been so sacred to her, just like this time with Andrew, so she did the only thing she could: she learned by heart his face, body, and smell, just as she'd committed to memory the layout of her childhood bedroom, the view out her one window, and the hugs her father had once doled out so generously.

If she slid from the bed and donned her clothes, she could slip from the house before he awoke…and hopefully, be gone from London before he came looking for her. It was the only way to keep him safe, but also protect Peter. It would hurt Andrew to find her gone— just as it would damage her to leave him behind—but those feelings would fade with time. One day he would forgive her many betrayals, though she would not be around to give him answers nor ever forgive herself.

Andrew breathed heavily and threw his arm over her, his fingers resting on her bottom.

Lorelei scooted away from him in the massive bed, his hand falling from her waist until her legs hung over the side of the bed. She stood as soon as her toes hit the cold floor, looking about the room. The only light came from the two open hearths and a single candle outside Andrew's dressing room.

She darted across the room, careful to keep her weight on the balls of her feet to soften the noise, and took the candle holder in hand. Holding it before her, cautious not to spill the hot wax on her exposed skin, she retraced their steps and collected her clothing: her dress and coat here, her shift there, and heaven only knew where she'd locate her boots and stockings.

A deep rumble came from the bed and the mattress creaked on its ropes.

Lorelei froze, prepared to hear Andrew call her name from the darkness behind her.

Thankfully, he rolled onto his stomach and continued his sated sleep.

Frantically, she searched the floor before the mirror for her boots and stockings. She couldn't bring herself to look into the glass, recalling what Andrew had done to her there earlier. She felt her cheeks flame with heat at the very thought.

"Where are you?" she said into the quiet room, hoping her belongings would see fit to answer her plea.

To her dismay, they remained silent—and hidden.

They must be close.

Had Andrew inadvertently tossed them into his dressing room? She tried to remember his actions but could only bring to mind the vision of his hands upon her body—and his lips caressing her every curve.

Deciding it was worth a try, she entered his most private space.

She immediately recognized her stocking draped over a long, cylindrical container in the back corner of the closet.

Lorelei rushed farther into the room and grabbed her boots, one lace stocking lay close by. When she pulled at it, the object behind it tipped over and rolled across the floor.

For the second time, Lorelei froze, expecting her name to be called from the other room. Again, luck was on her side.

She leaned down to pick up her lone stocking when the writing on the cylinder caught her eye. Scrawled across the case was the name 'Chastain.'

She set the candle on the floor and placed her pile of clothing next to it, but not so close that she'd start a fire.

When she picked up the case, a ring could be seen on the floor, as if it had sat in that very spot for years and years. The boards beneath still looked freshly polished.

The container, made of some type of hardened paper, was lightweight and appeared in excellent condition, obviously protected from the elements. She twisted one end, and the cap came off, revealing rolled paper within.

Breathless with anticipation, she turned the cylinder on its side and the scroll slid out and into her waiting hand. She need only peel one corner back to confirm her suspicions. They were the plans to Carcassonne.

But it couldn't be.

She staggered back, nearly allowing the plans and case to slip from her grasp. She could hardly believe her good fortune.

Lorelei had rebuffed Andrew's advances, turned away his kindnesses, all to gain access to homes that never held what she sought. She'd allowed Chastain to maliciously use her body, break her soul, and then act as if she and their child didn't exist. And all that time, Andrew had possessed what she sought.

This was likely why De Pez had failed in his mission all those years ago.

She concentrated on expelling the air that stuck in her chest and relieving the weight upon her.

Why hadn't Andrew told her before?

Simple: she'd never been honest with him. She'd kept her secrets, lied to him, and then thought he would tell her about a set of old dusty plans he kept in his dressing chambers?

Perhaps Chastain had brought them to Andrew, suspecting Lorelei's intentions all along. But from the dust ring on the floor, the plans to Carcassonne had been in this very dressing room for a very long time.

Andrew had just made the sweetest love to her, treated her as if nothing else existed but them and their pleasure.

He would never use her for his own gain—though she knew she'd done just that, sought her own release before preparing to disappear into the night, never to see him again.

Setting the plans aside, Lorelei hastily pulled on her clothing. The case in one hand and her boots in the other, she fled the room, slipping her boots on in the hall—though she still lacked a stocking.

She retraced the way to the main staircase.

The house was eerily quiet as she closed the front door behind her and walked into the early evening dusk.

Her freedom now tucked tightly under her arm, she only need exercise the proper amount of caution leaving town. Then—and only then—would she make arrangements for returning the plans.

She and Peter would be safely hidden away, Bonaparte would have what he needed, and all would forget about her.

The thought of handing the plans over to De Pez or her parents and returning to Andrew sparked a new hope within her.

Yet, the possibility of putting Andrew in harm's way did not appeal, no matter how much she wanted them to be together... To have a future.

She had every intention of departing London this very night, never to see Chastain or De Pez again. Peter would be safe, yet deprived of his inheritance; he would grow up alive and well and not at the mercy of others. That it also meant never knowing pleasure in Andrew's embrace again was the only thing that stung. But, like him, she would move on—though not to find love with another, she was certain. She would never trust someone so much again.

The walk to Chastain's townhouse was not a far one, but at dusk it would be risky with pickpockets and thieves lurking in dark alleys. It was only a few blocks to hail a hackney to drive her, however.

Two houses down from Andrew's townhouse, a set of footfalls fell in behind her, keeping pace with her, never coming closer. Cradling the case tightly at her side, she walked briskly toward the more populated area.

She could see the well-lit street not a block ahead of her. Lorelei lowered her head and once again increased her steps. The footfalls behind did likewise.

"Lady Chastain, where are you going in such a hurry?"

Lorelei didn't want to turn around, couldn't chance slowing her pace. Not much farther and she'd be safely in a well-populated area.

"My lady?" De Pez called behind her. His voice was

closer this time, as if he were only a few steps behind her.

Her plans to flee would never be realized if he noticed the case she carried.

"Does your *faithful* husband know of your indiscretions with the Marquis of Drake?"

She kept silent.

"No, I suppose he would not, although now that he has his heir, he is not as concerned about your activities. Though, I wonder if he'd be upset if his spare heir was actually the offspring of his best friend."

He prodded her. He knew her temper well, and baiting her into a fight was the most likely way of getting her to stop before she reached her destination.

"You do realize the need for a spare heir, do you not, Lady Chastain? For if something were to happen to the current heir, there would be another to step into his place." His threat was clear. "I certainly would never relish seeing something untoward happen to your poor babe."

He paused behind her.

But his threat was enough to make her pause, too.

"What did you say his name was? Peter?"

At last, she stopped and turned around.

He knew he'd chosen the correct wording and he laughed.

"Did you say *was*?" she hissed. He stood farther away than she'd expected, but there was no question he'd heard her. "You may threaten me, you may harass my family…but you do not, nor will you ever own my son!"

"He is of French heritage, regardless of where you gave birth." De Pez pushed his hands farther into his coat pockets, a satisfied smile settling on his face. "He belongs to the next head of France, which is now Napoleon

Bonaparte—and thanks to these plans, he will favor me and my allegiance to him."

"No." Her head shook in denial. "You will not have him—and neither will Bonaparte or whomever you align yourself with next."

"You silly, ignorant child. Napoleon is already in power." He took a step toward her, and she involuntarily moved back. "You still think you can control anything— that this mission was ever truly in your hands?"

Lorelei refused to back down. She'd put De Pez in his place on more than one occasion, and she may now have to pay for that, but she would not go without a fight. If he thought she was weak—of mind or body—he was wrong.

"And what have you got there?" She'd almost forgotten the container she clutched under her arm. "Have you actually succeeded?"

She took an involuntary step back.

"Give me the case."

She pushed it closer to her side, her coat shielding it from sight. "I will never hand the plans to you."

"Oh, yes, you will." He darted toward her and she sidestepped his advance. A narrow alley stood between two townhouses only twenty paces away. She ran to the safety of that darkness, hoping it led to a stable behind the grand house…and someone who could help her. Or at least scare De Pez away for the time being. "Come back here."

Lorelei only needed to get home. She could depart with Mrs. Dutton and Peter in a few moments' time and disappear into the night.

She ran as fast as she could, her soft shoes making hardly any sound as she moved down the cobbled alleyway.

Behind her, De Pez's boots thundered, the sound reverberating off the two houses that flanked the narrowing passage.

The alley finally ended, a stable on each side. She hurried to the closest one; surely a stable hand would help a lady in need.

"Help!" She ran through the open door—and was greeted by no one. The stable was abandoned, not a carriage or horse stood within. She panicked as she searched the low-lit room around her. Of course, no driver or stable boy would be about at this time. They would be awaiting their master outside another grand house.

De Pez followed her into the stable an instant later.

She moved farther in, toward an area littered with stable supplies and equipment. She threw the container into a large pile of loose straw and grabbed a pitchfork that leaned against the wall as she whirled back to face her pursuer.

"Do not come any closer!" she shouted. "Leave here, now."

Leery, he stopped, but circled where she stood, trying to get closer to the plans, nestled in the straw behind her. "You cannot win this, Lorelei. Step out of the way, and I will retrieve the plans and be on my way."

"You think me stupid?" She slid to the side to block him and shoved the pitchfork in his direction. She'd become a liability to him and his cause, for she would never conform nor serve this new man. "I know you will never let me walk out of this stable alive."

"I have underestimated you, *ma cherie*."

Her rage boiled over. They were the same words

Chastain had said to her that night at Covent Gardens.

The shout that erupted from her was more war cry than anything.

She watched alarm spread across his face when she charged forward, the pitchfork aimed at his midsection. He'd advanced so close to her that he didn't have time to sidestep her movement, nor did she have enough space to gain momentum.

But the spikes were sharp and penetrated his middle.

His eyes went round as he looked from her to the pitchfork embedded in his flesh.

Lorelei dropped the end of her weapon, and De Pez dropped to his knees before her.

If he weren't seriously injured, the pitchfork wouldn't keep him down for long.

She made a mad dash to the straw, digging around until her hands came into contact with the case. Her hands shook so much she had a hard time retrieving it from the pile. Glancing over her shoulder, De Pez knelt, the pitchfork removed from his middle and blood staining his shirt and hands.

He watched her through slitted eyes as she regained her feet and moved past him to the alley beyond.

"This is not finished," he called to her retreating form.

Lorelei was terrified it would never be over, no matter how far she ran or how much distance she put between herself and everything she'd known in her life thus far.

Chapter Twenty-Four

Andrew paced his stables, waiting for his horse to be prepared, the delicate undergarment resting in his coat pocket.

He'd be damned if he would let her run away again—let her act as if he meant nothing to her. Though the hours they'd spent in each other's arms weren't enough to guarantee them a future together, Andrew was willing to try, even if that meant living with the stigma of their scandal. It was nothing he wasn't used to, and many expected such behavior from him anyway.

After their short time of bliss, he'd awoken to a cold, empty bed. Not a trace of Lorelei remained but the lace stocking tucked deeply in his pocket. He'd thought for a moment he'd dreamed the whole afternoon: running into her on the street, whisking her away in his carriage, and then ravishing her naked body.

"What is taking so long?" he shouted. He'd almost taken into the night on foot to track her down. The silly woman, leaving at dusk—Mrs. Bee had informed him—on foot. Any sort of sordid character could have been waiting in the shadows for her. "Bring my horse, now!"

As he shouted the last word, a stable boy led his best stallion from his stall, saddled and prepared to ride.

He needed to track her down and make sure she'd arrived home safety. Then, he planned to lay out all the reasons why she belonged with him and no one else. They'd been so preoccupied with each other that he hadn't had the chance to tell her everything he'd learn at his solicitor's office. Not only could he offer Lorelei a future as the Marchioness of Drake, but little Peter could be made to inherit the title.

There was the matter of Chastain, but that could be dealt with. Andrew could publicly claim Peter as his son and heir, in turn forcing Chastain to file the necessary papers for divorce. It was risky attempting to force Chastain's hand in the matter.

"State your desires concerning my wife."

Andrew turned, holding his horse's lead, to face the man he'd once considered his best friend—as close as any family he'd ever had.

"Benji," he snarled. The man had mistreated Lorelei, not only before but also during their short marriage. "Do not come to my home and demand answers from me."

Chastain stood, his hands balled into fists at his side. "So you deny it?"

"I deny nothing." Andrew had anticipated this meeting, but had hoped it could wait until Lorelei was safely away and out of her husband's reach. "Unlike you, my desires are very clear, and are made with the utmost respect for Lady Lorelei."

"Lady Chastain!" Chastain took a menacing step toward Andrew. "And she is mine to do with as I see fit."

"Truly?" Andrew asked. "Is it because you pay her

so much mind that you knew she was with me, just this very afternoon?"

"Oh, no, her deceptive nature had eluded me," Chastain said. "That is, until her father saw fit to send word of his daughter's whereabouts."

Their months of strained meetings and ambiguous talks had come to an end, and Andrew was happy for it. He wanted answers…and only Chastian held them.

Andrew noticed the stable boy standing close by, his mouth open in shock, taking in the scene unfolding around him.

"Leave us!" The boy fled as if the very devil were on his heels. Again, Andrew addressed Chastain. "Why did you marry her?"

The man had the nerve to chuckle. "Because you wanted her, of course."

"All because I wanted her?"

"Yes." An odd expression—possibly sorrow— touched Chastain's features. "You were ready to forsake me…all for a woman. And worse yet, love."

The confession knocked Andrew off balance. "I would never have abandoned you or our friendship. Is that it, then? You did this—to me and to *her*—all because you were envious of my feelings for her?"

"It is so much more than that, and you will not steal her from me now. The whole of England will know your traitorous behavior."

"My behavior?" It was Andrew's turn to laugh. "You have mistreated her since the evening within the gardens." From his stunned look, his friend must have thought Lorelei would confide that to no one. "Oh, yes, she told me of your behavior, which is nothing less than criminal. I advise you to walk away, surrender your right to Lorelei, or you will not enjoy the outcome."

"You truly think she would favor you over me? She made her decision once, and I have faith she would choose me once again."

"You are wrong."

"She bore my child and heir," Chastain hissed. "If she left me, she'd never see her child again. I am confident she will see reason."

Andrew knew Chastain would make good on his threat, if only to cause distress and further hurt to Lorelei and himself.

"Do not forget that she is my wife—I could be persuaded to hand her over, but I will not lose my heir in the process."

"Persuaded to hand her over? Those are not the words of a man in love with his wife and caring of his son's future."

"As I said before, they are not your concern."

The men stood nose to nose, Chastain's eyes being slightly under his own, ready for the confrontation Andrew was bound to start—if Chastain did not do it first. "I can and will care for Lorelei and Peter better than you have."

"You will do nothing of the sort." Chastain shoved Andrew hard, and he stumbled into the horse behind him. "You will stay away from Lorelei and my son. Are we clear?"

Andrew was on him in an instant. His fist flew through the air and connected solidly with Chastain's chin, sending him reeling back. He landed on the hard-packed earth. "The only thing clear at this moment is that you care only for yourself—and that you are in possession of something I want."

A thin trail of crimson crept down Chastain's chin from his split lip.

"Stand up," Andrew goaded him, for this could very well be his last opportunity to settle this as men, with only their fists for weapons. "Show me you deserve her over I."

Wiping the blood with the back of his hand, Chastain gained his feet once more but kept his distance. "This is ludicrous. I have no reason to fight for my own wife."

Andrew grabbed Chastain by his shirt, bringing him close once more. "That is correct, for you have already lost her. Which is a pity for you." He eyed the man one last time. "You are not worth my time or her love."

With a quickness borne of his frustration, Andrew released Chastain and mounted his waiting horse.

"Where are you going?" Chastain called.

Andrew ducked his head as he rode out of the stable. He had only one person who mattered, and he hadn't any idea where to find her.

Chapter Twenty-Five

The hired hack stopped at the curb with a jolt as Lorelei ran her fingers through her tousled hair. Her hand came away with a few stray pieces of straw. She'd hurriedly picked off the pieces that had clung to her coat and shoes during the short ride. Thankfully, she hadn't gotten close enough to De Pez to get any blood on her.

A carriage with the Chastain seal on the door was parked in front of her. She hurried down, careful not to snag her dress on the exposed boards, while gripping the container holding the plans. Her whole body continued to tremble from the shock of spearing De Pez.

"I will return with your coin," she called to the driver.

"I knew ye wasn't good for da fare," he grumbled. "No good, lousy…"

Lorelei ignored his rant as she hurried up the front steps. The butler swung the door wide before she could grab the handle herself. She was forced back when her husband exited.

"Lorelei, whatever are you doing out here?" He

looked over her shoulder at the hack stopped behind his carriage and glanced up and down the street. Chastain's coat collar was raised, partially covering his face. "I do hope you made the necessary arrangements for your wardrobe."

"Oh, yes, I did," she stuttered, having forgotten why she'd left the townhouse earlier.

"Come on, lady. I ain't got all night."

Lorelei turned back toward the driver and held up her hand, signaling he'd only have to wait another minute.

"Do you mind paying the driver?" she asked.

Chastain eyed her suspiciously. "Why are you in a hack?"

"I do apologize, but I was dreadfully hungry after my fitting. I walked a block or two and found a tea room to take my supper. I lost my way and could not find the coach waiting for me." Lorelei wondered if anyone had noticed her absence—other than Mrs. Dutton, of course. "I hope the driver is not still awaiting my departure from the modiste."

Had the confrontation with her father only happened that morning? And this afternoon with Andrew? It felt like a lifetime ago.

"No, no, Charles returned hours ago." Chastain stepped around her and flipped a few coins to the driver. His coat collar fell a bit, revealing a cut lip and swollen cheek before he was able to pull it back into place. "I had figured to find you at the comte's home. In fact, I was headed that way now in search of you."

"Why ever would I be there?" she asked, pushing the cylinder farther into the folds of her coat, fearing it would draw Chastain's attention. The actual question she was burning to ask was why he hadn't searched for her sooner.

"Because," he paused, drawing out his next words as if she were too ignorant to understand. "They are your parents—and if you are not at *my* home, where else would you have gone?"

The question sounded like an accusation, yet no one knew she'd left her modiste to be with Andrew and had only just arrived home after hours in his bed.

Thankfully, Chastain hadn't noticed the case wedged against her side. For months she'd been apprehensive about overlooking it, for it wasn't all that large in size.

"Let me grab little Peter and we will accompany you." She didn't wait for him to agree before starting into the house. "I will only be a moment."

"Very well, I will wait in the carriage." Again, he glanced about, his nervousness clear. "Do hurry, I have somewhere I'd like to take you."

"Of course." Lorelei darted up the steps and into the house. That Chastain sought her presence at all was a surprise. She couldn't think of where he was taking her, but she needed to be away from the townhouse, and quickly, in case De Pez came for her—or Peter. But first, she needed to hide the plans somewhere no one would find them in her absence.

"M'lady, Peter done missed his ma," Mrs. Dutton said as soon as Lorelei crossed the threshold.

Lorelei was comforted by Mrs. Dutton words. They'd spent many hours discussing Lorelei's predicament and their plan should anything happen to her.

"Mrs. Dutton, Lord Chastain and I will be taking Peter with us. Please ready our things, we shall leave immediately."

"You be look'n a might frazzled, m'lady," Mrs. Dutton observed. "I be start'n ta worry when ye hadn't been home afore supper. Maybe I should be go'n wit ye and m'lord…ta keep an eye on Peter. You know how m'lord don't be like'n a fussy babe."

Lorelei wanted the woman with her, too.

"Ye know'n I be have'n things packed and ready in case we be need'n ta leave quickly."

She gave in to what she really wanted at Mrs. Dutton's comforting words. "All right, yes. We shall go with Lord Chastain to see the comte, then we are leaving town immediately."

"And what do ye be plan'n ta tell ye husband?" she asked.

Lorelei thought for a moment before responding. "I will tell him I fared better in the country and seek to return."

"Very well. I be retrieve'n the wee lad's bag and we be on our way."

"Oh, I will get it." Lorelei needed a moment before facing her husband. "Please, await me in the carriage."

She didn't pause to wait for Mrs. Dutton to exit the front door before making a mad dash up the stairs. Surveying the room, Lorelei looked for any nook that would keep the plans from sight.

"Lady Chastain?" a servant called from her open doorway. "I do apologize for this, but my lord requests your immediate presence in the carriage." The man had enough sense to look ashamed of how he spoke to her.

"I will be right down." There was naught she could do but take the plans with her. They were safer on her person anyways.

"I do apologize—" The man's eyes drifted over the container and a moment of panic filled her.

"There is no need for apologies." She smiled to reassure the servant he hadn't angered her. "I know more than most of my husband's impatience."

Lorelei spotted Peter's bag by his crib and stuffed the container in with his extra swaddling clothes and rattle. Who would suspect one great nation could be taken down—by way of their largest trading outlet—by a set of papers that easily fit in a child's bag?

No one would look inside a baby's satchel, she hoped and rushed back outside.

Mrs. Dutton stood outside the carriage bouncing Peter to and fro.

"He be a might fussy," she whispered when Lorelei approached. "M'lord near about threw us from the carriage."

With Peter safely in her arms, she motioned Mrs. Dutton to enter the carriage.

"M'lady." Mrs. Dutton paused. "There be a mounted man not far down the lane. He been watch'n me."

"Do move with some haste!" her husband leaned out of the carriage and called to her.

She hazarded a glance down the busy street, abuzz with people traveling here and there for the evening. Sure enough, a dark figure waited in the shadows a few houses down. Lorelei couldn't tell if he eyed her or was only loitering about. Surely, De Pez hadn't recovered so quickly, yet he was well-trained and normally stopped at nothing during his missions.

"Let us hope he does not have this carriage in his sights," she mumbled.

She climbed into the enclosed carriage with the help of a footman and situated herself next to Mrs. Dutton and across from her husband, who scowled at her in impatience.

"I thank you for joining us, my lady." His snide words cut the quiet of the carriage. "I would hope you understand that playing errand boy with your parents is not all I have planned for this evening. Let us be off," Chastain called to the driver with a sharp rap on the carriage wall.

Lorelei sat back in silence as the carriage gained speed along the cobbled street. Her hope was that this would all be over shortly.

Across the carriage from her, she once again noticed Chastain's swollen, cut lip, though she didn't care enough to inquire about it. Her nerves were still frazzled after her confrontation with De Pez.

"Where are we going?" she asked, handing Peter back to Mrs. Dutton.

"You shall see." Chastain stared out the window as the harnesses from the horses began to clink with their speed. "In time."

Lorelei was sick to death of his cold-shoulder act, and it seemed she could not control herself. "Do not tell me that. I thought we were bound for the comte's house. I demand to know where we are going."

He turned a chilling stare on her. "I know you would much prefer to be with your lover, but, as my wife, you go where I say you go."

"My lover?" Lorelei glanced to Mrs. Dutton, who busied herself with Peter, before addressing Chastain. "It is highly improper to speak—"

"Now, it is your turn to be silent."

"Then I demand you stop and let us out," she demanded.

"So you can run back to that coward?"

Lorelei tried her best to look confused; as if she hadn't any idea of what he spoke.

"Did you think I would not find out?" Chastain sat forward, staring straight at her. "I married *you* so he could not have you. And you see fit to give what is *mine* away? And that child…"

"What? Say what you want about me, but not your son."

"My son? How am I to know he is not Drake's bastard?"

Lorelei's hands clutched her dress, twisting the fabric to keep from launching herself at Chastain and clawing at his eyes.

"How dare—"

"How dare I, Lady Chastain?" he shouted. Mrs. Dutton cringed beside her and her hand came to rest on Lorelei's thigh to calm her. "Any man in my position would ask the same question."

"But you have also taken pleasure elsewhere!" Startled by the jostling of the carriage, Lorelei peeked out the window, only then realizing how fast they traveled.

"That is my right," he spat back. "Until you produce an heir you do not have that liberty."

Finally, she realized his anger came not from her unfaithfulness, but from the question of whether or not Peter was his true heir.

She could at least give him a bit of peace. "Do not fret, Peter is your child. Andrew and I were never intimate until after Peter's birth."

He leaned out the window and looked behind their

carriage before shouting at the driver to hurry.

Settled once more, he again contradicted what she believed lay behind his wrath. "You think I care who fathered your child? It is common knowledge that half the women in London have children fathered by men not their husbands. If a man says they do not have a bastard running about London then they are a damn fool."

"So, it is Andrew specifically you have cause to rail against?" The carriage slowed and took a corner, the road going from cobblestone to rutted dirt judging by the bounce of the wooden wheels against the ground. "That leaves only one question."

"And what would that be?"

She had to shout above the sound of the carriage and Peter's sudden cry of agitation. She wanted to ask why he'd accosted her at Covent Gardens that night, but thought if he was going to answer only one question, this was the more pertinent of the two. "Why did you marry me in the first place?"

"Because," he yelled, leaning close, "Andrew wanted you. And I could not have my best friend running off happily in love, leaving me behind!"

Lorelei sat back in utter astonishment, not wanting to know any more about the spiteful man she'd married.

Chapter Twenty-Six

Andrew maneuvered his stallion through the streets congested with *ton* members en route to a ball or the opera or a play. All unimportant, trivial pursuits compared to his.

As he rounded the last corner, Chastain's townhouse came into view. He watched a servant hand Lorelei up into the waiting carriage. She glanced around before entering. The servant waved to the driver, and the carriage took off.

He spurred his horse to a faster pace and zigzagged past slow-moving coaches. It grated on him to think that he could be caught here and have to watch her drive away—again.

His only hope was that Chastain hadn't made it there before him, for there were any number of dreadful things he could tell Lorelei to turn her against him and their love.

"Lorelei!" His shout was lost above the sound of carriage wheels and hooves on the cobblestone street.

He kept as fast a pace as possible, trying to gain on

the flow of other carriages and horses. As her carriage continued to gain distance on him, Andrew reined his stallion sharply to the right and onto the neatly swept walk bordering the road. There were few pedestrians at this time of day so he was able to get his horse up to a fast clip, enough to close some distance without jeopardizing anyone that may find themselves in his path.

"Lorelei!" Andrew waved with his free hand while holding the reins tightly in his other.

He managed to overtake a large wagon laden with goods from the marketplace just as someone leaned out Lorelei's carriage window.

Instead of slowing down when the other traffic thinned, pulling to the side of the street to await him, the driver snapped his whip and brought the two mares harnessed to the carriage to a run. Meant for more luxurious travel, the conveyance wasn't built for speed or agility.

With the walk ahead of him empty, Andrew coaxed his horse into a run on the even ground, fearing his stallion would turn a hoof, but knowing if he lost sight of Lorelei she could go anywhere and it would take him precious time to track her down.

"Watch out!" a merchant behind a cart yelled when Andrew flew by him.

He was past the vendor and another townhouse down before the man's shout was fully from his mouth.

Lorelei's carriage hit a bump in the street ahead, the two back wheels leaving the ground and landing once more with a loud crack.

The driver was pushing far beyond the capabilities of the carriage or his horses.

Finally, Andrew noticed the driver pull back on the

reins, slowing the horses slightly when an intersection came into view not far ahead. Carriages, horses with carts, and pedestrians made their way across the street in every direction, many not pausing for passing traffic.

At the cross street, a break in traffic appeared. With a last-minute tug, the Chastain coach careened sharply left onto the street, leaving Andrew on the opposite side, fighting the flow of the street to follow and keep pace.

He watched helplessly as Lorelei's carriage again increased its speed down the mostly deserted street.

He took his attention from the carriage long enough to navigate a path through the crowded road and onto the side street. Two blocks ahead, the carriage slowed once more and made an erratic turn into an area lined with warehouses.

The driver's path was unpredictable, leading nowhere Andrew could understand. If Lorelei sought to leave town, she wouldn't head toward the warehouse district by the docks.

What concerned him most was the dangerous pace the driver had set.

Once free of the overcrowded intersection, he rushed toward the next turn. His horse was more than capable of catching Lorelei's carriage with no one to get in his way.

"On," he encouraged the horse.

He slowed slightly for the next turn and leaned low on the horse's neck at the same time a loud crash echoed through the tall buildings, gaining volume as it reached him.

Whatever caused the sound was just around the next corner.

No one worked in the warehouse district after dusk,

the cost of wax candles too high for any businessman.

Andrew rounded the last corner—and was off his horse before he'd slowed to a reasonable speed.

Before him, Lorelei's carriage lay on its side. Skid marks in the dirt street led to the spot where it was wedged against a building. The perfectly matched mares that had pulled the vehicle ran at full speed down the road, their harnesses still attached and dragging the tongue of the carriage in their wake.

Andrew released the reins of his own horse and ran to the overturned carriage. The coachman had been thrown from his perch and lay prone and not moving a few feet from the accident.

Andrew clamored on to the side of the carriage, hoping to reach the door or at least the quarter light, which now pointed skyward. His only thought was that Lorelei was inside—possibly gravely hurt.

He pulled himself up easily then scooted across the upturned side of the carriage on his stomach. Andrew was sure to test that the carriage frame would not collapse, causing greater harm.

Looking about, he searched for anyone to help him, but all he saw were the fleeing backsides of the beasts that'd once pulled the coach. Not even the sound of their beating hooves could be heard at so great a distance.

Frantically, he realized he was alone—and only silence sounded from the enclosed carriage.

He made his way to the quarter light and peered inside.

"Lorelei," he shouted, though he was within feet of her.

It was then a baby cried and a woman moaned, as if time had stood still, the occupants of the carriage frozen until he'd called her name.

Staring intently, he waited for his eyes to adjust to the deep black of the carriage interior.

He hadn't seen anyone but Lorelei enter the carriage. He'd never thought that Peter could be with her. His heart ached at the harm he could find inside. He could not lower himself into the darkness for fear of landing on Lorelei or her son.

"Sir."

A group of men had appeared alongside the overturned carriage. Two peered up at him while one crouched by the coachman.

"Is there someone inside?"

Andrew didn't bother answering the man's question, for the baby's cries could still be heard.

"Give me your torch," he commanded, grasping the long wooden pole, careful not to touch the carriage with it, and leaned close to the opening. The new light cast a glow on the interior, and Andrew was able to see Lorelei unmoving within, her eyes closed and a trail of blood streaming down her face. An older woman lay on the opposite side, her eyes fluttering. In her arms, she held the screaming bundle. "Quick, lend me a hand."

One of the men climbed onto the carriage's side next to him and helped unlatch the door and hoist it open.

"Andrew," Lorelei's faint voice called. "Please, help Peter."

Chapter Twenty-Seven

"Please, help Peter," Lorelei said through her suffering. "Mrs. Dutton, you will see to him as we planned?"

"Help be here." The woman's words were slurred. "We be all fine, ye see."

Lorelei couldn't tell what pinned her down, only that it came in through the window and the pain came from her stomach. She ran her fingers across the rod-shaped wooden object.

The irony of the scene was not lost on her: only a short time before, she'd impaled De Pez in much the same manner she now was. She'd been crazy and reckless to think it had been De Pez chasing her coach, when in fact it had been Andrew. He'd come for her, even after everything.

And once again, she'd fled from him.

And Peter was out of her reach. She thanked the Lord above that Mrs. Dutton had insisted on holding Peter during the carriage ride. His screams could be heard above the loud men trying to right the carriage.

Beneath her, Chastain hadn't moved, not so much as the expansion and contraction of his chest. He was likely already gone. She only had a moment of despair at her involvement in his death, for she had the living to see to.

"But if I do not, take Peter and go. You still have the ring I gave you?" she whispered, remembering the heavy wedding band Chastain had given her on their wedding night.

Andrew was preparing to lower himself into the carriage and she only had a moment. When Dutton nodded, Lorelei continued. "Trust no one—not my family, no one. If I am well enough, I will meet you at your sister's home as we planned. If not, please take good care of my son."

Her focus blurred and she rubbed at her eyes. Her hand came back covered in her own warm blood.

"Andrew," she called again before it was too late. "Please, help Mrs. Dutton and Peter." She labored to bring more air into her lungs.

She felt the carriage sway as his feet landed not far from where she was trapped. The interior of the carriage, while seemingly cramped moments before, now felt bigger than her bedroom at Chastain townhouse.

A dim light came from above her, allowing enough illumination for her to see Andrew take Peter in his arms while Mrs. Dutton crawled to her unsteady feet. Before Lorelei's eyes, the woman was lifted out the open door above.

"Andrew, let me see him," Lorelei pleaded.

"When I have you out, there will be plenty of time for that."

She lay there helplessly as Andrew handed Peter to

a set of strong arms. The baby continued to cry, though softer now.

Andrew knelt beside her and she saw the torment in his face. "Lorelei, my love?"

"I am here."

"Why did you run from me?"

"It was not you…" She knew her time was limited. "Andrew, do you see a bag?"

"I am unconcerned with a bag—"

"No, you must find it." She desperately wanted him to understand the importance. "Please, take it with you and keep it safe—and hidden."

"Shhhh," he leaned in close and whispered. "We will have you out of here soon."

He set his hand on her forehead to calm her.

"Someone, hurry and get in here. We have more people." His shout was accompanied by a jerking outside the carriage.

The rod moved deeper through her, amplifying her pain.

"Have you got the bag?" she rasped.

Andrew finally gave in to her wish and looked about the carriage. "Yes, here it is."

"Is the case—" Her words stuck in her throat as she shifted. "…inside?"

He didn't immediately respond, for he must be searching the bag. Finally, he held the case in her line of sight. "I have it, now stay quiet and still. I beg of you."

She wanted to yell at him to open his eyes. She was trapped, a wooden rod through her side. Though she couldn't see beneath her, she knew her injuries were substantial, and no amount of shifting or jostling of the carriage would free her.

The pain was more than she could have imagined, radiating from her midsection to her fingertips, taking over the aching in her head.

She'd wanted to say goodbye to Peter, to hold him one last time—yet, Lorelei never wanted his only memory of his mother to be tainted by red.

At least Mrs. Dutton knew what to do: she would already be spiriting Peter away from the crash and would await Lorelei. If things transpired as she feared, then she'd made sure the nursemaid had the means to get Peter out of London and to her sister's house, far from France and Lorelei's parents—and the plans that had ruled her life.

Chapter Twenty-Eight

Her eyes glossed over and her breathing became increasingly shallow and labored.

"We will have you reunited with Peter very soon, my Lorelei."

The impossibility of the situation rocked him to his core. Lorelei was bleeding out before his eyes—blood filling her lungs—and the only damn thing he could do was reassure her that everything was going to be fine, though he knew well and true that she would not walk away from this accident.

But she must live through this—if he could convince her, perhaps he could convince himself, as well. Any future without her was unimaginable.

The carriage shook, and a man called down to him. "Send up the next!"

"Go, Andrew," she said, closing her eyes as if her energy to keep them open was gone. "Please...know I cared...for you."

Cared?

"I am not ready to let you go," he choked. "Stay

quiet and conserve your strength." They'd only just given themselves to one another, though Andrew had belonged to her for much longer.

"But you must..." She inhaled deeply, the fluid in her lungs making it impossible for her to gain a full breath. "...let me go." She squeezed his hand, the pressure of her grip hardly registering. "You must promise me...you will take that case, keep it close..."

She paused once more, her eyes shutting.

Andrew bent forward and brushed his lips lightly over each closed lid, hoping to give her strength to go on.

"...and destroy it as soon as you are alone."

"Why?" he asked.

"Just do as I request." With the little light that penetrated the closed carriage, Andrew saw a thin trail of crimson slip from the corner of her mouth and soak into his shirt. "And Andrew?"

"Yes?"

"Trust no one...else with this." The words were little more than a whisper, and he feared he hadn't heard her correctly. "You must go, get far from here."

He couldn't leave her. Not now, though he knew he was being selfish, as he'd always been. The right thing would be to send word to her family. Mayhap they would arrive before she took her final breath. But the moments it would take to send for them would be less time for them to be together, and Andrew would not give up a second.

"I cannot leave you." He brought their hands to his mouth and kissed her fingers softly—they were so very cold and slick with her blood. "Not now, when you need me so."

For him, time stopped. He wasn't crouched in an

overturned carriage, the man above wasn't shouting to get his attention, and most of all, Lorelei wasn't lying almost lifeless in his arms, her color fading as the life drained from her broken body.

He stared at her, her eyes closed. Was she past feeling the pain?

She truly was the most beautiful creature he'd ever seen, and would ever know. He swept the hair from her face and ran his fingers along her brow. This must be how she looked in slumber, completely at peace, he realized. Her face devoid of worry, pain, and anger—leaving only a flawless jawline, pert nose, and kissable rosebud lips. Her face no longer had the deep color of her French birth, but had begun to turn a dull grey. She lay as peacefully as she had in his bed, only hours before.

"I love you." He did not know what else he could say. He did love her, had known for some time, yet the words sounded meaningless in the shadow of such tragedy. "I only wanted you to be happy. I am sorry I pursued you thus. I never dreamed we would not have the future—our future."

He was rambling. His words tumbled over each other in an attempt to share a year's worth of sentiments in the few moments they had left together.

And there was so much he longed to hear her say.

"I will take care of Peter, you have my word," he whispered. Chastain, his best friend, lay motionless under the spot where Lorelei was pinned. He hadn't moved; no fluttering of his eyes, no agonizing moans, nor did his chest move up and down with shallow breath. "He will want for nothing. All I have will be his: my love, my home, and my title."

Lorelei's eyes flickered open at his declaration. "He

cannot be—" she paused, her lids becoming too heavy for her to keep open, "—for you."

"Shhhhh." Confused, he leaned down and set his lips to hers. "Just rest."

"No, I…must…tell…you…all."

"We have been through this, my love. I do not blame you for all that has happened. You did what you must." He needed her to know he understood, and he did not begrudge her the decisions she was pressed to make.

"Andrew, my family…and I are not here for the matter…you think." The words poured from her as if she knew if she didn't get it all out now, and quickly, she would soon be unable to say anything.

Lorelei coughed and more blood ran from her lips. "We were here to…obtain the case inside the satchel…you now hold."

He looked at the unsuspecting bag he held. He'd assumed within were Peter's things, the things he would need if Lorelei didn't make it through this.

"Please, take them. Destroy them. Keep them far from my son." She coughed once more and he saw her remaining energy drain from her body. "They are not safe, even with you. They will cause you nothing but grief, as they have me."

"But—"

"Andrew." Her moss-colored eyes stared intently into him. "Would you deny me my last request?"

"Never, Lorelei. I would deny you nothing; yesterday, today…and forever more. Nothing I would deny you, my love."

"I…am…sorry for involving you."

With one last effort, Lorelei expelled a deep sigh— and she was gone from him. Her head lolled to the side and the hand that had gripped his went limp.

"Come on, m'lord!" a man shouted from atop the carriage.

Finally, Andrew could no longer ignore the voices above him.

"There is no one left." She was gone—his reason for…everything, gone. "Help me up."

The men lifted Andrew from the wreckage to the sight of a dozen people milling about.

A man hurried toward him carrying a satchel, his hair and glasses askew. "Are you hurt?" he asked.

Andrew looked down at himself. In the lamplight and glow from the many torches, he could see his coat and undershirt were saturated with blood—Lorelei's blood.

"No." Andrew moved past the man without another word, the bag Lorelei had given him securely under his arm. "But please see to the child."

"Child, my lord?" the man asked.

"Yes, he and his nursemaid were lifted from the carriage a few moments ago." Andrew turned to a dock worker helping the coachman to his feet. "Where did the child go?" he yelled to him.

The man looked up and down the street. "They be over there not a few minutes ago."

Andrew searched the growing crowd for the stout maid and Peter, but they were nowhere to be seen. The crowd began to thin as interest in the accident waned, and the only work left to do was right the carriage.

The crowd was abuzz with news of the couple inside. "Is it true that Lord and Lady Chastain both perished inside?" someone called to him. He ignored the questions and kept moving through the crowd. Up and down the street—checking alleys, nooks, and doorways. But they were nowhere to be found.

He'd given himself one task, and he was unable to accomplish even that. Peter had disappeared.

Lorelei had begged him to get as far away as possible, destroy whatever was in the bag slung over his shoulder, and not to look for her son. But how could he not?

Peter was all he had left of his Lorelei.

He wasn't certain whether a fine mist had started to fall or if the moisture that soaked his face was from his own eyes. In the blink of an eye, he'd lost everything.

His months of dwelling on what to do without Lorelei seemed trivial now. She'd been alive—living with another man, true, but alive. Now, she was gone. No matter how many hours he pondered what could have been, it would never be.

No, he was left with this case and…

He hadn't even begun to work through the notion that Chastain had used her body when she hadn't agreed. All these months of hating his best friend and Andrew hadn't even known the depths of Benji's deceptions. The urge to tear the man limb from limb had been strong, but his need to love Lorelei had been stronger, knowing the time would come when he'd deal with Chastain. But first, he'd needed to have her, save her, keep her.

He hadn't been there to protect her that night in Covent Gardens.

And he'd failed to keep her safe once more.

Andrew didn't deserve her or Peter.

And she'd been a spy? He just could not believe her words. His task of taking and destroying whatever lay in the case seemed farfetched to the extreme.

With a hurried thought, Andrew rushed to his horse with a new destination in mind—but first, he needed to make one stop.

Chapter Twenty-Nine

After stopping at his townhouse to hide the case within and commanding his servants to lock every door and window, Andrew once again mounted his horse and departed for the one place he could find answers. There was nowhere else to go—and perhaps, he would find Peter, as well.

The night grew late, carriages having long since returned their masters to their homes for the night. Andrew rode like the fires of hell were nipping at his heels. If everything were true, his opportunity to find clarity in all that had happened could, at this very moment, be escaping his grasp.

Coming to a stop before the comte's townhouse, he saw that only a few candles could be seen lighting various rooms within. Either the comte and his wife were asleep, or they had departed in haste. For if they knew of their daughter's demise and their grandchild's disappearance, surely they'd be awake and mourning their loss—or searching every lane in London for their babe.

They would be frantic with grief, as Andrew was at

this moment. Surely they'd also be searching for answers to this tragedy.

That is, unless they knew Lorelei's secrets—possibly even shared in her deceptions. But then still they would grieve her death.

He dismounted his horse and took the front steps two at a time.

His fist upon the door echoed within the cavernous house as if nothing lay within but empty, hollow rooms.

When no one came to the door, Andrew grasped the handle and pushed, ready to take down the solid door himself if that meant gaining entrance and possible answers. But that was not necessary, for it swung open of its own accord, unlocked.

Stepping inside, Andrew listened.

He listened for the cries of an injured babe.

He strained to hear the soft singing of a nursemaid to calm an innocent.

After a moment, he still heard nothing.

Stilling his breathing and attempting to calm his racing heart, he listened once more. Footsteps could be heard moving somewhere in the large house. Andrew focused, realizing the sounds came from above.

Angry voices argued back and forth in French, confirming whoever was here was on the second floor.

Andrew rushed up the stairs. A thick rug muted his approach. Light came from a room far down the hall—the same window lit by the candlelight he'd seen from outside.

"Did you hear that?" Andrew knew enough French to make out the question.

"You are hearing things." Lorelei's father's voice was unmistakable. "He must have known something would be here or he wouldn't have come."

Andrew paused not far from the cracked door. Inside, Lorelei's parents rushed about—a pair of prone legs on the floor could be seen not far from the bed.

"Where do you think they went?" If one didn't concentrate so heavily on what was being said, the shrill nature of the comtesse's words wouldn't have been understandable.

"If I knew that, we would have departed by now." The comte's deep voice thundered through the room. "She may have them with her—and fled, leaving us to deal with things."

"Oh, Mathis," the comtesse cried. "Lorelei would never deceive us, would she?"

"She is not our concern any longer. Your daughter has abandoned us."

"She would never," the poor woman moaned.

They thought Lorelei had abandoned them? Andrew wanted to tell them the truth, but hesitated to enter the room.

A groan sounded.

"Quiet," the comte hissed at the man on the floor. "If you refuse to answer my questions, then remain silent and accept your fate."

Andrew realized then that Lorelei had been correct about the comte and comtesse.

"Keep searching. If there is something to find it is either with her or here. Lorelei would be a fool to retain the plans in Chastain's own house."

"But why would she bring them here and not tell us?" The comtesse sounded close to hysterics.

"Perhaps our child knew she'd soon be departing London."

Andrew applauded his own foresight in dropping the case at his townhouse before continuing on. He'd risked missing the comte, and possibly never seeing Peter again, but Lorelei had been carrying what they sought with her, not the man lying on the floor close to his demise.

Drawers opened and closed, and the creak of bed ropes could be heard from within. "We must depart. Someone will search for De Pez soon, or the servants will return and find him. Perhaps Lore did the smart thing by disappearing; we were sent on a fool's errand. How do we even know the plans still exist, or that Bonaparte will spare our lives if we fail?"

"That is not for us to question, Camille," the comte said. "We were given a task, and we failed."

Andrew had heard enough. Lorelei's parents were willing to forsake her for their own lives. It was clear no one had been round to tell them of the accident, and Peter most certainly was not within this house.

Still, Andrew listened, though he should be out the door and back on his horse searching—there was a great chance Peter was badly hurt. His nursemaid could have, in her daze, wandered off and gotten lost.

Andrew pushed the door open, revealing a feminine bedchamber. Hair brushes, clothes, and ribbons were scattered about. The bed sheets pulled from the straw mattress lay in one corner. The dressing room had been completely emptied of belongings, as well, and they were now piled about the floor and tables.

The comtesse yelped like a frightened pup when he stepped into the room and glanced to the man lying motionless on the ground.

The comte was instantly on guard. "What are you

doing within my house? I shall call for the magistrate immediately."

For once, Andrew knew he had the upper hand. "Oh, I will quite relish regaling the good magistrate with tales of French spies and espionage—not to mention the man bleeding to death on the floor there."

They all looked to the pool of blood that would likely soak through the floorboards.

The man was familiar to him—he'd been the one leaving Lorelei's home not long ago. Had she said who he was or how he knew her?

"Lorelei told me all," he said, yet he knew barely anything. "Tell me, what do you search for?"

"It is none of your concern," the comte said in English. "Where is Lorelei?"

No one moved, as they each assessed the others. The comtesse looked ready to hop over the man on the floor, skirt past him, and flee. The comte eyed him and then the area around himself. It was then that Andrew noticed the blade clutched in his hand, likely used on the man on the floor.

Andrew should have found his own weapon before climbing the stairs. But he wasn't here to hurt anyone, and he most definitely would not allow anyone to harm him. He'd seen enough death and blood to last a lifetime.

It was at that moment that the comte noticed the dark stains that saturated Andrew's riding pants. "Are you covered in blood?" Odd that he wondered about the blood covering Andrew, but hadn't looked to the prone body on the floor, the man's eyes staring lifelessly up at the ceiling.

But Andrew was here for answers, not to give them. Ignoring the comte, he asked, "Why Chastain?" He hadn't thought much of it until now. They'd certainly chosen Chastain for a reason, and Lorelei had said she'd felt responsible for what Chastain did to her.

"Ah—so you know, but not everything. She's fled—used and discarded you—and you think we will give you answers."

"Lorelei did not discard me." His defensiveness was heard by all in the room. "We loved one another."

"Is that what she told you?" The man laughed. "Lorelei does not give her emotions so freely. She has been taught better."

"You mean *trained*."

The comte shrugged. "If that is what you would like to believe, but I see no reason to mince words. What do you want?"

Andrew took in the room, letting the comte's question hang unanswered.

"Did you come here looking for her? As you can see, she has betrayed her family, as well."

"Never say that, Mathis," Lorelei's mother said.

"It is—"

"No," Andrew silenced them both. His need for answers drained from him. "I know exactly where Lorelei is. I came here looking for something else, but I see it will not be found here."

"You know where she is?" the comtesse asked. "Please, tell us where. We must find her and leave England."

Andrew felt pity for the woman, realizing he could not keep it from them—they were her parents and must, at some deep level, have some affection for their offspring. Now, he only wanted to find Peter—and start to process all that had happened.

"If you know where Lorelei is, tell us." The comte meant it to be a threat, but all Andrew heard in his words was relief.

"She is in the warehouse district by the docks."

"Does she hide from De Pez?" Camille glanced at the man on the floor nervously. "She should know he is no longer a threat to her safety."

"No, she has nothing to fear now." There was finality in his voice.

Camille took in his bloodied clothes, and the comte stared intently into his eyes.

"Is she hurt?" they asked in unison.

Their desperation was clear. It was only then that he realized they cared about their child beyond their mission.

"She is gone."

"Gone? But you said she was in the warehouse district." Puzzled, Camille moved toward the door, her words coming in a mix of English and French. "We must go to her, Mathis. Find a way out of this for all of us."

"Yes, you must go to her, but she has found her way out," Andrew said.

"What do you mean, boy?"

"Her carriage…it was traveling too fast—the corner was too sharp, and the driver was unprepared."

"What are you saying?" Camille once again gave in to her tears. "Is that Lore's blood upon your person?"

Andrew couldn't stand to tell them he'd been the one to cause the crash. "Yes. I made her comfortable in her last moments."

"But…that cannot be." The comte looked to his wife in disbelief. "It was not supposed to be this way."

"Why has Lord Chastain not come to us?" Camille asked, directing her question at no one, but hoping someone had the answer.

"He was in the carriage with her."

"And baby Peter?" she asked.

Lorelei had told him to trust no one, not even her own parents. "He was with his mother as well." He did not lie to them, for the babe had been in the carriage, but Andrew hoped Peter would be far from London by the time the comte discovered his grandchild's body was not within the wreckage.

"You are certain?"

Andrew only nodded.

"We must go to her, Mathis." She collapsed to the floor, not far from the ever-increasing pool of blood. The comte was instantly at her side, taking her into his arms as she cried. Overwhelming sobs filled the room as a mother bemoaned the unfair and cruel world she had created for her only child.

Andrew longed for someone to hold him, allow him to weep in agony. To call into question every unfairness that had been dealt to him in his life. He wanted to go to them, seek their embrace to soothe his own pain.

Yet, he did not belong here.

On unsteady feet, Andrew fled the room, hurried down the stairs, and out of the house.

Epilogue

"Andrew?" A familiar voice fought to break through the haze that surrounded him.

He looked up from the plans he'd been studying since the night Lorelei left him, to see Mrs. Bee in the doorway, his blurred gaze bringing her into focus.

"Are you still awake?"

He only nodded. Sleep had eluded him for months. He was exhausted, yet when he closed his eyes the nightmares started. Even when he opened them the images kept invading his sight. He'd sworn off anything harsher than sherry, as well, for any slumber was torture. He'd settled on staring at the plans for hours on end.

"Can I bring you anything before I retire?" she asked.

"Just go!" Frustration, incompetence, disappointment, fury, hopelessness—they all coursed through him at once, fighting to dominate his movements and speech. "I am sorry—"

"Do not apologize to me, my lord." She stood, hands on her hips, ever the scolding mum. "You should be ashamed of how you have been treating the servants, however. Me—I will survive, as I always have. Now, I can barely stand the smell of you. Do seek your quarters and freshen up."

Andrew's drive to do anything other than sit behind his desk was nonexistent. He wondered if anyone would notice if he never left this very room again. What would be the point of any of it? He'd given his love, unconditionally, and he'd been scorned for it.

Stomping her foot, Mrs. Bee again gained his attention. "Your eyes are redder than redcurrant. You look about to collapse."

"I can care for myself." And he had, ever looking over his shoulder. He dreaded the day the comte or his associates would come for him, too. He had his servants running to and fro double bolting doors and windows; his paranoia only grew as the days passed, though. "Do check the kitchen door before you retire."

"Always something," she muttered. "Scared of the dark, a grown man. Anything further, my lord?"

"No, thank you." She'd given him space since that night, never disturbing him during the long hours—and sometimes days—he'd spent locked away in his study. "Do seek your rest."

He returned his attention to the papers before him after she quietly closed the door. It had been several days before he'd realized the case had been the one that had sat in his own dressing room all these years, virtually unnoticed by him. The thick leather cylinder had been left over from when his father had used the suite of rooms.

Two months—well, eight weeks and four days actually—staring at them, and he'd garnered no knowledge of their importance. He'd gone to bookstores and map collectors, but none recognized the place portrayed in the drawings. They were decades old and were already fading. He'd been careful not to damage them, for they'd meant something to Lorelei—and the men who had sent her to find them.

Andrew had hid the plans well, though he trusted no one with their existence and whereabouts.

He'd hoped by decoding them he'd also locate Peter—or someone who could tell him of the child's whereabouts. What he did know was that Lorelei hadn't been the woman he'd thought she was. In a rash move, Andrew had sent word to France, addressed to the Comte of Epernon, but had received word that the title and estate were absorbed decades before and no longer existed. There was no record of her name or that of her parents.

It was as if she'd never existed—their love had never happened. She'd deceived him so fully, he truly questioned his own memories of her, if he even had the right to be angry or confused or lonely. She had begged him over and over to forget her, to leave her be, but he'd been unable to do that one thing for her.

Andrew wanted to blame her, or the comte, possibly even Benji for the pain his betrayed heart suffered.

He could look at the plans before him, go over the response from France, or speak with others who'd met the comte and his daughter—but those accounts were all too factual. Set in stone, unchangeable. Meaning nothing.

His emotions were a tidal wave of unexpected change, evolution, and regression.

One moment he wondered how he could live without her.

The next he cursed her existence.

And then still he relived every moment they'd shared from that first glance when he'd spied her silent sobs through the crack in that study door to their afternoon of passionate, life-changing lovemaking only hours before she would be forever gone from him.

If he'd known what was to come, would he have done anything differently? Begged her not to leave him or barred his doors?

The questions only kept piling up the more he searched, with no one to give answers. There had been no official inquiry into Peter's whereabouts, as the new Lord Chastain—a distant cousin of Benji's—had no motivation to find the child since Peter stood to inherit instead of him.

So, as his men scoured the countryside from one end of England to the other, Andrew locked himself away. He studied the plans—and met with his solicitor. Anything to give him some semblance of a mission, the ability to truly believe he was worth something, that his actions would someday grant him that which he sought.

The official documents had been drawn up and signed that very day. For when Peter was found, he would be the keeper of much—all that Andrew had. Peter would be the future heir of the Marquis of Drake. He would have property and wealth far beyond most men of the *ton*.

It was the least Andrew could do for Lorelei… For he'd promised to give her everything, and though he'd failed her in so many ways, he would use his every breath for the remainder of his life to uphold his pledge to her, to find her child and do for Peter what he could not do for the child's mother.

A knock sounded once more at the door.

"Enter," he called. His servants knew not to disturb him. "I said I do not need anything."

"My lord?"

Andrew looked up to see his butler shifting from foot to foot in the doorway.

"Yes." He knew irritation over his failed attempts to find Peter clouded his every waking moment. "Do spit it out, I am busy."

"Errr, Mrs. Bee said I should have you come to the foyer with all haste."

Andrew sighed, but rolled the plans up and slipped them back into their case. After putting them in a drawer and locking it, he followed the man from the room.

"Whatever is that noise?" As they approached the foyer, a loud crying could be heard. "Is that...?" He walked faster, passing the servant and finding Mrs. Bee standing before the wide-open front door.

"Do move aside!" he shouted.

Could it be?

Had they found him?

Andrew wanted to demand why they hadn't sent word. There was still much to prepare for a child in his home. The nursery needed refurbishing, and he required time to think about schooling and such.

Looking out the front door, he saw no one.

His men did not cradle a baby upon his stoop.

"What cruel jest is this?"

"Andrew." He looked to Mrs. Bee at his side, and she nodded for him to look again. "Lower."

There! He saw it...him...Peter.

A basket was nestled in the darkened corner.

How long had he been there, unheard and vulnerable to the elements?

Andrew could not get out of the house quickly enough. He scooped up the basket, surprised by the light weight of what it held, and brought the babe into the warmth of the foyer.

The baby was tucked tight within a green blanket, and a sheet of paper poked out of the side.

Puzzled, Andrew set the basket upon a small side table and grabbed the paper. His fingers shook with relief. He was unsure if he'd likely harm or thank the person who'd kept Peter hidden from him—but had ultimately returned him.

Mrs. Bee cooed to the baby as Andrew unfolded the note and read:

My Lord,

As promised, here is your child. If you are receiving this then I have succumbed to childbirth, as I feared. Please take care of him or her. Love our child as only a father can.

~E

Andrew looked back to the baby. Sure enough, a sprout of red hair peeked from beneath the blanket tucked tightly about it. This infant was not Peter, nor did it hold any blood of his beloved, only a symbol of his darkest hours—and a weakness he was determined to overcome.

Dropping the note, Andrew took in the sight of the baby before him as he stepped closer.

Just as he inspected the tiny bundle, the babe also narrowed its eyes, staring back.

Leaning in, Andrew noted the large hazel eyes with

hints of green flakes, which looked suspiciously like his own—and his mother's before him.

As he scrutinized the tiny face, so delicate, the babe's mouth parted in a gummy smile and a giggle echoed in the hall.

"Oh, my," Mrs. Bee sighed beside him. "What a pretty little thing."

Andrew felt himself falling, spiraling downward into the depth of his child's eyes, losing himself in the light laugh that still rang about the room.

His child.

His flesh and blood.

Not Lorelei's offspring, but something much more.

Something that solely belonged to him.

His first instinct was to turn away, block his ears from the sound, and lock himself securely in his study until the child was disposed of. He knew he should send word to Craven House. The child was rightly Madame Sasha's responsibility, not his. Its mother was likely now sheltered within Sasha's sanctuary, oblivious to the turmoil Andrew fought.

But he could not take his eyes from the babe.

There was a pull—an invisible draw—to the creature, one Andrew assumed most felt for their offspring, but he'd only just seen the child. It seemed unlikely to his rational mind that a connection could be formed so quickly, yet he sensed it was irrevocably there, as real and concrete as if he could touch it.

Andrew grabbed the handle of the basket that housed the babe securely. The sudden movement startled the child, who immediately hushed, the smile vanishing and a pensive expression taking over his face.

His face? Andrew did not know for sure that the

infant nestled in the swaddling clothe was a male, the small face and tuft of red hair gave away nothing.

"Whatever shall we do with this young?" Mrs. Bee set her fingers atop his hand, which still grasped the basket, his knuckles white for his hold. "I can take it to the kitchen while a nursemaid is called for."

Andrew shifted the carrier and his own hand away from Mrs. Bee. "The fire in my study is much larger than the one in the kitchen. It is best to keep the child warm, is it not?"

"I suppose you are correct, Andrew." Mrs. Bee paused. Her hands fell to her side and she stared at him as intently as the child had moments before. "You are very clever to think of that."

Without another thought, he returned to his study. He lightly set the hamper next to his desk, closest to the warm fire—and sat heavily in his chair.

Andrew took in the room around him before removing the plans from his desk once more. They'd been no help so far in gaining any new information about Lorelei's past or her child's whereabouts.

He feared his state of perpetual unease and failure would continue as hopelessness set in once more.

In his frustration, Andrew swiped his hand across the desk and the rolled papers he'd removed only moments before shot off his desk and through the air—directly toward the fire. He pushed his chair back in haste and moved to grasp the pages before they rolled into the open hearth.

Kneeling on the wooden floor with the plans safely in his hands, Andrew heard soft laughter behind him. It didn't sound as loud, nor bounce off the walls as it had in the open foyer, but the melodic sound dug straight to his heart, for it reminded him of his mother's laugh.

Not Lorelei's throaty chuckle, but still a familiar sound—one that hadn't been heard in his home since he was a boy—before so much agony, disappointment, and death had entered his life.

And the sound infused Andrew with—hope.

For a future.

For his future.

A better future for the child before him—and another he would one day find again.

Other Books by Christina McKnight

A Lady Forsaken Series
Shunned No More
Forgotten No More
Scorned Ever More
Christmas Ever More
Hidden No More
Loved Ever More (Exclusive Bonus)

Craven House Series
The Thief Steals Her Earl
The Mistress Enchants Her Marquis
The Madame Catches Her Duke
The Gambler Wagers Her Baron

Lady Archer's Creed Series
Christina McKnight writing with Amanda Mariel
Theodora
Georgina
Adeline
Josephine

Standalone Novellas
The Siege of Lady Aloria
A Kiss At Christmastide

About the Author:

Christina McKnight is a book lover turned writer. From a young age, her mother encouraged her to tell her own stories. She's been writing ever since.

Christina enjoys a quiet life in Northern California with her family, her wine, and lots of coffee. Oh, and her books . . . don't forget her books! Most days, she can be found writing, reading, or traveling the great state of California.

Email her: christina@christinamcknight.com
Follow her on Twitter: @CMcKnightWriter
Keep up to date on her releases:
www.christinamcknight.com
Like Christina's FB Author page:
ChristinaMcKnightWriter

Christina McKnight

Author's Notes

Thank you for reading *Scorned Ever More, A Lady Forsaken (Book Three)*.

If you enjoyed *Scorned Ever More*, be sure to write a brief review at
Amazon, Barnes and Noble, or Goodreads.

I'd love to hear from you!

You can contact me at:
Christina@christinamcknight.com

Or write me at:
P O Box 1017
Patterson, CA 95363

www.ChristinaMcKnight.com
Check out my website for giveaways, book reviews, and information on my upcoming projects,
or connect with me through social media at:

Twitter: @CMcKnightWriter
Facebook: www.facebook.com/christinamcknightwriter
Goodreads: www.goodreads.com/ChristinaMcKnight

Sign up for my newsletter here:
http://eepurl.com/VP1rP

There are several people I'd like to thank for staying with me through the emotional journey of writing this book.

To Marc, my amazing boyfriend, who nursed me through countless weeks of self-doubt, missed deadlines, and utter chaos. Thank you…your love and dedication never ceases to amaze me. I hope to one day be as selfless and compassionate as you are.

To Lauren Stewart, my critique partner and best friend, you pushed me to explore new avenues of thought that I never dreamed possible. When I told you my outlandish ideas for this book you encouraged me to write from my heart, even though it might not be popular to the masses.

I'd also like to thank the wonderful women who've supported me in both my writing career and life, including (but not limited to): Jeannine Meador, Renee Bernard, Angie Stanton, Sharla Metheny-Ybanez, Debbie Haston, Roxanne Stellmacher, Laura Cummings, Annalisa Nicole, Dawn Borbon, Suzi Parker, Jennifer Vella, Brandi Johnson, and Latisha Kahn. I know I'm forgetting people…You have all been very patient and wonderfully supportive of my eccentric ways.

A very special thank you to my editor, Chelle Olson with Literally Addicted to Detail, your skill and professionalism surpass all that I expected. Chelle Olson can be contracted by email at literallyaddictedtodetail@yahoo.com.

My proofreader, Anja with Hour Glass Editing did an amazing job fighting through her tears to make sure not a coma was out of place.

Cover art and wraparound cover design credit to Sweet 'N Spicy Designs.

Finally, thank you for supporting indie authors.